THE FIRST BATCH

Dustin Dreyling

Cover Art and Interior illustrations:

Elden Ardiente of Lungga Creatives

Acknowledgements

First and foremost, Christofer Nigro and Zach Cole at Wild Hunt Press for giving me the chance to write for them and bring this project of mine to fruition. Neil Riebe and Elden Ardiente at Lungga Creatives (visit them on Facebook and Instagram!) for really helping me to get it off the ground, along with Dan Delgado (https://www.d2voice.com/). Your help means a lot to me!

Second, my Mom (Sandy), Dad (Mike), and better half (Melissa), for all their love and support. My sister, Heather Hageman, and the rest of our family for their continued support. Posthumous credit definitely goes to my Grandpa George. He lit the fire. After that, there is a list of people who have influenced and encouraged me in so many ways. Forgive me if I miss anyone.

Jeremy Robinson, Jeff Strand, Brian Keene, and Tim Curran, for being the biggest reasons I love reading, and the individuals who made me want to start writing this book. Right behind them are J.F. Gonzalez (R.I.P.), Kane Gilmour, Sean Ellis, Kent Holloway, Aurelio Rico Lopez III, William Meikle, Max Hawthorne, Eric S. Brown, Rick Chesler, Rick Jones, Xander Weaver, and too many more to name here.

Also thanks to Josh Beane, Jym Donovan, Kevin Jones, Nick Rotter, Tom LaCroix, Chris Olson, David Hernandez, Kelly Allenby, Kyle Mohr, Tim Giossi, Virgil Churchill, Deb Fairhurst -- for her encouragement and proofing very early on -- and finally, all of the ARGH!ers (you know who you are). You have been more of an influence to me than you know… yet. Mwahaha! Stay tuned.

To my mom and dad. Thank you for everything.

Table of Contents

PROLOGUE

1980-something
Transantarctic Mountain Range
Antarctica

The ice ax sank into the surface of the final rise like a champ, and Sadako Sōzō used it to pull herself up onto the flat, rocky ledge. The exhausted seventeen-year-old-woman took in the sights that the last rise had to offer her. She was ecstatic to be so close to discovering one of her father's last secrets.

The landscape mesmerized Sadako. Giddiness bubbled up inside of her, attempting to overthrow the strong sense of decorum that had been passed down to her by her late father. The teenage part of her protested the stifling of her emotions, but she tamped those feelings down when her father's displeased face appeared in her mind's eye.

Screw him, look where I am! Even my father could risk cracking his face with a smile at this view!

While she pensively gazed at the shadowed, sun-deprived valley, three men wearing the same gear as Sadako reached the summit and stood with her. They were all prime examples of her most trusted protectors, one of whom she had known her entire life. She smiled at each of them in turn before re-securing her faceplate, as the snot was just beginning to freeze around her nostrils.

They had found the valley. At last.

Sadako raised both arms in the air, turned to face the expanse behind her and let out a wild whoop of a victory cry that was snatched up by the wind before it could even echo. Then she turned back to her associates.

"We found it, boys!" she shouted, arms still raised in triumph.

Five years of research, development, and fundraising had paid off. It was not without cost; getting to where they now stood had cost Sadako most of her formative years. Ishiro Sōzō had left his daughter the coordinates to the valley upon his demise. This was in addition to his journals, countless hand-drawn maps, and control of his nefarious company. His simple description of the valley, "rocks scattered all around like a child's discarded toys," was more than enough to confirm their successful arrival. The geologic formations on the valley floor did indeed resemble a child's messy playroom floor.

She looked up at Captain Bruce Hodder as he stepped up to stand next to her. He was her most trusted employee, and the tallest of the trio she had brought with her on the climb. The former marine's ugly eviction from the military branch had been less than honorable, but her dad had welcomed him with open arms. Bruce worked for Sadako's father for eleven years until he died, whereupon she had "inherited" him as her bodyguard, for all intents and purposes.

He was the leader of her newly acquired forces of cutthroats, mercenaries, and orphaned children who had been reared under the guise of a global family. Never mind the masses of scientific outlaws they employed to create the kinds of things that were formerly only real in nightmares or science fiction movies. The multitude of miscreants employed by the company were now *her* minions.

Hodder was hers to command, offering strategic advice and personal commentary only when asked or when he knew it was needed. When the man did choose to give her input, he was rarely wrong. There was only one instance she could remember, and that was merely an incorrectly ordered cup of coffee from a gas station. Botched coffee orders aside, she trusted him completely. Just as her megalomaniacal father had.

"Bruce, please radio Captain Englund and tell him we are a go," she said. "I want a base camp operational by this time tomorrow evening," she said.

2

"10-4," Hodder nodded and barked orders into his gigantic walkie-talkie, relaying the new commands to the oceanic vessel, *The Spriggan,* standing by in the waters just off the southern coast. He turned to the two men behind him. "Cunningham. Romero. Fetch the rest of our crew at the bottom of the rise. Drive the Cats into the valley and set up the tents. We stay in the valley until the rest of our supplies and personnel arrive tomorrow morning."

"Yes, sir!" Cunningham yelled with a salute before he and Romero started back down the rocky slope to the caravan of Sno Cats.

The weather resistant vehicles were waiting with needed supplies at the bottom. A low spot next to the rise they were on would provide them the opening they needed to gain passage into the hidden valley. Hodder and Sadako watched the Cats drive through the narrow opening before starting their own descent back down from the ledge.

Two hours later, the caravan had disembarked, and the small crew was nearly finished setting up heated shelters for themselves as well as the people coming in from the *Spriggan*. The summertime sun had gradually followed them into the valley, which made their work easier. Soon it seemed more like they were in the midst of a fine winter's day in Minnesota, rather than at the bottom of the world. The congregation of Hidora Neo elite were surrounded by snowy, ice-covered peaks and rocky cliffs, with the one low spot being their entrance to the resting place of Ishiro Sōzō's last obsession. The surrounding isolation gave them all a feeling of security that their actions would be hidden from the prying eyes of the world.

Sadako and Hodder searched each of the rock formations in what they were calling the "playroom," while their crew continued construction. The pair eventually came to stand in front of an odd, wedge-shaped hunk of limestone buried in the snow. It looked unnatural the way it was embedded in the ground, as if some god had driven into the earth. It was the bright red paint on the rock that had originally caught their attention, however.

"Sadako" in Japanese.

She locked eyes with the big man next to her, even though she could not see them through their tinted goggles.

"This is where we dig."

***

15 hours later

BOOM!

The explosion scattered chunks of Antarctica in all directions. Smoke billowed out of the hole where Sadako's boulder had been mere moments before. She followed Hodder and his men as they approached the ten-foot diameter hole, their mouth pieces all hanging open. Plumes of visible exhalation raced through the air around them.

"Look there," Sadako said, pointing down at a tin can that was crushed underneath a chunk of rocky debris from the explosion.

The infamous red and white logo of the reigning cola champion of the world shone in the meager illumination from Cunningham's flashlight.

"My father was a certifiable addict of that carbonated swill," Sadako said with a somber face. "It is just like him to leave his garbage laying around for me to clean up."

Hodder was the only one of them who dared to chuckle at her comment.

"How the hell did he cover up this hole with that gigantic chunk of a mountain?" Cunningham asked his question reactively, garnering a quick head snap and glance from Hodder.

"Cunningham, rope ladder, please," Sadako asked. "It is better if we do not speculate on that aspect too much. I am certain we would go insane trying to figure it out. My father was far more mysterious than any of us will ever genuinely understand -- save for Captain Hodder."

Hodder laughed heartily. "Oh no, little Miss Sōzō, he was into *far* more things than I ever wanted to know about. I just did my job and kept his ass out of trouble."

He held up a gloved finger as an afterthought struck him.

"Although now that you're the big boss lady, I'm sure we will both be finding out what those things were." He went silent and stared down at her with a serious face, the implications of which were not lost on the teenager he had voluntarily dedicated himself to.

"As long as you have my back, Captain, I am positive we can handle it," was all she said.

"I am going to oversee the workers constructing our new facility, Sadako," Hodder said. "Cunningham and Romero will accompany you below."

"Very good, Captain," Sadako said.

Hodder headed off towards the beginnings of their new base on the continent.

Cunningham stepped to the edge of the hole. Producing a small hammer from his coat and a rolled-up bundle from under his other arm, he knelt down and pounded securing spikes for the ladder he was holding deep into the snowy ground. He then threw the roll over the side, the ladder unfurling down as it was designed to do. Then the man stood up and swept his arm out towards the hole and bowed.

"Your palace awaits, Milady."

"Smartass," Sadako muttered as she climbed down the ladder. Before disappearing completely, she stopped and looked up at Cunningham.

Cunningham handed her a flashlight. "I'm right behind you," he said.

When she reached the bottom, she shone her light down the dark, quiet tunnel. The light was swallowed up a dozen meters in. She heard Cunningham's boots on the rocky debris as he stepped down off the ladder behind her. It was at least twenty degrees warmer in the hole, the warm air wafting up to meet them making the air shimmer slightly from the temperature collision. It was warm enough to make them sweat in their arctic gear, but not enough to melt the snow. She pulled the can out from under the rock it was stuck under and stuffed it into her coat pocket. Then she turned to Cunningham.

"We need more lights… and Dr. Dyer. I want his expertise down here," Sadako said as her flashlight exposed the rock ceiling and walls lining the downward sloping tunnel. "We need to know the structural integrity of this passage before we venture any further."

Minutes later, Dr. Randy Dyer was standing next to Sadako, appraising the rock walls with his much brighter beast of a spotlight, similar to one that a scuba diver would use.

"Limestone, I think," Dyer observed, his moustache twitching back and forth as he spoke. "It's hard to tell, as embarrassing as that is to admit. This rock looks *melted,* yet also looks like something bored this tunnel out with an absolutely savage bore head. But it seems strong, and I see a line of what I expect to be basalt underneath. So, I believe we should be good to continue. All the same, rope off and take it single file and slow. I can't wait to see where this tunnel leads."

Cunningham led the way at his own request, followed by Dr. Dyer, Sadako, and finally Romero. They followed the tunnel down at a 20-degree angle. The melted, horribly uneven walls were strange to even look at, let alone use as hand holds in their descent through the uneven tunnel.

"What the hell made this tunnel, Dr. Dyer?" Cunningham asked the geologist, with the tone of an eager elementary school student. "It almost looks drilled out from the straightness of the angle, but the walls are jagged more like it was dug out with claws or something."

The mustache twitched again. "I don't know. It *is* very strange," Dyer said.

Sadako stopped suddenly. "Turn off your lights, gentlemen."

The three men complied, plunging all of them into darkness.

Gradually, their eyes adjusted to the faint blue glow that emanated from further down the long tunnel. They headed down again with the lights back on, until they reached a crude archway that opened up to a massive chamber. The cavern glowed with the blue light they had followed down like a beacon, and the source of the illumination took their collective breaths away.

A minute quickly passed by in silence before Dr. Dyer finally croaked, "Is that what I think it is?"

"It is, Dr. Dyer, it is indeed," Sadako confirmed. "You are looking at my father's greatest discovery. We will build our new headquarters here, and for some, a new home. The first of many more Hidora Neo stations. If the incredible claims in my father's journal are even close to legitimate, what is waiting inside that craft will change everything for us all. With this discovery, Hidora Neo will take back this world from the corrupted societies running it, and mold it into *our* vision of a better future. The future my father wanted to see become a reality."

Sadako removed her headgear and shook her head back and forth, loosening her silky, black hair. Anger and triumph shone in her electric blue eyes, enhanced by the similarly hued glow inside the cavern. The quartet gazed in wonder at the gigantic object that was embedded in the ice and rock on the opposite side of the immense cavern. The object's size was that of a professional football stadium and was also the obvious source of the radiance that filled the chamber.

It was a bio-luminescent type of glow that was strange for the craft's presumably metallic hide. Its *alien* hide.

Ishiro Sōzō had found an actual UFO beneath Antarctica and had successfully concealed it with a geometrically shaped boulder that was impossible for any man to move without heavy machinery.

Sadako had just inherited it and a successfully covert organization that was a force to be reckoned with. If what her father's journal had to say about the alien ship's contents was to be believed, and with the entirety of Hidora Neo at her disposal, anything was possible.

Oh, what fun she was going to have, capturing the world's attention and making all its governments see the folly of their ways. Her company would get to work, repurposing society to fit Hidora Neo's vision and needs -- *her* needs. Someday, it would all belong to Sadako.

Someday.

Sadako Sōzō's journey to that day had only just begun.

CHAPTER 1

40 years Later
Duluth, Minnesota
North America

David Goodman looked towards downtown Duluth from the curtained window of his Whirlpool suite in the Waterfront Plaza hotel, located in Canal Park right on the harbor. The post-coronavirus morning sun's rays spread out over everything in sight. The white IMAX dome of the theater located a few blocks away was irritatingly bright from the reflection. The deep blue sky met the treed hill and rocky bluffs Duluth was built into the side of with a contrast that was pleasing to David's tired eyes.

The view of the city was still a beautiful sight to him. David had always been a city boy at heart. It was going to be a gorgeous day… once it started. Still tired and groggy, he looked at the clock in the corner on the bedroom nightstand. 8:02 a.m.

Coffee.

Now.

He turned away from the window and began walking towards the kitchenette. Halfway there he was dropped to his knees by the deafening sound of metal being torn apart in the most antagonizing way. It was like Freddy Krueger's glove on the boiler room pipes multiplied tenfold. The aging metal fillings in his teeth reminded him of their presence in response to the sound. His ears throbbed like they were going to start gushing blood from the pressure the horrible noise was creating behind his eardrums. David screamed, but his agonized cries were rendered moot by the metallic assault outside.

Suddenly, the noise ceased. David got up, breathing heavily, and ran to the window. His wife Madeline screamed at him from the bed. She pointed a rigid finger out the window behind him. The finger was warped from the intensity she put into it and it resembled an old decrepit woman's hook, like the Old Witch from the vintage *Haunt of Fear* comics David had read when he was thirteen.

"David! What the hell is *that*?"

David looked from his wife back to the view out of the window. He froze in place, slack-jawed and gaping stupidly out the hotel window at the *S.S. William A. Irvin* docked in the harbor behind the hotel. And the living *thing* atop it.

A gigantic turtle with a prehistoric nightmare of a head sat perched atop the retired ore ship turned nautical museum. The horrible wrenching noise that had brought David to his knees was from the monstrous animal's claws digging into the ship as it hauled itself up out of Superior. The thick, jagged shell poured water down in torrents due to its massive girth as it rose from the lake. Dark greens and browns colored the giant chelydrid's shell, its rigid surface was covered with sharp pointed scutes that stuck up like conical teeth.

The beast's skin, darkest green and wrinkled like an octogenarian's pruned bath fingers, hung loosely where it exuded from between the shell. The webbed feet sported massive, curved talons, the black keratin that they were comprised of displaying a dull sheen in the morning light.

The chelonian beast's head was not that of the alligator snapper, nor any other turtle species. Instead, its round, blocky head was that of a snout-less demon shark. The smooth skin on its face was a mottled black and silvery gray and covered in armored plates. Giant, round eyes were mounted near the front of the monster's head. Each orb consisted of a dark sclera with an ancient iris in the middle, grayish-blue doughnuts with pitch black pupils. Neither human was an expert on prehistory, but this was the head of a *Dunkleosteus*.

The kaiju's mouth looked more like a demented bear trap than a set of teeth. The top jaw blade was jagged in the front at symmetrical points, like a pair of front fangs. In reality, however, the seeming incisors were part of one big, serrated length of bone. The similar bottom jaw had more of a toothy saw blade appearance. It resembled a lumberjack's hand tool instead of Nosferatu's mouth as the top jaw did. Yet it too had a pair of canine tooth deviations.

Heat shimmered from its slightly agape maw and David could clearly see quicksilver waves billowing out from it even thirty yards away.

"Oh my god, what in the actual *fuck* is that?" David's wife screamed again from behind him at the terrifying sight looming before their eyes.

David spun around in a panic. "We have to go, Maddy. Now!"

***

As David and Madeline scrambled to save their lives, the monstrous, aquatic horror lumbered out of the water completely, crashing down on the opposite side of the *S.S. Irvin*. In front of it was the movie theater and the gigantic sports-entertainment complex next door. The beast's plated head looked back and forth indecisively at the buildings in its path.

Cars and people, though few in number for this time of day on a Saturday morning, scattered in a panic. Human screams and automotive squeals filled the air as hysterical citizens tried to escape the giant creature. It paid them little mind, its eyes quickly darting to and fro, but not yet reacting; it was as if the giant beast was trying to make up its mind which building it wanted to destroy first.

The wicked mouth blades clacked together with a sharp, resounding crack that sent some people sprawling and a few screaming while holding their ears in pain. Windows in the direct path of the vibrative attack shattered from the force the action threw at them.

The beast charged.

The theater complex never had a chance. The monstrosity bull-rushed through the theater's smaller screen before it slammed into the giant IMAX screen at the backside of the building. The walls gave way as though they were made of Styrofoam. Chunks of building rained down all around, some of the debris causing human and collateral damage in the process. Fires soon ignited all over the ruins of the movie house.

The turtle thing seemed to be in a state of euphoria as it continued stomping all over the already decimated theater complex. As it stamped and pummeled the building into dust, the chelonian terror turned northeast towards downtown Duluth. Its spiked, reptilian tail swung back and sliced a long, ragged gash through the arena next door. Without warning, things inside the ruined buildings began to explode as flammable gas and liquids met open flame. In less than a minute, both structures the monster had demolished were engulfed in flames, while the thing from the lake stomped through the freeway beyond to destroy the rest of the city.

Three Duluth PD squad cars raced down Superior Street towards the prehistoric terror as it smashed through a mercifully empty school. The kaiju gnashed its jaws and hissed as the school fell to ruin under its assault. The three squads screeched to a stop in a parking lot less than 75 yards from the rampaging daikaiju, at the exact moment a gas line inside the school went up in a bright orange plume, searing the monster's left flank. It emitted a high-pitched wail while thrashing around in agony.

The creature's outer epidermis sported a raw, stippled burn that marred the skin and shell, still fresh and wet looking in the morning sun. The monster reared up on its hind legs in protest to this new pain, crying out just as a second explosion let loose and knocked the nearly standing creature back across the demolished lanes of Interstate 35. The turtle beast tumbled ass-over-tea-kettle directly into the stadium conflagration burning fiercely in broad daylight.

The three squads remained untouched where they had stopped. Five doors opened, an officer stepping out from each. They all stared, dumbfounded, as the turtle-giant righted itself without difficulty -- *so much for the turtle on its back theory,* one of the officers thought unexpectedly to himself -- and stampeded directly towards them in a rage. They each raised their pistols and fired desperately at the thing. If the enraged turtle beast noticed their resistance before smearing them all over the asphalt, it gave no indication before crashing into the mortgage bank behind them.

After leveling the bank building and turning northeast once again towards the shops of downtown, the monster abruptly stopped and gazed out at the frigid waters of Lake Superior. Its head twitched once, and it clacked its jaws again, almost as if in response to someone or something. It inhaled deeply, and the beast's flesh swelled up until it was squeezing out from between the marginal and vertebral shells like it was a squished marshmallow s'more.

A noisy jet of blue-white flame blasted out of its mouth when it finally exhaled. The fiery force instantly charred and cremated everything in its path. Everything not reduced to cinders and ashes was completely engulfed in flames. A series of explosions blasted through the cityscape as combustibles ignited from the damage. Burning buildings on both sides of Superior Street soon went up as well, one after the other, hazards igniting in the chaos. Downtown was a raging inferno.

With a shrieking hiss, the monster charged forward. It obliterated every burning building unfortunate enough to be in the way on its new path. Undeterred by the burning hot wreckage it plowed through, the kaiju came to a halt in front of the neon lights of the untouched Fond-Du-Lac Casino, smearing some fleeing people into the asphalt as it stopped itself in front of the glowing structure.

It gazed at the hypnotic lights for a full ten seconds. In that small amount of time, four more squad cars pulled up. The foolish but dedicated officers opened fire after the initial shock of glimpsing the beast up close. The standard police issue pistol shots had no hope of penetrating the thick hide or shell, and the kaiju ignored the puny humans and their pop guns. The frightened officers knew their weapons' deficiencies but were fueled by the optimistic hope that the military would take over soon. That is, until a lone female officer adjusted her aim and shot directly into the monster's mouth with her .40 caliber Smith & Wesson. The tiny bullet shredded the back of the abomination's throat, the first real injury the creature had sustained since coming ashore.

The pain caused the shelled goliath to immediately snap out of its daze and begin shrieking out. It then rose up on its hind legs and stood partially bipedal like a grizzly bear. Blood ran out of the corners of its constantly flapping mouth. Its dark shadow loomed over the fear-stricken officers as it finally saw them as a threat. One of the bigger cops pissed himself and ran. His coworkers quickly followed him, but the escape attempt was ultimately futile.

Whitish-blue flame erupted from the kaiju's throat like a jet engine and erased the officers, along with the block of buildings they had parked in front of. Their cars exploded, spinning haphazardly through the air in a dozen different pieces and directions like cheap bottle rockets all shot out of the same container at once. Cars up and down Superior Street detonated when the white-hot flames greeted their fuel tanks and lit the gasoline inside. Flying pieces of the vehicle shrapnel smashed through the surrounding buildings, doing massive damage to the aging structures. Fires burned everywhere in the aftermath.

Unfortunate people within range of the destruction were crushed by the falling debris or skewered by pieces of the destroyed automobiles. One unlucky man ran in between two buildings, just as a smoldering Prius crashed through the front corner of the structure he had been standing in front of seconds prior. The damaged building buckled and fell into the restaurant next door with a loud boom. Chunks of brick and mortar collided as the two edifices mashed together and buried him where he hid in the alley.

Down the street, the twin high rises of the Graysolon Plaza were ablaze as well, the fires visible across the lake in Wisconsin. A few of the people trapped on the upper floors by the flames found swan diving into the asphalt to be preferable to burning to death and leapt to their doom. Groups of more level-headed people escaped from back doors, fire escapes, and the windows of the lower levels.

Amongst all the destruction, the kaiju had yet to even touch the Fond-Du-Lac Casino. It just stood there watching everything around it burn. It suddenly slammed back down on all fours from its grizzly bear stance, the seismic backlash affecting everything within a one-mile radius like a split-second earthquake. Car alarms shrieked. Building foundations cracked and buckled. Several structures crumbled to the ground, while others fell seconds later, all

13

collapsing in on themselves from the ground-shaking assault and gravity's pull.

With surprising speed, the monster tore into the casino walls, annihilating the bright, neon lights of the casino's namesake sign with the act. It burrowed into the building vigorously. Much of the walls, furniture, slot machines, employees, and casino patrons were all scooped out and flung aside like dirt tossed carelessly from a freshly dug hole. It continued to tunnel until it reached the basement, screams from the people that managed to hide in the lower level splitting the air as they were discovered by the turtle from Hell.

In one fluid motion, the monster thrust its maw into the newly created hole. The juicy morsels inside were devoured. The beast's jaws clacked noisily as it chewed them up and slurped them down. When it was finished, the satiated kaiju turned back towards Lake Superior.

Countless screams, alarms, and sirens had surpassed the sounds of the burning, misery-ridden city. Without warning, the shelled behemoth charged back towards the shoreline it had originally emerged from. The monstrous thing destroyed many of the structures that it had missed on the first trip through, as well as Canal Park in its flight. The beast slipped back into the cold depths of Duluth Harbor, seamless and effortless like a relative ejecting itself from a sunny log at the first sign of trouble.

The Devonian-headed terror disappeared as quickly as it had appeared, the wake from its submergence rocking the *S.S. Irvin*, and causing the lower decks to flood. The whole catastrophe took less than fifteen minutes. The *Irvin* would sink into Lake Superior ten minutes later.

Hours later, emergency crews would pull David Goodman and his wife from the Canal Park rubble. Some cuts and broken bones aside, David was hysterical, ranting and raving about "that stupid turtle from *Mystery Science Theater* being fucking real," and how he would never eat turtle soup again.

***

Superior X Station
The Depths of Lake Superior miles away from Duluth

"That was awesome!" Dr. Herbert Brundle exclaimed excitedly from his rolling desk chair.

The scientist looked away from the giant screen of multiple monitors, mostly made up of satellite images, hacked CCTV screens, and various national and international news sources. He swiped up his energy drink with a quick arm snap from his desk and dumped a bunch of the ginger ale-colored liquid down his throat.

Brundle had a severe addiction to the things, the humor of this specific energy drink being stocked readily in the complex not lost on the young scientist, especially given the monster they had unleashed on poor Duluth. He scratched the small zit on his cheek before running his fingers through his mop of red hair.

The young man then turned to his colleagues, his green eyes radiating joy and a hint of malevolent glee behind his hipster-frame glasses.

"Do you two not agree? That was the shit!"

The other two scientists -- Doctors Seth Brown and Emmet West -- only looked down their noses at the much younger biologist of multiple fields and shook their heads. The long-haired, bearded Dr. Brown -- looking like Jesus with Santa Claus' white hair -- spoke first.

"It was a borderline disaster, Brundle. Shellshock damn near blew himself up taking out that school. He clearly still has an immature brain. He wasn't ready, and we should have waited at least another week, but far be it from me to tell Sadako Sōzō 'no!'"

Dr. West -- a clean-shaven, bespectacled man with a creepy demeanor and black hair -- chuckled a little. His side part reached back from the right corner of his receding hairline, distracting from the widow's peak hiding under the bangs he combed to the left. He

15

flashed a smile that seemed wrong on his face and followed up his chuckles.

"He is just a juvie, Dr. Brown. We simply ran out of time. Once he is secured back in his kennel, we'll start him on phase two hormones and supplements. He will grow up a bit by next weekend, anyway. Physically. Mentally speaking, he's like that simpleminded phrase, 'Young, dumb, and full of --'"

"It is imperative you do *not* finish that statement," Dr. Brown pointed a liver-spotted finger at West. "You know my stance on that kind of talk," the 75-year-old geneticist said in a voice dripping with venom.

"Fine, *Methuselah*, excuse me all to hell," West shot back with a look of irritation. "The point is, Shelly wasn't ready. He has a fish brain sharing DNA with his simple turtle brain." The obvious use of layman's terms showed Dr. West's contempt.

"What is your problem, West? Did Hodder shit in your cereal again?" Brundle taunted. "This was a trial run. Y'all have been working on this project for over thirty years. I thought you would be happier with the results. This *was* a success, after all, was it not?"

"It was successful in the loosest sense of the word, Dr. Brundle. If the National Guard had shown up, things may have gone quite differently. Had our little pet done anything more to deviate from the original plan, things may have gone poorly. We were lucky. That's all I'm saying." West crossed his arms to further drive his final thoughts on the matter home.

"Fair enough, man," Brundle said. "We do still need to go over our report with Sadako, Tsuburaya, and Hodder. Then we'll get our report cards. Although I don't see why Hodder is always there. He's not exactly our boss."

West growled, becoming impatient and irritated with the confident millennial. He changed the subject.

"I am very anxious to work more with the Mesozoic and Cenozoic samples, as well as the foreign specimen samples. Modern-day samples are boring." He looked up from his laptop screen with a pouty face. "We've been messing with those for a few decades now. It has been over forty years since Sadako discovered the site in Antarctica, and we have plenty of specimens to utilize.

Theropods, Sauropods, Thyreophora, Cerapods... these should be our base models for daikaiju creation. We've waited long enough to incorporate them!"

"What about the *Dunkleosteus* head? That doesn't count?" Brundle said defensively as he spun back and forth in his chair like a hyperactive child, his hands linked together behind his head. "That was our first successful splice with prehistoric DNA. That's not something to just dismiss!"

"A giant turtle with a Devonian shark's head is not what I'm talking about, Herb," West retorted. "I will admit, though, I was elated we did go with that particular specimen! His 'teeth' are very impressive. That jaw snap attack it does is a happy biproduct. It appeared to hurt the people running away." Dr. West frowned. "I still wish we understood how its blow torch works. That has got to be from the foreign DNA. Nothing else makes sense. Now, if I could just be left alone with some samples for even just a weekend, why I could take a *Liopleurodon* sample and --"

"We need to perfect the process first, my old friend," Brown interrupted.

"It *is* perfected, Seth!" West exclaimed with disdain. "I am just the only one here who wants to accept that."

The scientist got up from his workstation and walked through the open doorway that was the one exit to their command room. The space beyond was the beginning of their living and recreational area. West's destination – the kitchen – lay just beyond.

Having been renovated months before their latest "tour of duty," the game/living room consisted of three separate but linked entertainment centers. Each flat screen was hung on a triangular pillar in the center of the area, positioned at an angle so you could not see your neighbor's screen without standing behind them. A comfortable, but fully game-worthy reclining chair was situated below each television. A short console shelf stood against the pillar beneath on each side, loaded to the gills with the apparatus needed to enjoy many forms of media, from video games to audiobooks.

They would pass their down time playing the multitude of games provided, from *Pong* to *Red Dead Redemption 2* (the most current game they had), and everything in-between. They usually kept to the old school '80s and '90s games for Brown's sake -- when he cared to play. It was during a session of playing *Teenage Mutant Ninja Turtles: The Arcade Game* that Brundle came up with the name Shellshock for their chelonian creation. West thought it was childish and demeaning but had no better suggestions.

Now, months later, Brown had surpassed West on several of the games. West had played a lot in the arcades in the last decades of the twentieth century, but it did not help him much. The exception was when Brown's arthritis was acting up, which happened more and more all the time these days, most likely from the activity of gaming itself more than his age.

Nevertheless, the friendly competition helped to focus them, and anticipation to the next game night kept their remaining sanity. It was funny how scientists striving to achieve the impossible with their work were so dependent on video games to stay on task. Brundle grew up with the older video games as well, so he was used to them all, and was the reigning champ for weeks now.

Dr. Brown's computer chimed repeatedly, announcing a phone call. They all looked at each other.

"Parent-Teacher conference time, boys!" Brundle said, then made a big show of gulping nervously as he pulled at his collar like Curly from the Three Stooges.

***

The three men sat in the tiny conference room next door to their individual dorm rooms. Brundle drummed his fingers on the conference table to the music being pumped into his earbuds. West gave him a condescending look and turned to Dr. Brown.

"Where the hell did he pull those damn things out of?" West queried. "Never mind. I don't want to know. Think about what I said, Seth. We have been working on this shit too long to make giant turtles with primitive shark brains. They will continue to be disposable and stupid. We need a good base creature, so we spend less effort on increasing size. The extraterrestrial creation system will require less DNA from the base, as well as the extended species included in the mix. Efficient and economical."

18

"I know that, Emmett, but we have to do things one step at a time. In case there are any malfunctions or genetic time bombs. Until we completely perfect the creation process, using species we are not really familiar with is dangerous and very unpredictable. Let us not forget how dangerously easy it is to make these monsters; the possibilities for disaster are ever-present! I am sorry, but I agree with Dr. Sōzō's method. Sadako really does know what she is doing, trust me, please. We will get there!"

"Dr. West, I am most inclined to agree," Sadako Sōzō's face suddenly appeared on the conference room screen.

Next to her sat Dr. Tsuburaya, her head bioengineer. The man's gray-streaked hair and sparse mustache were punctuated by a pointed nose and a pair of dark eyes framed in spectacles. Behind them loomed Capt. Hodder and Campbell, his right-hand man. The former was a grizzled, gray sonuvabitch who was still violently relevant even past seventy. Campbell was a big pug-faced man with blonde hair and blue eyes. Both stood with feet shoulder-width apart and arms crossed.

"I share your anticipation and restlessness, Dr. West, which is one of the reasons I value your expertise," she said. "However, do not make a habit of doubting my methods. It would be a... mistake."

Sadako's aging, yet still exquisitely beautiful face twisted into a vile glare, making Emmet West's insides cringe. Her blue eyes bored into him like step drill bits through wood.

"Now, that being said, gentleman," she continued, "you have done well today. There is vast room for improvement, but that will always be the case. The three of you must improve your strategy more than anything. Just sending the beast on a childish rampage cannot be the standard operating procedure for future endeavors." Sadako paused to stare at each of them individually before resuming her spiel. "All the same, I thank you for your efforts today. You have not only entertained me but have also made me very proud. My father would not have said so -- that would have been a sign of weakness to him -- but he would have been proud of your work, nonetheless."

Sadako turned to Tsuburaya before continuing, an unreadable look passing between them. Not a pleasant glance. "That being said… Dr. West, I grant you permission to make one Mesozoic based kaiju, with one rule besides the normal extraterrestrial DNA percentage cap." She smiled in her evil, cunning way and said one final thing before the feed disappeared faster than they could blink. "It must have *three* heads."

West jumped and whirled on his older colleague after the screen winked out. "*Yes! Yeah!*" he yelled. "*You like that shit, old man? Huh? Now it is my turn, Seth! Watch me blow you out of the water!*"

West pointed dramatically at Dr. Brown and then did a very awkward happy dance, his legs and arms flailing spasmodically, all the while grunting with his lips tucked in between his teeth. It was a white guy overbite, standard for Caucasian men with no dancing ability. He reminded Brundle of a cross between Elaine from *Seinfeld* and Beavis or Butthead dancing to a music video that did not suck. Brundle burst out laughing.

"Congratulations, West," Brown stated. "Do not waste this chance! Of course, if I can help in any way, let me know." Brown paused for a few seconds, appearing deep in thought, then continued. "This is your time, however, and I will not interfere unless you require assistance. I am sure Dr. Brundle feels the same way."

Brown's humble face belied his disbelief and frustration that West had gotten his way. He looked at Brundle, expectantly, as if to say… *do not leave me hanging*.

Brundle looked at the eldest of them blankly. Then he looked at West, who was sitting in his chair with his fingers laced behind his head, grinning like a fool.

"Uh, look West… you know I'm totally on board with whatever you're doing, right?" The look of hopefulness was like that of a dog whose master has said the magic words that come right before "walk."

West chuckled. "Of course, but I am completely in charge, remember that. My say is final!" He stopped smiling and resumed looking like his normal sour self once again as he stood up from his chair and walked towards the hallway. "Gentlemen, I suggest we stuff our faces and play some games. I feel like kicking your asses tonight, and I mean that in the nicest way possible!"

Then West vanished through the bulkhead archway and headed to the kitchen. He planned on pouring a glass of Shiraz and fixing himself a microwaved dinner before retiring for the evening.

Brown turned to Brundle after West had left the room. The look on the man's face was amused, but his eyes screamed concern.

"I'm staying out of his way for his ego's sake, as well as any remnants of the friendship we had up until the turn of the century," he said. "Emmett is a very... driven man. Very loyal to Sadako, and to us, but he is an edge-walker, Herb. The edge of madness.

"We all are, of that there is to be no doubt! We run a secret, underwater lab that creates and controls city-smashing monsters and is owned by a brutally cold Japanese woman. A woman who is hellbent on dominating the world as revenge for her father's illegal corporate betrayal at the hands of his own board of directors." Brown took a breath and continued. "We do it because it was his dream as well. Why?"

"Holy crap, Doc, do you need a drink after that mouthful?" Brundle replied. "Also, how many times are you going to repeat all of that to me? I get it, already! She wants Hidora Neo to rule the world. Geez, back off the dead horse with that bat, will ya?

"As far as your question... this job gives my life and my work meaning. That's why I do it. Creating new life forms from practically nothing…that is *wicked*. My childhood imagination comes to life."

He stood up and walked around the table to where Brown and the door were. "Now, as far as the super-villainess that we work for…well, shit, Seth." He walked out the door and turned back to face Dr. Brown. "'We're all mad here. I'm mad. You're mad.'" He stretched his mouth out in a cheesy attempt at a Cheshire grin. "Mad scientist sounds legit to me! Embrace it, man. Not to mention these creatures we create might come in handy someday.

"Who's to say our legatees from God-knows-where won't return, pissed off and looking for revenge for usurping their technology? Or some other entity? We might actually be doing mankind a favor in the long run." Brundle smiled at the older man. "C'mon, let's go get some grub. I think we both need a beer."

Brown sighed. "It's easy to forget how young you are sometimes, Brundle. But I will relent. Plus, I am starving."

21

He followed Brundle out of the room, shutting the lights off as he left.

***

The world heard about Duluth minutes after it happened. After a state of emergency was declared, the Coast Guard began sweeping the harbor along with the National Guard. The Guard had also set up a base of operations in the city, positioning troops and vehicles at different points along the shore, in case of reemergence. FEMA was notified, and the Red Cross had arrived quickly. Bionautics, Incorporated -- rival to Hidora Neo -- had just lost one of its board members in the attack, and deployed field operatives in the area. The rival organizations' agents had already scoured the ruins for samples of the giant turtle monster before the emergency crews had begun to rescue the injured, dead, and dying on Minnesota's north shore.

Hidora Neo continued forward, putting the next phase of their plan into effect as the government scrambled to alleviate the disaster-stricken city and its people. At the bottom of the world, however, the origin of the rogue company's empire would give up new secrets that would change everything.

CHAPTER 2

Ripley Station
Somewhere Beneath the Transantarctic Range
Antarctica

Louis Donovan and Jean-Paul Beane were screwing around again. The two engineers were the top tech experts at Hidora Neo's Antarctic base. The complex was a bare bones facility and its sole purpose was to guard the ship and its secrets. It was a completely separate building that housed everything from labs and scientists to weapons and soldiers. Connected to it by a series of hallways was Ishiro Sōzō's buried craft from another world.

Both mischievous technicians had been stationed there for just over a decade, and it was not until this particular moment in time that either of them had given much thought to the ominous door in the bowels of the spaceship. A week prior, Donovan had brought the unopened chamber up to Beane. That and the fact that only a skeleton crew was running things at the southernmost headquarters for the company.

The two of them could rig up the surveillance cameras and make their move when the patrols were the farthest out on their security checks. Plus, as Donovan was quick to point out to Beane, Hodder's men never went down to the Pangea machine room anyway. Soldiers have little interest in genetic engineering, even on such a user-friendly scale. So, the two friends and coworkers prepared, pilfering what they needed -- or thought they *might* need -- and waited for this very moment, seven days later.

They had taken up residence just past the cavernous room that contained the remaining creature creators, the Pangaea machines. The contraptions' inventors had yet to be seen anywhere aboard the parts of the ship Hidora Neo had explored so far -- exploration which had ceased the moment they had discovered the insane devices that could create genetic aberrations so easily. For decades, countless arguments ignited over the prospects beyond the sealed room just past the incredible creature creators.

The Pangea machine room itself was a large, atrium-like space, with balconies running around its misshapen perimeter for eight floors above the ground level. Hidora Neo had installed some lighting of their own throughout the ship, but the bulk of portable strip lights were in this space. Illuminated in LEDs, a climate controlled cold-storage building stood apart from the two remaining Pangea machines. The three empty spaces next to them told of the former locations of the alien contraptions they had moved years before. This transport was only possible after more than a decade of reverse engineering the alien technologies to better understand how to disassemble, move, and then reassemble them at a different place. Hushed voices fretted over the ease of this task – alien technology should not be so comprehensive to human beings – but progress continued, regardless. Eventually, the dream became reality, and the trio of Pangea contraptions were relocated to stations in North America and one in Japanese waters.

The separate storage room held countless specimens from throughout Earth's history and prehistory. It was a round blob of a room that seemed to bubble up out of the dark floor from the way it appeared to be constructed. It was constantly kept frozen by a still undetermined source that some of their experts hypothesized to be below the room's floor. Apart from ripping the floor apart, they had no way of knowing. Ultimately, the storage room was their best find in the derelict vessel, though many of its stores had been depleted as Hidora Neo relocated a vast number of the samples to other facilities.

The genetic material stores had contained *millions* of biologic samples, and still did despite the genetic material the company had already removed. The variety of species spanned the planet's *entire* living history. The most recent sample had been determined by the lab techs to be from the nineteenth century. The oldest uncovered so far was Pre-Cambrian. They had barely touched the DNA that was *not* of Earth origin. The scientists first wanted to get a proper handle on the process before they meddled with the genes of other species from different worlds. Only one foreign sample had been used so far. That was all they had needed to create their monstrous army, anyway. Sadako was known for her default answer whenever prompted to utilize the other alien cells.

"Why fuck with things we don't understand more than necessary? If we have already achieved what Hidora Neo set out to accomplish, then we must forge ahead and reach our glorious destination as rulers of the world. It would be foolish to risk everything just so we can experiment with alien DNA for shits and giggles. That's how bad science fiction movies start."

Of course, some of Hidora Neo's scientists *had* been messing with the other samples, but that would come to fruition much later.

The immediate focal point in the room, the two remaining Pangea Machines, were giant, womb-like tanks. Stretching nearly eighty feet into the air, the majority of their makeup was spherical. A gathering of tubes, cables, and wires occurred at the top of each round container. These were made mostly from a titanium offshoot the experts were unable to identify. One of the techies had jokingly nicknamed it "space titanium" in lieu of correct terminology. Sadly, it stuck.

A small, ovular room sat on the equatorial side of each Pangea machine like a wart. This was the main monitoring area to observe the residents of the growth chamber. From the control room, a crude ladder in a sealed tunnel that descended down to the main entry for the machine's inner workings. This room contained a simple workbench that appeared to be made of stone but was actually composed of the same strange titanium found all over the ship. Besides the main entrance door and the ladder to the control room, there was one other portal. It was marked up and down with alien language pictograms and guarded with an easily operated airlock.

It was in this room that one could play with DNA like molding clay. One could make a monstrosity from either a dream or a nightmare via a three-dimensional, holographic display. The controls were simple and consisted of descriptive pictograms and easily deciphered number symbols to operate. It occurred to even Beane the one time he had been inside of a machine that it was almost as if they were all designed to be used by humans in the first place. Sadako had come to a similar conclusion years before, when she was first introduced to the devices.

Once the specimen was created on the 3D display, it was then established in the laboratory by manipulating the gene sequences of each specimen in an eerily comprehensive program. Once satisfied with the formula and a predictive preview of what the machine computed the animal would look like, the creator would then transfer the embryo into the chamber beyond. This happened with a system of tubes not unlike the drive-thru teller at a bank.

The holographic creation program enabled a monster maker to pick a base animal. They would then add or tweak specific features of one or more specimens to said animal via anatomical models. Donovan and Beane had no idea how the rest of the process was done. The painstaking steps in growing the creatures were unimportant to both men.

Donovan and Beane were instead more interested in breaching the doors that all were forbidden to open for forty years, per Sadako's strict orders. The pair of doors were gigantic and made of the black metal. They were currently bathed in the multitude of strip lights that had been installed in the corridor leading up to the doorway. The doors themselves seemed constructed in the same fashion that a human set would be, only much larger. The two portal covers opened from the middle via something that was akin to an odd-shaped handle or latch. The opening hardware paired up in the center where both slabs of space metal met. One obvious thing made it immediately apparent that people did not manufacture these doors. The latches were two feet higher than any man-made entrance.

The strange set of doors was also mysteriously sealed shut -- from the other side. An incredible amount of a foreign metal alloy covered what appeared to be the actual lock. It was conveniently situated where a human door's lock would be. It was even at the right height, unlike the higher door latches. Lastly, there was the most obvious reason for Sadako's apprehension to ever open them.

Something inside the sealed room had made a bulging dent in the door. From the shape of it, it looked like something had tried to pound its way out. This was very intimidating, considering the dent bulged three feet out from the door, and had a diameter of about eighteen inches.

A *very* big fist lurked on the other side of the entrance, owned by God knew what.

Stretch marks were visible all over the strained bulging metal, seemingly of the same makeup as the stands of the Pangea machines. Whatever had been trying to get out had come damn close to doing so. But… what was it? What hell would be unleashed? How stupid would they be if they tried to find out? The debate raged for the first three years of Ripley Station's existence.

Eventually, it was decided to leave the sealed room the way it was.

Sealed.

Someone or something had tried very hard to keep the fist's owner inside of that room when it was sealed many years prior. Sadako was stringently clear on it being left alone and off limits to *everyone* -- Donovan and Beane included. Bottin, who was Ripley Station's commanding officer in charge, was very thorough about patrolling the door daily. Sergeant Bottin and company were out doing the perimeter patrols, fortunately, and they would not be back underground for at least an hour yet -- never mind the unlikelihood of them going down to the Pangea machines.

The lock and key scrutiny for the sealed door was thrown aside by the impulsive engineers, for as the saying goes, *when the cat's away, the mice will play*. The bored, mainly utility workers were all mice at the moment. All the cats were watching the city-stomping festivities, working on new monsters oceans away, or patrolling their frozen home for intruders or spies that would likely never show.

Who knew what fantastic new technologies the two men might find inside?

That alone made it worth the risk for them, both wanting desperately to breach the door for a decade now. As Beane's cutting torch finally seared through the upper part of the strange solder-covered locking mechanism, a quick burst of air signified the breaking of the door's seal. A rank odor, organic and completely indescribable, flooded the hall they stood in and made both men retch.

"There. That did it! We're through! But holy hell, what the fuck is that stench?" Donovan slapped the torch wielding Beane on the back and continued. "Good job, my friend! I'll get the 'bots!"

Donovan stood up and turned to the pile of tools sitting on a hand cart they had wheeled down to the small open corridor that transitioned between the Pangea room and the formerly sealed one they were about to open. Beane stood up and killed the acetylene torch. He hooked the torch back on a hanger attached to the dolly carrying the gas cylinder that fueled the cutting tool. The still quiet man raised his welding mask, giving his bearded face the chance to void perspiration.

"We aren't through all the way yet, Lou. Get me the drillbot first," Beane said.

"Right on, daddy-o! One Hidora Neo diamond carbide drillbot, version Lou-point-oh, coming up!"

Donovan's enthusiasm mirrored Beane's own, yet both men conveniently ignored the internal alarms their minds were blaring at the risks of their endeavor.

They were going to open a sealed room that smelled like organic filth from the stars.

Donovan opened a large composite case resembling a tackle box, drops of sweat from his own scruffy beard dripping onto its surface. The case was full of tiny, fully functional robots they had designed and constructed, each with its own specific purpose. Donovan scanned the trays for a second before scooping a unit out of its storage space.

He pulled the first drillbot out and thoroughly checked it over. Looking like a rifle cartridge with a wicked drill bit for the bullet end, the miniature robot resembled some contraption from an old sci-fi movie, like *At the Earth's Core*, or *The Last Dinosaur*. A "Polar Borer". Donovan knew most people would not know the movie references, but that is what search engines were for, after all.

The cylindrical back half of the miniature machine was lined with tiny tank treads. The treads were positioned in five places all around the circumference of the cartridge casing look-alike. This assortment of momentum apparatus meant it always had purchase, even more so within the hole the 'bot was boring into.

He set it down in front of the rapidly cooling, liquefied hole. Beane had made in the ancient lock. The drillbot went to work immediately, and wisps of smoke started to drift out of the hole before the little machine disappeared into it. Bits of chewed up metal spat out behind the little autonomous device. Ignoring the high-pitched whine of metal on metal, Donovan turned to Beane.

"You think maybe we should have brought some guns? Or, one of the badasses roaming the complex?"

The balding, stocky man that had been Donovan's equal at Hidora Neo for years looked at him with a mischievous gleam in his eyes.

"I've got the guns right here," Beane giggled and slapped both his biceps. "Maybe *you* need guns!" He laughed heartily and pointed behind him on the floor. "Plus, what do you think is in that duffel bag?"

Donovan ran giddily to the huge bag and unzipped it. He squealed with delight as he pulled out a Mossberg 590A1 Tactical shotgun. The pistol grip, pump-action beauty had an adjustable stock, ghost ring sights, and held 9 slugs. Donovan worked the pump-action, racking a slug into the chamber with the satisfying *ka-chunk* that was synonymous with shotguns the world over.

"Fan-fucking-tastic," Lou said as he stared at the firearm like it was an ancient relic of immense power.

Beane rolled his eyes, then glanced back behind them in the direction of the large door they had come through to get into the Pangea machine chamber. His paranoia at being here, against explicit orders was increasing. Beane had installed the cameras in the creation chamber himself, however, so it would take a while for any of the current staff to figure out the deceptive loop they were on.

Once more, Beane's eyes crawled over the otherworldly architecture of the room, luminated everywhere by lights installed by Hidora Neo years before. The artificial rock walls and ceiling of the atrium spanning above their heads. The tentacles upon tentacles of hoses and cables made of unknown bio-metallic materials that ran everywhere around the Pangea machines. His eyes reluctantly crept to the creature makers, themselves. How they made the things they made, he would never understand -- he didn't think anyone *truly* did -- but they were veritable scientific wonders.

Someday, he hoped to putz with one. A giant millipede of some sort would be his monster of choice. After checking the cameras and finding himself satisfied they were still covert -- even though he had no way of actually knowing -- Beane turned back to the task at hand. He looked at the door lock -- steam, metal pieces, and sparks spitting out of the hole the tiny boring device had disappeared into.

"Five minutes, Lou," Beane said. "There are several flashlights in the duffel; attach one to the brackets on the front of your Mossberg. It's gonna be dark in there."

Donovan sarcastically saluted him and dug back into the bag.

Once Donovan had found a light, he began attaching it to the shotgun's barrel. Beane moved to the duffel bag and picked up a bulky object from behind. He slipped on backpack straps then pulled the cumbersome, box-shaped object onto his back. It was an olive-green metal frame housing three different compressed gas bottles; two cylindrical and one spherical.

The two cylinders' hoses merged together into one hose, and the sphere had a hose of its own. The two gas lines ran down to the bottom right corner of the frame, where they came together but were still separate from each other. After about five feet of slack hose exuded from the bottom corner of the backpack and connected into the stock of a weapon resembling a rifle. It sported pistol grips at both the front and back ends. The back grip was also paired with a trigger. The barrel of the weapon ended in a large cone with a two-inch diameter opening.

"This is an M9A1-7 flamethrower, Lou," Beane declared proudly in response to the wide-eyed, slack-jawed Donovan's face. "U.S. used them in 'Nam. This one is a special request I called in to Capt. Hodder last year when we were doing the final debugs on the drillbots. I planned on using it specifically for today. Woot! Woot!"

Donovan scowled at Jean-Paul's attempt to be hip, declining to comment on how easily he had gotten Hodder to obtain the antiquated weapon. "Fuck you, Bean-curd. Don't be using that magnificent bastard in close quarters. I don't want to get roasted." He pointed to the duffel bag. "I saw Petunia in there; I'm sure Daisy is, too. Put the char machine down and pick up at least one of those Eagles."

Beane grinned mischievously and tipped his head in a nod down to his side. Moving the flamethrower still clasped in his hands aside, he revealed the .50 Desert Eagle in a hip holster. Each of them had received plenty of combat and weapons training from the Captain himself, and Beane had talked Hodder into showing him how to handle the massive caliber pistols. After trying to train with them for a week with near disastrous results, Hodder made the bearded engineer do some strength training as well. This made the engineer at least competent with two of the massive weapons, though he rarely fired more than one at a time. An old scar on his forehead was his reminder of the reason for that discretion.

"Daisy is right where she belongs, you loopy fool," he said. He made no move to take the flamethrower off, however. "The torch stays, 'cause we don't know what's in there. You need another gun, though. Grab something semi or fully automatic."

Donovan reached up and stroked his curly beard that was mostly pepper with some salt. His long, wavy black hair, also lightly salted, snaked out from underneath the folded bandana skullcap on his head. After ten seconds of thought, Lou looked up. He grinned and snapped his fingers.

"MP5! Love the three-round burst and fully auto options! Penetration is shit, but it will complement the Mossberg."

Beane rolled his eyes at Donovan's comment. The only thing nerdier than the way he talked about firearms was the browser history on his PC.

Donovan was back in the bag and back out again in the blink of an eye, now with a submachine gun in his hands. Slightly less than two feet long with the collapsible stock extended, the MP5 could fire around 800 rounds in a minute, making up for the small 9mm cartridges it fired. Checking the magazine and then slamming it back into place, Donovan looked at Beane and nodded at the door.

"Let's do this."

Beane laughed and strode slowly towards the door, the awkwardness of the flamethrower painfully obvious. Donovan followed closely behind. They looked at the spot where the drillbot had gone to work, boring through the door's security device in an attempt to free the seized-up locking mechanism. The drillbot's whirring was barely audible from its current position inside the thick piece of metal.

"It's almost through," Donovan said. "Let's hope this works. I'm having a tough time with how easy this has been. I mean, what are the odds that an alien door is similar enough to ours for our 'bot to open it?"

"Not too shabby maybe, if they're a humanoid species, but I know what you mean," Beane replied. "I feel like we're getting away with murder. Or, playing the story mode on a video game."

"Are those two things similar to you?" Donovan joked.

Beane glared at him. "No, you fuckhead! This is just too easy for how naughty we are being."

"*'You naughty kittens, you lost your mittens, and now you shall have no pie.'*"

"Exactly," Beane said. "Wait. What?" His face scrunched up in confusion at the children's book quote Donovan had volunteered. "What the hell does that have to do with this?"

"*'We're not in Kansas anymore, Toto?'*" Lou's face held a crooked smirk.

"Don't start with me, Dorothy," Beane warned Donovan, who started to giggle. "Besides, you look more like one of the flying monkeys' asses, anyway."

Donovan's face fell into disappointment, and he opened his mouth to retort.

A muffled clink from the other side of the door erased the flippancy he had been about to unleash on his platonic better half. The sound was followed by the small robot's engine revving as it retreated from the hole. Beane grabbed it and instantly dropped it by the composite case, shaking his gloved hand, furiously. The smell of burnt leather joined the rancid organic stench still lingering in the air. Bile rose up to both men's' throats at the combination of the two scents. Beane shook his hand faster.

"Hot! Holy crap!"

Donovan laughed at him. "Of course, it is, dumbass! Thanks for making the bog of eternal stench angry. God, that smells!"

"Shut up, Lou. Get the crowbar."

Donovan reached down by the cutting torch at his right side and plucked up the thick crowbar waiting there. He walked to the doors and swiftly jammed the wedged end in between. The metal groaned in protest as he dug in and pried back and forth. Eventually, it yielded to the simple human tool.

Suddenly, the fist-dented door cracked open with an incredibly loud thunk, stopping dead after opening only about a foot. A groaning metal noise warned them before it suddenly flew open wide as if on automatic. The large door squealed like a tortured dog the entire way before it smacked into Donovan, knocking him to the floor. The rank air inside quickly flooded the hallway instead of just the mere trickle the scent had been before.

"Shit!" Donovan yelled as his ass hit the ground, one hand immediately going to cover his nose.

Getting back up again, he let the MP5 hang at his side as he rubbed his keister with his other hand. Meanwhile, Beane just *stared* into the dark room beyond. The room's putrid, rotting smell -- like a great white shark's breath after a fish and excrement dinner -- hit them both once more. This time it was seemingly a fresh wave of stench, and both men had to swallow the bile rising in their throats from the pungent fumes the mystery room had expelled.

Yet, the stubborn engineers – in truth a pair of Sadako's much-beloved Orphans – were somewhat stupid for such intelligent men. A sealed door with a punch mark the size of a beach ball accompanied by the organic stench of death was not enough of a combined warning sign for the evil *Big Bang Theory* rejects with beards. They had transformed metaphorically from playing mice to that of curiosity-stricken cats. And as everyone knows, that affliction kills.

"What in this universe could smell like *that?*" Donovan asked while still holding his nose with one hand.

"Ugh. Whatever it is, it's dead," Beane declared. "Nothing alive could smell like that."

Donovan shone his shotgun-mounted flashlight into the unlit room. It did not reveal much, the blackness inside was refusing to give up without a fight. Somewhere inside the room, something shuffled with a wet, scraping sound. After a moment, they heard it again, the second time from a different direction. The second sound's faintness indicated that the chamber beyond must be another massive room, also given how both noises had echoed in the unseen space past the open doorway. Neither of the sounds were all that far into the dark Pandora's box they suddenly realized at once they had opened.

Beane backed up. "Get back, Lou. Let's light this place up first," he quietly said, fear edging his voice. "Something's in there, I can feel it -- like it's fingering my brain or something."

Donovan also retreated away from the yawning doorway and quickly met his friend at the composite case. The men moved their equipment and supplies out of the open corridor and back into the Pangea Machine room. They organized everything half-assed, then Beane went back to the composite case full of 'bots.

Beane was lifting out trays on the collapsible racking they were connected to. He then pulled three things from the largest compartment at the bottom. The Orphan engineer came away with two small, six-wheeled vehicles, and what looked like a video game controller with a retractable antenna. He pulled the small tapering antenna out and turned on the device.

Each vehicle he had removed from the case looked like a housefly's eye on wheels. Each 'bot's multi-faceted dome contained a variety of different light spectrums. They included, but were not limited to; UV, Infrared, night vision, blinding daylight, and even one that Donovan called "glow stick" for its phosphorescent green luminescence. Beane handed one to his fellow Orphan, and the men walked out and placed them both in the hall where the gaping, black doorway of death waited like the jaws of the Abyss. Beane looked at Donovan, who switched on the controller he had been handed.

"Ready?" Beane looked his adopted sibling and best friend in the eye, all business.

Donovan readied his MP5, awkwardly balancing the controller so he could switch the weapon to fire semi-auto, then clicked off the safety.

"Do it." His fear-laced eyes did not hide the readiness in them.

Beane nodded in response and pushed forward on the stick on his own controller.

Beane drove the glowbot he had placed on the floor into the dark. The three LED readouts on the controller told him how far it was from the remote-controlled devices. When it reached twenty yards, it stopped dead, an audible thunk sounding from inside the room. Beane hit the button on the top left of the remote.

The black room came alive in a toxic green glow. The two men stood frozen in awe at the sight before them, even standing as far back as they were from the doorway. The room's ceiling was easily fifty feet up and comprised of a series of truss-like archways. They were pitch black and made of some smooth, obsidian-like material along their entire surface. That was except for a series of reflective spots positioned in the archway middle and at symmetrical, rigid intervals in the center of each side truss. They clipped the controllers to a handy bracket each wore on their belts, made to secure a variety of tools. Then the two Orphan engineers advanced, walking right up to the doorway with their weapons raised, and gawked further.

The reflective spots on the trusses reminded both men of the material used in the safety vests, warning signs, and high-visibility equipment used by construction crews. Barely refracting the electric-glowstick-on-wheels' dim illumination, the spots on each truss told more of the room's length. Both men could see the spots shining back at them for at least 100 yards. Donovan gasped and the sudden intake of air was loud as thunder in the silent, empty chamber past the opening.

Beane looked at Lou in wide-eyed alarm. He shook his head slowly in disbelieving contempt, taking the other glowstick-bot's controller from the loose-lipped man's belt clip. Not needing it, Beane placed the controller he originally had on the floor next to him. His head turned and glared at Donovan like a scornful teacher taking a student's smartphone away in class.

Beane hit the accelerator on the second bot and it shot out and into the chamber, veering around where the first came to a stop – the obstruction likely an uneven protrusion in the floor that was barely visible in the faint light -- and rolled past the incapacitated first 'bot into the darkness. The sound of the little electric motor suddenly ceasing told them it had stopped somewhere past where the reach of the previous 'bots' light ended. Donovan glanced at the controller in Beane's hands, the remote-control display reading a distance of 100 feet for the second 'bot. Beane playfully raised his eyebrows up and down twice, looking devilish in the meager green glow, his finger flirting with the button to activate the light on the second machine.

He mouthed, "1...2..."

A gigantic form tore into the dim light of the glowbot and plowed into Beane where he stood in the gaping doorway. The remote control flew out of his hands, hit the wall behind Donovan, then clattered onto the floor. The two LED displays were still lit. Donovan turned back to the monster on top of his good friend and brother from a fucked-up family.

"Jean-Paul!" he yelled.

He unleashed the MP5 and a torrent of 9mm firepower ripped into the hulking, twelve-foot mass before him. The bullets tore countless holes into its flesh, and thick cobalt ichor sprayed out from each new wound in the monster's hide. It let out a loud, baritone screech like a lower pitched eagle's cry.

Then the creature stood up to its full height -- which was probably closer to twenty feet. Its form cleared the height of the ceiling-less hallway's walls - then turned around to face Donovan. The man almost pissed himself when he glimpsed the mind-scrambling face.

Its head was shaped like an acorn, wide at the top and curving down to a pointed chin. That was *all* there was, however. There was no nose or mouth to speak of -- just a slimy-looking, featureless face.

The top --or cap -- of the acorn-shaped head consisted of five long protuberances, similar to an Asterozoa (starfish). These each stuck out at angles almost identical to the oceanic comparison. At the end of each of the appendage-like stalks glared a blazing red eyeball. The identical blood-colored orbs contained a jagged pupil that glowed with a prismatic hue and zig-zagged vertically down the middle of every respective oculus.

In between each of the main eye stalks sat globular piles of a snot-colored, mossy-like substance. It was a greenish goo that seemed to be growing from the spaces in-between the five stalks like hair sprouts from an armpit. Out of each mound of grossness was a multitude of smaller eyes. Every one of these orbs and their stalks looked similar to writhing maggots the size of fat caterpillars.

In place of a voracious head, they instead ended in an almost human eyeball. These smaller eyes had the same white sclera that *Homo sapien* eyes do, making up most of the ocular spheres. An iris and equally human-like pupil filled the center of each eye. The irises, however, were a color that Donovan had never seen before. A shimmering, liquid… *colour.* One that seemed to suck him in…

Beane groaned on the floor behind the creature, Donovan snapping back to reality at the sound. The standing man brought the MP5 to bear on the hulking brute and pulled the trigger. Numerous rounds of ammunition ripped into the thing's muscular chest, liquefying it in a matter of seconds, but not deterring the monster. A rock-solid, meaty fist the size of a twenty-pound propane cylinder struck a concussive blow to the side of his head, sending Donovan spinning through the air. He landed ten feet away in a crumple on the floor, his weapon flying from his hands. There he lay unmoving.

Satisfied, the lumbering hulk turned back to Beane but found the man standing again, though on visibly shaking legs and sporting a bloody, smashed face. His nose was clearly broken, given the odd angle it jutted out from his face, as well as the blood pouring from the nostrils that cascaded down his beard. He spat red from his mouth and raised the business end of the flame-thrower attached to him. The backpack was a couple of feet behind him on the floor. There was an audible click as he engaged the ignition, and a small flame flared to life from the end of the weapon's nozzle. The thing bent its head and looked quickly at the plume of fire, just as Beane brought the nozzle up to greet its hideous face.

"Mwahahaha, fucker!" he shouted, and squeezed the trigger.

Flames vomited out of the nozzle, instantly coating the thing with the burning mixture of gases as if it were liquid fire. The star-headed thing backpedaled, flailing like a severed worm, and the ear-shredding shriek it emitted hurt Beane's ears almost enough to drop the flamethrower to cover them. The panicking monster tripped over Donovan's prone form behind it and fell clumsily to the floor just inside the newly breached room, where it was bathed in the green light of the 'bots on the floor.

The flames burned down quickly, however, soon snuffing themselves out entirely -- no doubt thanks to the thing's slimy skin coating. The Starhead barely moved where it lay inside the room. The top half of its body was now mostly black char, and blue blood covered everything else. The fungal eyes growing between its central eyestalks were gone, melted down to solidified syrup. A gory portion of the eye remnants covered the strange black floor on either side of the doorway's threshold, the melted sludge knocked loose from the burnt face when it tripped over Donovan's body.

"Gawdamn Starhead," Beane muttered in an obvious imitation of southern drawl.

Beane dropped the incendiary weapon and ran to the man's motionless form. He checked for a pulse and -- finding a good one -- pulled his cohort back down the small corridor to the Pangea room. All the while he trained one of his Desert Eagles -- Daisy -- on the heap of alien laying barely inside the breached room. *Pandora's room,* he thought.

Beane managed to drag Donovan just outside of the corridor and into the Pangea room proper. His own beaten body made the task somewhat difficult, but he persevered.

"Just what the fuck *are you doing, Orphan?"* An angry voice shouted behind him in the expanse of the Pangaea room.

Beane looked back over his shoulder. Five men from Ripley Station's security team were running his way, all armed with M-16's.

CHAPTER 3

Ripley Station
Antarctica

The soldiers were dressed in dark black ops gear with forest green stripes running down each side to the waistline. These were the main force in the complex, save for two men that were absent from the group surrounding him.

The man who had barked at Beane was Sgt. Bottin. A tall, uncomfortably lanky man, he reminded Beane of one of the blue people in that *Avatar* movie everyone loved so much over a decade prior. Long, gangly limbs were the soldier's identifying characteristics when they all wore the same gear. He was a reserved man, only talking when it seemed necessary, but was usually angry when he did.

This was one of those times.

"Who the hell told you two gearheads to come down here and breach that door? God only knows what you've done!"

The bald man's face was beet red, with several veins trying valiantly to pulse their way out of his forehead. Then he saw the dark mass lying greenlit on the floor inside the wide-open room that had previously been sealed for centuries. His jaw dropped, and his rifle came up. The other four men mimicked their superior and raised their weapons. Beane reached the security team's position with his unconscious friend's limp form. He laid Donovan down and stood up, still pointing Daisy at the downed creature.

41

"Don't fucking help me or anything, you assholes," he muttered under his breath as he looked down at his fallen friend.

Then he turned to face Bottin.

"Well, Sarge, I'd say we activated a security system when Lou and I breached that door, releasing that guy on the floor over there," he pointed towards the downed creature with his Desert Eagle. "Either that, or he's been stuck in here for thousands, if not millions of years. Conscious, alive, and locked up in the buried part of the ship." Beane met the tall man's furious, grey eyes. "I'm pretty sure the former is the case, sir. I'm almost positive he wasn't alone, either."

A deeply muted eagle's shriek exploded from the unexplored room, confirming the statement. The five soldiers jerked like they had been shocked by the loud sound. Their weapons locked themselves onto the open doorway, trained on the downed creature who had yet to stir. Seconds ticked by feeling like minutes, until sweat beaded on everyone's foreheads.

The second alien exploded out of the dim green light and covered half the distance to the soldiers before any of them could react, stunned by the sight before them. One of the men pissed himself but kept his aim. Fear jerked his trigger finger before he could center the sights on the thing's head, and he unleashed a premature hell storm of bullets. Spurred by the gunfire, the rest of the squad followed suit.

Hundreds of rounds pierced the charging beast's flesh. Its rich, ocean-colored blood sprayed the floor and nearby walls of the corridor it charged down to get to them. It shrieked again but did not slow. The star-head plowed into the pissed pants soldier, stepping on him in the process. Its clawed, heavy tree trunk-like foot pierced the man's dark armor and punched straight into his abdomen. Crimson spurted out from between the thorn-like toes as the soldier's body was smashed into the floor.

The squashed man's bones crunched under the Starhead's weight as it stopped to pull both mighty arms back behind it. Then it launched both huge, rocky fists into the two soldiers who were standing behind the first soldier. Both men flew backward through the air, arcing up slightly before landing in two motionless heaps thirty feet away with a sickening, wet crunch.

Thick, cobalt blue blood gushed from the multitude of bullet holes decorating the lumbering thing's body like sadistic acupuncture. Its five red eyes darted back and forth at the remaining four men, including Donovan on the ground. The dozens of fungal eyes in between the main eyestalks not damaged in the gunfire whipped around, constantly keeping tabs on the remaining men as their hypnotic hues swirled and shimmered.

The remaining member of the security team besides Bottin -- a man named Miner -- pointed his rifle at one of its bony knees and proceeded to blast the hell out of it with his M-16. The rounded leg joint practically vaporized under the concentrated fire. The mighty beast was brought down to one knee. A huge, armored hand shot out and grabbed Miner in its crushing grip. He cried out in pain as it squeezed.

Beane roared in an adrenaline-fueled fury and leaped onto the thing's broad back. He growled in agony as he managed to climb up to the monster's shoulders. There, he brought Daisy up to its fiendish head, and buried it into the fungal eye mass. A muffled whump resonated from within, accompanied by kickback that Beane almost forgot to brace for, and was followed by an eruption of dark fluid from the opening on top of its head. Beane could see jagged, triangular teeth-gnashing within the gore pouring out of the orifice on top of its skull. It was the alien's mouth.

Suddenly, a long tentacle shot out of the tooth-filled opening. It flailed about, trying to grab him, but Beane pushed off its back, landing harshly on his ankle with a shout of pain. He pulled himself away from the thing, sliding backwards on his ass like a dog. Before he could get out of the way, the twenty-foot creature toppled towards him and landed on his legs -- pinning him and eliciting another painful howl. Bottin ran to him, along with a gasping Miner, and the two men pulled the huge body up far enough, giving Beane room to free himself.

"You okay, Beane?" Bottin asked as Miner took to checking Donovan's pulse.

Beane nodded. "Yeah, get him to medical, though." He jerked his thumb towards the unconscious man on the floor. "He took a good hit when the other one first attacked. He was thrown into the wall in there."

Miner picked Lou up and threw him over his broad shoulder. The former was a huge guy, looking like a defensive tackle from the NFL, and the engineer was a sack of potatoes to him.

"Will do. I'll brief the nerd squad in the labs, too." The giant, German American man grinned and started towards the door leading out of the Pangaea machine room and the spaceship itself. The medical facilities were just outside of the spacecraft.

"What the fuck did you guys do?" Bottin asked Beane after Miner had left. "Sōzō is going to kill you. And Captain Hodder will if she doesn't."

"Yeah... I kind of realized we made a mistake when we heard these ugly buggers moving around in there. Lou and I figured we'd get some answers to the forty years of questions everyone has had since Sadako found this."

Beane looked up at Bottin, bloody cuts and scrapes all over his face, as well as a good shiner puffing up his left eye. Never mind the twisted thing that used to be his nose.

"We didn't get far."

"No shit. You got three of my men killed for your curiosity," he said, pointing to the dead men laying in pools of their own blood on the floor. "There had better be something damned important in that part of the ship, Beane. Or else I'm going to add to your cuts and bruises. You got that?" He locked eyes with the remaining engineer, fury radiating from them. "I know you're one of Sadako's adopted kids and you and Lou are the golden boys for figuring out what the golden geese run on."

Bottin pointed at the Pangea Machines before he leaned down and stuck his face in Beane's. Coffee breath made the Orphan's eyes water. "But I don't like it when disobedient, spoiled *brats* get my men killed because they were messing around where they had no business being! If it were up to me, I'd have shot you already." Spit flew from his mouth as the big man growled down at Beane.

Bottin's big head flew forward, smashing into Beane's face and crushing his nose again, which had never actually stopped bleeding.

Beane dropped to the floor, screaming while holding his nose as blood poured out from between his fingers.

"You dirty sheep fucker! What the fuck is wrong with you?" Beane clutched his spurting face, trying vainly to staunch the flow.

"Now get the fuck up and get to medical before you bleed out. I don't want to see you again today." Bottin's hand went to his earpiece. "Miner, this is Bottin. Round up some of the lab guys and pull Coscarelli and Hansen off their rounds. We need to secure these things and the Pandora's box that our resident jesters opened."

"Yes, sir," Miner confirmed in Bottin's ear.

Beane was up and limping towards the exit door. "Be careful, asshole," he shot back over his shoulder. "We don't know those that Starheads are dead for sure, or what else is in that room. And now you're all alone."

He pushed through the swinging door and made his way out of the ship towards the medical building.

"Fucking punk-ass Orphan," Bottin mumbled under his breath after the door had closed behind Beane.

He looked up and into the room twenty yards from where he was. The green light was still lit in the front part of the newly opened room. That was it, though. No prone monster to be seen illuminated in the green glow that emanated in the open doorway the things had come out of.

Where the hell did it go? The beast that Donovan and Beane had felled was completely gone. A pool of black ooze was all that remained. *How did it get up without anyone noticing?* His blood ran cold. Bottin keyed his mic.

"Miner, this is Bottin. Come in. Over."

"Go ahead, Sarge. Over."

"What's your current ETA? Over."

"Five to ten minutes, sir," Miner's voice chimed back into the headset. "Just waiting for Hansen to get back. He was about as far away from base on his rounds as is possible. Over."

"Well, tell him to meet you down here. I need backup, A.S.A.P. The thing the monkey-wrenchers shot up is missing. Over"

"Copy that, sir. Coscarelli and I will head down now, with a couple of the eggheads. Be there in three. Over and out."

Bottin exhaled in relief. He could not believe it, but he was scared as hell. The way that thing moved, the way it crushed his first man Jackson like he was thin ice on a street puddle... that would never be unseen. He looked down at the poor man's disaster of a corpse. *No man should ever be reduced to a pulp like that.* Then he looked back at the piles of limbs that used to be Polanski and Cameron. Bile rose in his throat.

The way they looked reminded him of a video game he played in the late '90s in his college dorm room on his PlayStation. It was about an Indiana Jones rip-off of a woman from England with better firearms experience and ridiculous mammaries. *Tomb Raider*. He liked to save his game when he got frustrated with the anal-retentive controls, placing her on top of cliffs. Then he would make her swan dive to her demise. When she hit, she would crumple into a heap of broken limbs, just like his men were now. The nostalgic comparison his brain had put together released the bile from his throat and he vomited onto the monster's legs.

The fallen thing sat up immediately, snagging Bottin's entire head in one massive hand. It began squeezing. Crushing pain and severe panic were all Bottin could feel. His vision and breathing were cut off by the huge palm covering his entire face and chin. With the last of his fight, he brought his rifle up to the thing's smooth, acorn-shaped chin, and emptied his clip. The bullets ricocheted all over the room -- some bouncing back and into Bottin's chest and appendages, some deflecting off the hard, chitinous shell of the thing's acorn face. He felt his own skull begin to fracture and pop, ratcheting the pain up tenfold. His already high-pitched, muffled cry turned to a piercing shriek.

The massive amount of point-blank gunfire finally cracked the thing's smooth face, and it split open, allowing ten or so of the M16 rounds into what was its braincase. Its grip finally broke the man's skull, imploding Bottin's head to chunky mush before dropping the lifeless body to the ground.

The thing swayed back and forth like a shitfaced drunk as brain matter fell out of the gaping hole in the protective cover for its larger, but almost human-shaped brain. The beast up and dropped like a lead balloon, landing on Jackson and Bottin's corpses, further crushing them both.

Seconds passed. Nothing moved.

The green light in the newly opened room that Beane and Donovan had first lit was abruptly snuffed out, coupled with a glass and metallic crunching noise. Pandora's room was plunged back into darkness once again.

More seconds ticked away.

Silence.

Suddenly a muscular, hammer-like fist reached out, grabbing the door's edge and slamming it shut, the loud noise echoing throughout the ship.

CHAPTER 4

Nippon X Station
Somewhere off the coast of Japan

Somewhere in the confines of the organization's northern Asiatic headquarters, the Hidora Neo elite were stationed at their controls for world domination through kaiju. The room resembled the command bridge of a certain starship created by Gene Roddenberry. Sadako had requested the customization personally. The late 1960s show was a staple of her childhood up until her mother's demise.

There would be a reemergence of her fondness for it once again in the '80s, but her personal views on life made the next generation of enterprising crew members seem so blind and ignorant to her. Even then Sadako was already up to her neck in the rising waters of evil she was immersing herself in with her family's legacy. There was little room for choice in her life, but she had accepted the life God or fate had delivered to her.

Round in design, with multiple view screens at the front of the room, and containing a crew of seven, the Japanese war room for Hidora Neo was very simply decorated, imitating the science fiction show. The control room was painted a neutral, bluish-gray color, from the floor to the ceiling. In the middle of the rotund space sat Sadako's chair, designed like a throne. It was an elaborately carved frame, with plush, red velvet upholstery, in stark contrast to the room's colors. The armrests had various controls and switches, as well as a detachable wireless keyboard. The mix of old and new eras made Sadako look almost otherworldly when she sat in it.

In front of Sadako, past a small grey wall bordering the throne's elevated dais, Tsuburaya sat at his own elaborate workstation on the lower front level, nearest to the screens. His chair was functionally futuristic looking in comparison to his leader's. Tsuburaya was her main man in the room, even though both he and the bloke across from him were the same age as her father would have been.

While Tsuburaya was on her left, to her right sat Dr. Ifukube at a virtually identical workstation. He was Dr. Tsuburaya's own assistant. Both men were also positioned facing the gigantic wall of view screens, which were showing multiple angles of Duluth's recent destruction at the hands of their first ever daikaiju assault.

Behind Sadako, four of Tsuburaya's minions stood and ran diagnostic programs at separate stations. The students from Hidora Neo's secretive university and training center were monitoring each of the vital signs for Nippon X's own menagerie of grown daikaiju. The three young females and one male spoke rapidly back and forth to each other as they compared the pages of data. The bevy of computers they stood at cast multiple colors across their determined faces as their fingers flew faster than some of the best receptionists.

"All specimens are resting comfortably, Dr. Sōzō. Our welcoming party for the mainland of Japan is on track for our surprise visit," the lone male student declared. "All kaiju have healthy vitals and optimal DNA blending… foreign strands remaining at 2%. The genetic structure is still sound."

"Very good, Dr. Kaneko. Continue to monitor them. I want readouts every four hours."

"Hai." Kaneko bowed and resumed the flurry of fingers across his keyboard.

His three co-workers followed suit, relaying statistics to him constantly. Sadako turned to the man sitting across from Tsuburaya.

"Dr. Ifukube, I want you to find the six strongest specimens from this batch, and work with your team on stimulating additional growth. Is that understood?"

Ifukube nodded once in confirmation. Sadako stood up from her chair, stretching her spine and back muscles out as she did so. A yawn tried to escape her, but she suppressed it.

Sadako sauntered up to the wall of screens and stood gazing at images galore of the giant turtle monster with its primeval fish head. Her hands remained clasped behind her back and her legs stood shoulder length apart. At '5'6", she was slightly above average for a Japanese woman. Her hair was pulled back in a bun and staked through the middle with a pair of silver hair sticks. One thick strand had escaped and traced the contours of the left side of her face. Sadako's uncharacteristic blue eyes shimmered like icy Arctic ocean, betraying her less than pure lineage. It also explained her Germanic nose and full lips, cause for unspoken disdain among her countrymen.

Her mother -- a strong, German-born American immigrant with a razor-sharp wit and cunning intelligence -- had been ripped from her when she was fifteen. The tragedy had preceded her father's ousting from Bionautics, Inc. The company was formed during World War II by her grandfather, Toshio Sōzō. The elder Sōzō's unexpected fatal heart attack in the following decade passed control of Bionautics to his heir. That was her father, Ishiro, in the late 1950s. For twenty odd years, Ishiro Sōzō made Bionautics into a successful biologic and technologic innovator, especially given the time period. Their research and developments in multiple fields changed the biotech game several times over.

Once the company went corporate in the 1970s, however, the board of directors and the company's principal shareholders began scheming to remove Ishiro from his CEO status and take his company from him. Once he was dethroned, they could make deals with other countries besides Japan and America. This was something Ishiro was hesitant to do, for fear of the technology falling into the hands of terrorists or communist dictators.

Things finally culminated in the mid-'70s when Sadako's mother was killed in a car crash on her way to pick Sadako up from school. The spring day had been sunny, with no fog or precipitation present. Her car was found *fused* with a tree -- the Toyota Corona physically touching itself where it had wrapped around the far side of a giant oak. A matching series of skidding tire marks indicated she had swerved to avoid something, but no further evidence as to what that was could be found, and the investigation into her death had been considered closed.

Upon examination of the disastrous wreck and its mangled contents, however, a series of cooked accounting books were found in the trunk. The ledgers were seemingly records of embezzlement and fraud on Ishiro and Gretchen Sōzō's behalf. Although forged as hell, the planted accounting ledgers easily gave the board the evidence they needed to exile him from his company and land him in jail for ten years. Four years into his sentence was as far as he made it.

In 1980, Ishiro was hospitalized from an inoperable brain tumor. The last seven months of his life were spent contacting all his loyal former employees from Bionautics and current employees from his new private organization, Hidora Neo. In those months, Ishiro and his army of trustworthy employees who saw his vision on "helping" the human race -- and making a lot of money along the way -- had put a contingency plan together for his only daughter Sadako to take over immediately upon his passing.

The new Hidora Neo then initiated the insane Daikaiju Directive. Through the directive, they financed and sponsored the expedition to Antarctica, as well as the building of the on-site labs. Hidora Neo earned its way from what was basically black-market science and was more than able to cover the equipment, scientists, and motley crew of assorted ex-soldiers, assassins, and mercenaries that protected her and her team of geniuses, all supervised by Bruce Hodder.

When Ishiro Sōzō lost his fight and finally passed on, everything had already been up and running smoothly for over a month. Assets from various accounts, funds, and sponsors of all legalities began flowing and Sadako was in business. Medical technology was becoming big business at the beginning of the last decade of the Cold War... especially the illegal kind.

After some extensive Antarctic survival training with Hodder and his troops, they had gone to the seemingly barren frozen wasteland, following her father's notes and journal. Sadako's rage and ambition

51

fueled her desire to find this great discovery that Ishiro had been unable to harvest. Since the "accidental" death of her mother five years prior, she had prepared on her own, and her family members and friends soon consisted of hardened mercenaries and deranged scientists.

She knew Captain Hodder well before they had begun the Antarctic training. Trained in a mixed bag of martial arts, melee, and firearms combat, Sadako was a regular badass by the time she reached the age of nineteen. When she was not developing her physical prowess, Sadako studied Academics. Rigorous homeschooling had begun after her mother's death and father's subsequent incarceration. All manner of math and sciences -- different fields of biology in particular -- were her forte. She was also taught everything she would need to excel at running the family business, quickly becoming adept at investing in the world markets in the process and locking away a personal nest egg outside of the company.

When Ishiro Sōzō passed his legacy onto Sadako, her schooling was put on hold until after the discovery at the bottom of the world and then once the Antarctic station was fully operational. Then she went to college officially. Only taking five years to graduate, she excelled at classes, being rewarded with early advancement for her efforts. Testing out of many classes from several different scientific fields in her freshman year at the University of Tokyo, she shocked her professors and intimidated most of her classmates. Her teen years spent in the labs with her father's best had paid off immensely.

Accomplishing in five years what took most much longer, she walked away with Ph.D.s in several of the biological and neurological sciences. She began working in Antarctica with Tsuburaya, Ifukube, and Brown daily until new stations had been built. By the early '90s, they had learned how to use the alien machines and had successfully created several living creatures purely from combining any DNA with a minuscule amount of the foreign genetic material that the still functioning cryo-storage units contained.

Fortune had smiled upon them the day they realized the source of power that ran the strange alien splicing machines. The freshly acclimated rookies Donovan and Beane -- her now crack engineers -- figured out the damn thing ran on freshwater. Parked on a continent covered in ice and snow, the reason for its continued operation became clear.

Staring at the screens of the chaos Hidora Neo had begun orchestrating forty years later, Sadako reflected on those first creations they had grown, with both joy and sadness.

They had created four living, breathing chimeras. The first was mostly made up of an anaconda, but they had given it large bat wings, as in the flying fox variety. Once the simple-minded thing figured out how to tuck its tail up, it could fly. It latched onto things with the chiropteran claws at the "elbows" of the wings, and the small mammalian feet growing out of its serpentine body three-quarters of the way down, right before its true tail started. It was not meant to be anything more than a successful creation.

The second such hybrid was a half saltwater crocodile, half brown bear. With a burly, shaggy body and legs of a grizzly bear, the creature had an armored, crocodilian head. Its thick, leathery skin ran down and protected the beast's back as well, finally ending in a crocodile's long, reptilian tail. It looked a like a grizzly wearing a crocodile's hide and head for a costume. However, when you saw the speckled eyes of a prehistoric remnant looking back at you, it did not look like just hide anymore.

The third chimera was also made with a bear, but a panda bear this time (at Sadako's giggly request.) The creature received a spinal adjustment, making it able to stand fully erect like a human. They also gave her two more arms... from a fiddler crab. Her name became Bearclaw amongst much laughter in the labs. Bearclaw was feisty, however, and was never taken lightly when it came to feedings and examinations. Two scientists had been ripped limb from limb by the genetic monstrosity. As a result, five guards supervised any human-to-kaiju interactions with the female panda chimera, instead of the usual two. This ferocity pleased Sadako more than she let on.

The fourth, also Sadako's favorite, was a gorilla with the head of an elephant, including its tusks. The most intelligent of the four specimens, the beast learned how to open doors within his first month once his height had passed three feet. King Pachy, another bad Sadako joke, soon learned sign language. Shortly after, the two were nearly inseparable. Sadako became very attached, much to her colleagues' dismay.

One horrible day, exactly 392 days later, the four impossible creatures owned up to their probability. All four literally melted right before everyone's eyes, the sounds of which kept Sadako up for months after and still plagued her dreams. Her failure and helplessness, coupled with the beasts' painful demise, hardened the scientist and made her colder than ever. She vowed to do whatever it took to never fail again. She also promised herself that she would never love the creations, only respect and admire them from afar.

The team of brilliant, yet slightly mad minds found out through grueling trial and error that they needed a minimum of 1.34% "foreign" DNA to eliminate the shelf life on the specimens. This changed when they unlocked the secrets of the foreign samples later in the second half of the '90s. This new discovery also increased growth potential in the newly spliced creatures, something they took every advantage of, with minimal failed prototypes in the years that followed.

Twenty years and many creations later, Sadako stood on the precipice of vengeance, the burning images of Duluth on the news leaving little doubt. While only one of her father's mutinous board members had been devoured so far, Sadako had begun realizing her father's megalomaniacal dream: world domination; control over the fools who knew nothing yet ran everything.

The military had marked off restricted sectors and quickly constructed headquarters in Duluth's disaster zone. Soon after, a groundswell of medical aid and disaster relief followed, preceding an ugly wave of verminous reporters, looking for misery to feed upon in the name of informing the masses. As they did this, Sadako looked to the location of the next phase. Dr. West's progress report had been promising, and she looked forward to the next attack.

With the use of Mesozoic DNA, coupled with her specific conditions, West's monster would fall into the kaiju category, maybe even daikaiju, if she was lucky. Chicago would fall hard. With a happy little squeal -- barely heard by a smiling Dr. Tsuburaya

54

-- she turned and walked out of the control room, down the long corridor to her plush quarters. The schoolgirl spring in her step belied her fifty-some years as she practically skipped down the hallway to her small apartment.

***

At 3:15 a.m., Sadako's phone vibrated all over her nightstand, the irritating noise more than enough to rouse her from her sleep. She swore as she scooped it up from the table and answered.

"Yes? Why are you calling me at the witching hour?"

"Sadako, I apologize for waking you. This is Miner at Ripley Station. We have had a breach of the sealed door in the Pangea Chamber room. Donovan and Beane opened it after sabotaging the camera feeds. I don't think they were betraying you; I believe that curiosity finally killed the cat."

Sadako ground her teeth and dug her nails into her palms, her pulse quickening.

"What did they find inside?" She was trying to suppress her excitement, regardless of the fate of Donovan and Beane.

"Well, they found what, in my expert soldier opinion, seems to be the aliens the ship belongs to," Miner said over the muffled reception. "Or, at least their gatekeepers. Big fuckers, too."

Miner gasped then, his obvious realization that he had dropped an f-bomb to the woman who was basically his queen evident over the line.

Sadako smiled. "Relax, soldier. You do not offend me with your curses. I enjoy the crudeness of it, sometimes." She stopped with the pleasantries. "But why are you contacting me instead of Sergeant Bottin?"

"I brought Donovan back to the infirmary, and Bottin and Beane stayed back. Three of the squad that went down there to intercept besides Bottin and I were killed by a huge star-headed thing with five eyes. It had these globs of what looked like goo but had more eyes growing out of it. They were a really fucked up color, too. Looking at them made me want to rip my own face off a little."

"So Bottin was left with Jean-Paul? Alone."

The last part was a statement, and Miner must have caught that, as he did not reply.

Sadako continued. "Bottin hates the Orphans. Please go check on Beane at once, Miner, as a favor to me. I will owe you one." the smile influencing her voice was clear to the grunt down in Antarctica.

"Anything for you, ma'am."

"You may call me Sadako when it is just the two of us. I feel you've earned it during your time with Hidora Neo. Thank you for your service. I will see you in a few days."

"Yes, ma'am. Safe travels and good night."

CHAPTER 5

Superior X Station
Lake Superior, North America

Dr. Emmet West was in absolute awe, mostly of himself. The mega-sized beast floating in ochre-colored amniotic fluid in front of him was beyond his wildest dreams. The small viewing room that West stood in was a small station full of monitoring equipment, as well as an extension of the station's main computer system. The scientist stood before a fifteen-foot-long, eight-foot-high viewing window. In the immense chamber beyond the thick, reinforced plexiglass, slept a monster. He had literally created a prehistoric chimera… with some modern and out of this world tweaks.

Now, soon after the world had survived a worldwide pandemic of a virus seemingly named after a beer, he gazed upon the greatest thing he had ever done. Actual tears of joy welled up in his eyes. Emmet Jeffery West had created a chimera.

A giant, city-stomping monster.

A *daikaiju*.

And it was beautiful.

It was a Mesozoic masterpiece of genetic engineering spliced together with the borrowed alien technology. With plenty of injections of growth hormones to go around and the added extraterrestrial DNA, it had grown to bc 110 meters long, or about 362 feet. Even though a quadruped, it would still stand 235 feet tall.

For the base creature, he had used a *Paralititan*, a gigantic sauropod like the formerly named *Brontosaurus* - now called *Apatosaurus*...or was it back to *Brontosaurus* again? He couldn't remember anymore. There was also *Camarasaurus*, *Diplodocus*, or better yet *Brachiosaurus*. The family of long-necked, massive herbivores were the migrating wildebeests, giraffes, and elephants of the Mesozoic age. *Paralititan* was a broad-shouldered, tank of an animal. Its front legs were taller and longer than the back pair - which were thick and sturdy, making it possible for *Paralititan* to rear up on its hind legs for very short periods of time, although some said that was a myth generated by the film, *Jurassic Park*.

West's monster did not have the head of a long-necked dinosaur, however.

It *did* have the three heads Sadako had asked him to produce at the end of their video conference.

Dr. West had grinned ear-to-ear and giggled like a hysterical schoolboy when he finally decided on his heads. Looking at all of them now as he reflected, the man was very happy with himself. In the center was the massive head of a *Tylosaurus*, a prolific, prehistoric marine predator. Its long dinocroc of a snout was filled with a full set of sharp, conical fangs that would make a *Tyrannosaurus Rex* jealous.

Stemming out on each side from between the main head and shoulders of the creature, West had added the long necks of two *Elasmosaurs,* complete with the smaller, needle-toothed heads of the plesiosaur family. They were fish-eating prehistoric marine reptiles that, like the *Tylosaurus*, normally sported flippers but possessed long, snake-like necks. The *Elasmosaurs* normally had a reach capacity with their hooked teeth that was longer than two-thirds of the creature's entire body length.

Emmet also marveled at his success with the monster's back plates. There were two rows of *Stegosaurus* plates. These misshapen pentagons ran along either side of its spine and continued down each length of the two tails West had given the beast. One sported the Gary Larson named thagomizer of a *Stegosaurus*. The other belonged to an *Ankylosaurus*, its business end all armor plating and tipped with a mean bone-club.

Just because he could, Emmet also added some extras. Using a sea urchin's genes, he was able to grow sharp, thick spines from the monster's already scaled back. They were not very long but looked to serve the intended purpose. These gave it some deadly protection for its dorsal side. Still somewhat mystified by the foreign DNA they used for creating monsters, West had no idea what, if any, sort of "breath weapon" or other strange natural weapons his creation might possibly have. He was still unclear of how Shellshock's strange blowtorch came to be. *Not that it would need it*, he mused, *but the little bit of my own DNA I incorporated might give this monster a couple of surprises.*

West took out a small, cylindrical device and pushed the one button positioned on the side with his thumb. It lit up, and he inhaled, puffing every now and then, and billowy clouds of vapor burst from his mouth. Soon the air smelled of the sweet electronic cigarette vapor that passed for "tobacco" flavor. West preferred an old fashioned, Sherlock-style pipe, but smoking wasn't allowed anywhere in Superior X. However, even with the almost banning of a valuable smoking cessation option, vapor was practically harmless to the life support systems and almost unnoticeable by the fire alarms, so he had gotten away with it since he'd arrived. His stash was rapidly dwindling, unfortunately.

While he puffed and let the vaporized nicotine flood his system and appease his addicted receptors, he again thought about what he was doing – although what Sadako and Hidora Neo were doing -- to the world. All the innocent people already trampled, burned, and eaten at their hands so far. Were their deaths necessary? Sadako was surely insane, as her father had been. His megalomaniacal goals had been nothing short of world domination through advanced, unstoppable technology. Biotechnology.

When he had been hired by Hidora Neo in the mid-eighties, West realized right away this would be his last job, ever. Retirement, getting fired, or quitting all would equal death. But the opportunity to find alien DNA was too good to be true. Now, he grinned, it *was* too good, and it *was* true.

West put his e-cigarette away and took a sip of his rapidly cooling coffee which was sitting on the small table next to him. He looked back out into the enormous metal womb before him, containing his very own Frankenstein's monster. As it floated in the orange amniotic fluid filling the chamber, he could see the chest rise and fall as it took breaths.

Three giant, hood-like air regulators came down from the ceiling of the chamber and were attached to each of the creature's heads, designed after the original machine's layout. He had given it three pairs of lungs, with each head getting its own set. It was a precaution put into place to help possibly save the other heads, should something put one or two out of commission. Dr. Brundle had thought he was crazy to try, but it was a success. The three esophagi came together after the lungs and emptied into a large, shared stomach.

Pushing his glasses back up the bridge of his nose in a very nerdy fashion, the five-foot-seven scientist turned and walked towards the hallway door opposite the observation window. The track lighting overhead reflected off his black hair as he walked under it. This lit up his spreading bald spot where the whorl of his crown once was. His deep brown eyes displayed his fierce determination -- and a little of his madness -- as he strode out of the dimly lit room, exiting into the hallway.

He turned left, walking down the series of connecting corridors to his room, where he began to get ready for bed. Tomorrow would be a big day for everyone, especially Emmet West, *monster maker*. He chuckled evilly at the juvenile title he had given himself. A little giddy, the normally reserved man suddenly burst into an acapella version of the late 70's TV show, *Three's Company*, belting out the ridiculous show's suggestive title theme as he climbed into bed for the night.

***

On the surface of the moon, some 238,000 miles plus from the Earth, the warrior awoke. His cryogenic chamber opened, thrusting him from his suspended animation like a space marine in a bug hunt movie. The door of the tubular chamber rose, flooding the small space with recycled, yet still fresher air, which caused his hard skin to crawl from the sudden change in temperature. Groggy and sluggish, the warrior practically fell from his resting place of the last thousand years, give or take. Eventually he stood, his four bare feet practically ice blocks on the cold, unforgiving floor. Glancing around and doing a mental check of his surroundings, the alien life form found everything as it should be.

Quickly approaching a bevy of oddly shaped monitors and strange computers at the front of the cramped room he was in, he sat down at the main console. He started to activate the different sensors and readouts available to him. Efficiency returned to the warrior, and it was like he had never been in a state of torpor.

While the sickness that commonly followed re-awakening from hypersleep began to take hold of his nutrient-starved body, the alien soldier typed several commands into the system. This brought up status reports and multiple types of video footage of what had caused his early defrosting. The last line of defense for his species stationed in this solar system -- as well as for the Earth itself -- was greeted with a steady, blaring alarm. Red lights flashed as the room shook. Then things clicked into place and the buried cockpit began its ascent to the surface of the moon.

Once the room he was in had risen to the full extent of its upward motion, the alien being left the cryo-chamber and walked briskly down the short hallway to the preparation area. There, he donned his environmental suit, consisting of a helmet, and thin, flexible material that made up his armor. From the prep area, he passed through the only other door in the room, entering his new home for the duration of his mission.

The relatively small cockpit, although bigger than anything humans were capable of designing, would serve him satisfactorily in the coming days and possibly weeks ahead. More screens and advanced consoles greeted him with their many lights, touchpads, buttons, levers, and switches. Smiling at the nostalgic familiarity of technology he hadn't touched in ages, the alien pilot sat in his chair - a slanted, ergonomic piece of functional furniture that allowed him maximum comfort with peak efficiency regarding his four legs. Strapping in and flipping switches to pull the room's contents closer and within his reach, the pilot activated the connection to his war machine.

A symphony of gears and machinery commenced as the modified room advanced along the moon's barren surface a few hundred feet before locking into place with something else buried beneath the surface. Lights and sounds signaled a successful merging and told him of a perfect connection, and suddenly the view out of the main screen dropped as he rose to the top of the mechanical monstrosity he was now a part of.

Automated beeps and rotating lights further confirmed his attachment to the main body of his mech, as he brought up the weapon systems checklist on the small screen to his left. He began to check and prime the various armaments located throughout the artificial husk's entirety. Finding everything to be as it should, the alien warrior nodded once in satisfaction, then took to the manual movement controls like he had never left them.

The giant mech's body lurched forward as it took its first steps in hundreds of years. Its metallic form walked awkwardly at first as he got used to the controls all over again, his place in the robotic defender's head giving him a nearly 360-degree view of the darkness shrouded landscape around him. Grinning through pointed teeth, the alien soldier went through the normal warm-up routines every operator was required to do upon initial assimilation.

Within minutes, he was confident in his abilities and ready to make the relatively short trip to the blue planet. His four arms with their six-fingered hands flew across the controls, initiating the appropriate sequences to begin his flight down to the larger life-filled planet below. To maximize the warrior's stealth, he switched on the cloaking technology, effectively bending light and invisible waves of every spectrum to camouflage his vessel from the many mechanical sensors orbiting the globe.

After the mech had seemingly dissolved into the air, its pilot took it up into space, shooting out towards Mars with a burst of the jets in the overlarge legs before swinging back around to head towards his destination.

The humans had opened doors they were never meant to, unleashing the life forces from two vastly different, very sinister species. Both were mortal enemies to all life in the galaxies, and his race existed solely to stop them in their conquests. The infernals that the company known as Bionautics had made bedfellows with concerned him slightly more than the near mortal elder race Hidora Neo had activated. Both were of major concern, regardless.

The best mech pilot currently awake in the universe, Volk'narr began his approach to the primitive world below, preparing to fight anything that threatened the balance he had been placed on the moon to keep so many years before.

As he made the journey to the surface, he familiarized himself with all that had transpired since he had last been awake. Calling up every available piece of information he could through his own computer's databases, as well as the cornucopia of data he happily hijacked from the planet itself, Volk'narr educated himself on the humans' history. He waded through the humans' massive information and communication networks, commonly known to them as the internet. He quickly skimmed through thousands of files every five minutes or so, learning and memorizing various events, inventions, people, and a host of other things -- far quicker than any human being could. Within an hour, Volk'narr had caught up to the twentieth century.

Then he discovered that century's music.

Starting with the big band and swing era, his alien auditory canals were almost instantly addicted to the merging of sounds from different instruments and voice boxes, all powered and operated by the still evolving species of primates' lungs. The audible bliss he experienced made him *happy*. It was a feeling he had almost forgotten about; he had been on duty for so long.

He wandered through decades of music, listening to songs here and there along the way, exploring different genres and subgenres. The reflection of the social and political environments affecting the music through the years was fascinating to him. Especially intriguing was the way their prejudices, relationships, vices, and protestations influenced so much of the way the general populace perceived and integrated the collection of sounds and voices into their everyday lives.

The deepness that the humans took their thoughts and emotions to was so advanced compared to his own race that he had found respect for some of the cruel, polluting, "rulers" of planet Earth. Their love and hatred towards one another was shocking, and yet made him envious at the same time. To feel about another being the way they sang to their friends, their enemies, their loved ones, and their heartbreakers in so many songs was almost unimaginable to Volk'narr. But he was already starting to get it. As he began to research the 1960's and 70's, slowly approaching the planet, his knowledge of the Earthicans, their history, and his newly found taste for their music only grew.

CHAPTER 6

Duluth, Minnesota
North America

The city of Duluth was in shambles. Numerous city blocks had been destroyed by the monster Shellshock or burned in the immense fires afterward that took most of the downtown and Canal Park areas. These regions were charred, and in some places, still smoking ruins.

The National Guard arrived on-scene with troops and guns twenty minutes after the giant reptilian kaiju had disappeared from Duluth Harbor back into the cold, deep waters of Lake Superior. The Coast Guard was already patrolling the harbor and surrounding lake area for any signs of where the turtle monster had fled to. The nearby Air Force base had also sent some helicopters to scout for the beast by air, with equally frustrating results. Soldiers in and out of their armored personnel carriers were positioned all over town amongst the blackened ruins of what used to be some of the best sights and sounds the picturesque but aging city had to offer.

FEMA, The Red Cross, The Salvation Army, and a host of various other disaster aid groups had originally set up many tents and shelters just outside of the disaster zone that used to be Canal Park. The assortment of medical field staff was originally bombarded by victims of Shellshock's rookie attack, but with hospitals in close vicinity, the patients were not on-site long. The media camp of tragedy-circling vultures popped up very close to the

65

FEMA tents, their news vehicles creating their own lot where a small park had once been. Things had calmed down a lot in the last day, however, and many already had or were beginning to clear out and leave.

Various medical personnel rushed back and forth in these areas, most people carrying boxes or equipment. They were packing up the unneeded supplies and moving them out of the disaster area. In the three days since the attack, everyone had been relocated to better facilities and the field crews were no longer needed. As such, it was time to go.

Miranda Shepperton was making a pile of boxes twenty feet out from the Red Cross tent that had been her home the last 48 hours. She made sure to conceal the small cube-shaped cooler in the middle of so much cardboard and so many plastic storage containers. Mostly everyday equipment -- syringes, gauze, bandages, and other basic emergency first aid items -- amongst it all hid a cooler full of dry ice and the already decomposing cells of the kaiju not publicly known as Shellshock. It was only a slightly burned chunk of skin she had found scraped on some of the remnants of what used to be a school, but it was invaluable. Miranda had covertly removed it quickly, without attracting any attention, and immediately encased it in ice.

Now, waiting for her ride, she nervously chewed on her lower lip, worried about the specimen's viability in the cooler. It had been stuck to the building for two days before she had found it. The deterioration was already settled in. Her ride had better show soon, or it could become a useless hunk of flesh. She was glad no urban critters had gotten to it. The thought of what *that* could result in scared her a little.

She sat on one of the large totes and pulled out her smartphone. Swiping away the lock screen, she brought up the text message app and quickly tapped a message to her ride announcing her readiness for pickup and the importance of transferring the cells to a better storage facility as soon as humanly possible.

His response popped up on the screen, heralded by the quack of a duck.

I see you.

Miranda looked up to see a large, cliché SUV -- an Escalade -- rolling into the parking lot of the park where the disaster relief zone had been situated in.

Really? A fucking Escalade? God, I hate them sometimes, she thought to herself as she smiled at the approaching vehicle.

It pulled in, turned to the right sharply, and began backing up to where Miranda and the cargo was. Two large Caucasian men dressed in black suits with white ties got out of the vehicle from the rear doors and walked to the back door, one throwing it open. Then they proceeded to fill the Escalade until everything was in it except for the cooler, which Miranda snatched up quickly in paranoia.

The man who opened the back looked at her for the first time and said, "You and the specimen have shotgun." Then he and the other man climbed back in the SUV and closed the doors.

Shepperton walked up and got into the front passenger side, clutching the handle of her prize's container like a woman who has narrowly avoided having her purse stolen. She looked at the driver, a ferret-looking man with a crazed look on his pale face. A dirty lip mustache and triangular soul patch decorated his mug, adding to the crazy effect. She smiled.

"Martin Keene, I should have known." She buckled her seatbelt and glanced back at the thugs behind her. "Who are you two?"

"Miranda, meet Ellis and Gilmour. Two of the Three Stooges, as Strand likes to call them," Keene said as he looked in the rear-view mirror at them.

Gilmour, a steroid-raging version of Richard Gere with a week's worth of beard stubble squinted his offense taken back at Keene in the mirror. Ellis, a dark-haired, sunglasses-wearing man with a Van Dyke goatee, merely stared out the window.

"Robinson --their boss -- is with Dr. Strand and Dr. Curran at our destination."

"Which is where?" Miranda asked as Keene pulled out of the parking lot and turned right, heading towards the interstate that bisected the partially ruined city.

He chuckled and said, "The Greater Lakes Aquarium, actually."

Just as Keene said this, Shepperton noticed they were avoiding the freeway and turning down a half-wrecked street covered in

Guardsmen -- who looked at them suspiciously but did nothing -- merely a block away from the disaster zone. To the left were the remains of Duluth's gigantic theater and arenas. To the right, a lakeside building comprised of many trapezoidal sections sitting atop a small hill, its walls mostly unscathed.

The aquarium, built in the year 2000, was the subject of much criticism at the time, many locals and other Minnesotans alike thinking it a waste of the taxpayers' money and time. Inside it contained many animal exhibits -- local, state, and international. One of the Major attractions was a giant tank spanning multiple floors and filled with Lake Superior fish. From the prehistoric sturgeon to the invading lamprey to the Mata turtle from South America, freshwater denizens were everywhere in the building, as well as select oceanic species of aquatic fauna. Otters, a bald eagle, and a macaw topped the small but detailed list of other animals residing there. It was a more worthwhile facility that the state's citizens gave it proper credit for.

The luxury SUV pulled up unimpeded by the military to the front entrance. Keene backed the Escalade up into the first handicapped parking spot. He noticed the look Shepperton was giving him.

"What? If there's a sudden rush of customers with disabilities, I'll move it, I promise!" He threw his hands up in the 'excuse the hell out of me' gesture, then turned off the engine. The four got out and walked to the front door, just as a man with curly auburn hair to his shoulders and a clean-shaven baby face walked out, grinning.

"Dr. Shepperton, I presume?" The six-foot-tall man stuck out a sausage-fingered hand in her direction. She took it and he pumped her arm up and down vigorously. "Dr. George Curran, at your service."

She smiled grimly back at him. "Pleased to meet you, Dr. Curran."

He let go of her hand, turned and opened the door, grinning and beckoning inside with his free hand. "After you," he said with the squinty-eyed smile of a happy housecat.

Miranda entered the building with Keene, Gilmour, and Ellis following behind. They walked into the unsecured area that was the lobby, ticket counter, and gift shop. A giant water wall dominated the scenery, gallons of H_2O cascading down a colorful wall depicting many of the residents of the aquarium before it disappeared into the floor. Several giant replicas of fish hung from the ceiling by wires, and colorful pictures of Lake Superior and Duluth Harbor adorned some of the other walls in the entryway. A staircase ran up the left side of the two-story, circular room, leading to the exhibits' entrance.

"This way," Curran said and walked ahead of her to the elevator at the base of the stairway set into the adjacent wall.

He pushed the button and the doors opened, the five people all entering the large car. Curran pushed a button at the bottom of the panel that was unmarked and a mustard yellow color. A second, hidden panel opened underneath the small array of elevator buttons, revealing a green-lit thumb-print scanner.

The thumb mold that was the scanner flashed red as a robotic male voice said, "Please press thumb to pad for fingerprint identification," repeatedly until Curran complied.

After accepting his print, the light turned green, and a "Thank you, Dr. Curran" replaced the looping request.

The car dropped slightly as it began its descent. No floor number lights lit up above the door, and it felt like about three or four floors down to Miranda before the car lurched to a halt. *Strange. Why so many underground floors in an aquarium? This is going to be interesting.* Still carrying the cooler with the cells, she already had an idea of what she was going to see when the doors opened.

Sure enough, a clinical white hallway with a monochrome checkered floor greeted her. Curran led them down the corridor past four doors to the room at the end of the hall. This chamber was marked only with a symbol. It was a trident spear, but the three prongs that made up the business end were DNA strands that ended in barbed points as the normal tips would have. It was the Bionautics' company logo.

Dr. Curran scanned his fob key and the door buzzed as the lock released with an audible noise. He pushed the door open and led her into the room. The smells of tidepool, swampy pond, and humid jungle floor -- along with formaldehyde and various other laboratory chemicals of different applications -- hit her in the face with gusto. Bile threatened to make its appearance from the immediate overstimulation to her nose. She held on as she gazed in wonder at the room before her eyes.

The room was filled with specimen tanks of all shapes and sizes all along two long walls. Creatures both living and dead filled these and represented many regions and climates all over the world. A door marked "Filter Room" was right in the middle of the main wall of cages housing the non-aquatic specimens -- mostly reptiles, amphibians, bugs, and birds. The adjoining wall was almost all aquatic life, fresh and saltwater alike.

Fish from all over the world, as well as crustaceans, jellyfish, starfish, and many other species filled the tanks, some almost to bursting, with lifeforms of all kinds. On the opposite walls, just about every type of equipment necessary for biologic work lined the walls on many heavy duty, stainless steel tables. Microscopes, centrifuges, specimen refrigerators, row upon row of dissection equipment, an autoclave or two and many others took up every available inch along the far wall. A few tables were set up like islands in the room, allowing four-sided access, as well as drainage underneath them set into the floor.

Standing at one of the island worktables was a tall African American man wearing a lab coat failing to conceal the black suit and white tie he wore underneath. He had a buzzcut of gray hair covering his head, and a similar gray mustache covering his upper lip like fur. A wicked, gash of a scar bisected his face across the bridge of his nose, which hung off his face at an odd angle - most likely from a bad break that healed wrong. Miranda Shepperton knew this man all too well.

"Hello again, Dr. Strand," she said, trying to keep as much contempt from her voice as possible. "It's been awhile, hasn't it?"

Strand looked at her with annoyance before smiling in a mockery of an honest facial feature. His faked happiness was scary, expressing some of the mania that lived behind his eyes. Gooseflesh immediately broke out all over her skin.

"Dr. Shepperton, am *I* glad to see *you*! I trust those are the cell samples in your beer cooler there?" He nodded down at the blue box she cradled like it contained nitroglycerin.

"Yes, Ivan, they're right in here," she said as she hefted it up onto the lab table he stood at.

Her eyes finally noticed Robinson, the third of the Three Stooges Strand kept around as his bodyguards. He sat on a stool behind Keene, wearing a red beanie cap, and reading a novel called *Torment* by Jeremy Bishop. He would glance up every now and then at them, a sign that he was paying attention, somewhat. She noticed he only looked at her, Strand and Curran. Turning her head, she realized Keene and the other two stooges had left or not come into the lab with them.

Strand opened the cooler and removed the Styrofoam containers encasing the cell samples. He put them in the nearby fridge, leaving one of the seven boxes out on his table. After putting the others in the fridge, he opened the one he had left out, whistling like a construction worker upon seeing its contents.

"That's a good chunk of turtle there, my dear!" he exclaimed loudly in an ecstatic manner.

Strand grabbed a pair of tweezers and a scalpel from a tray on the edge of the table and began to cut a piece of the green flesh chunk inside the container. With steady hands, he placed the tiny piece he removed onto a waiting slide and secured it with a coverslip. Strand hurried to the nearest microscope and placed the slide underneath the ocular, securing it with the clips provided. He looked in and gasped.

"No fucking way," he stated matter-of-factly. His language had thrown her off.

"What?" she asked, confused.

Strand looked up at her and beckoned to the microscope. "Take a look. Not only is it turtle DNA, but there are at least two other kinds in here. I think Ms. Sōzō has finally become the problem we feared she might."

71

***

Later

"Dr. Strand, I've managed to isolate the three types of DNA. However, there are actually four. One of them is unidentifiable. It's like nothing I've ever seen."

"That's... interesting, Dr. Shepperton. I'm also not surprised. There must be a recent technology at work here to combine prehistoric and present species' DNA, as well as for making the creature so large."

"But Doctor, where the hell did she find *Dunkleosteus* DNA? That's impossible! I question my ability to confirm 100% that it even is *Dunkleosteus*!"

"Only slightly more impossible than you knowing what kind of DNA it is, my dear. We shall find out soon, Dr. Shepperton. I will say, however, that it sure as hell looked like a *Dunkle* head to me, my dear. Dr. Curran, please ready the splicing lab. I think we have enough of each DNA sample to begin testing. I would also like you to retrieve these samples I have listed here from the cryo-storage and bring them as well."

"But Iv-- Dr. Strand, are you sure you want to start with these specimens? We don't have a proper containment facility yet, and--"

"Just make it so, George. I am fully aware of our current facilities' capacities. Or, do we have a problem?"

"No! No problem, sir! I'm on it!"

"Miranda, please bring me the four samples you have separated along with you. Those will be our backups for this experiment."

"You do know this one is not from Earth, right, Ivan? No life on earth has that many base pairs in its genetic code. It has to explain the growth rate, cell merger success rate, and most likely, the flame that thing melted a portion of downtown with!"

"Agreed, Doctor. Let us move to the next room and begin. That is where our artificial wombs are. I am... glad you are here, Miranda. I know how much you hate me for what I did to you."

"Good. Don't you ever forget it, Strand. You made me completely sterile. Do you have any fucking *clue* how devastating that is to a creature capable of growing life inside themselves? Having that equipment and never being able to use it? To have a gaping void where once was capable of miracles? Yes, I fucking remember, Ivan. I will *never* forget."

"Miranda, you make me smile! I hear the hatred in your voice, the homicidal intent! I do believe we shall kill each other someday. I've no doubt you want to slit my throat as much as I yours. Once we abolish Sōzō and her precious Hidora Neo... and their monster army, we shall finish this between us. Until then, we are the world's best chance of stopping this."

"Agreed."

"Then it's a date!"

"Fuck you, Strand."

"Not on the first date, my dear. Have some self-respect."

CHAPTER 7

Golden Gate Bridge
San Francisco, California
North America

Traffic on the Golden Gate bridge was flowing smoothly for a Wednesday afternoon. Vehicles of all kinds drove steadily back and forth across San Francisco's claim to fame. Chunky cirrus clouds were the minority in the blue sky dominating the day, the rich azure hue bold and inviting to the eyes. A light, salty breeze blew in off the Pacific with just enough push to make the local seabirds work for the scraps they scoured from around the bridge's foundation and Fort Point nearby.

Erin Rasmussen and her boyfriend, Peter Anderson, were just beginning the drive across the bridge, heading back to the city from the Marin Headlands. Driving her blue Ford Taurus, Erin looked over at Peter with his bare feet propped out of the open window. She momentarily lost herself gazing at the tan, muscular legs he owned that she loved so much. Peter suddenly sat up and pointed out the window towards the other end of the bridge.

"What's that?"

Erin looked back at the bridge in front of her. Cars and trucks drove towards their destinations on the other side like normal, with nothing out of the ordinary.

"Peter, what are you--"

Then she saw it.

The creature climbing out of the water dug its primordial claws into the rocky embankment on the ocean side of the bridge. The monster worked its way up onto the road with a minimum of effort. It stood up to its full height and greeted the traffic at the 'Cisco end of the bridge. The impossible beast stood between the abutment and toll booths that were just a bit further south down Highway 101, blocking most of the thoroughfare.

Erin slammed on her brakes like the fifty other southbound cars, resulting in only a few smashing into each other as a result. The exceptions were the few vehicles that had just exited the bridge when the... dinosaur, or whatever it was, stepped up onto the 101. A semi, several cars, and a couple of SUVs slammed into the massive thing's legs.

The monster's jaws splayed open, expelling a pants-wetting roar as vehicles crashed into its shins. Even in their car, Erin and Peter had to cover their ears to dampen the sound. The multiple impacts were nowhere near enough to drop the kaiju, but they had obviously pissed it off. Its tail lashed back and forth like an angry feline. One of the SUVs at its feet caught fire, burning the prehistoric nightmare, and further increasing its stress levels. It kicked the flaming wreck to the side, and it went rolling off the embankment the creature had ascended.

Standing at least 160 feet high, the monster's head was the size of a small building. A building full of salivating, razor-sharp teeth. Drool dribbled from its mouth, the slimy shoestrings quite visible in the sunlight. The couple both thought of their dog. Then their minds flashed to *Jurassic World* or *Godzilla vs. Kong.* It looked like a velociraptor or tyrannosaurus, but the head and snout were longer. It was more like an alligator or crocodile. Unlike any of those reptiles, however, wicked horns stuck out from all around the thing's skull, which was thick and armored with bone. The kind of skull that rammed things.

The halo of horns gave the impression of a crown. The thick cranium ran forward on the monster's head until just before its eyes. From there it tapered into a pair of symmetrical ridges that covered the monster's two pairs of peepers. The monstrosity had *a quartet of eyes.*

75

On the sides of its head, the first pair of eyes under the bony ridges were reptilian. Their slit-like pupils stared vacantly, cold and unresponsive to the chaos its arrival had created. The second pair of eyes were set in the front of the skull a bit more, positioned just below where the tapered ridges came together over the snout. These eyes were eerily mammalian, tracking movement erratically. There was an intelligence in them and the way they moved, almost human, but not quite, like a dog.

The monster's dinosaurian body sat atop two powerful hind legs and leveled out with a thick tail. Both body and tail were naturally horizontal while it moved, as carnivorous dinosaurs were known to do for balancing purposes. A mass of writhing tentacles that were crazy long and too numerous to count in their stupor flailed angrily from the thing's chest. It was an army of grasping, boneless arms. As if displaying their potential uses, the beast turned halfway around and began grabbing the cars that had piled up from the toll booths behind it and tossing them in all directions. Erin noticed a pitiful set of three fingered claws typical to a dinosaur buried within the angry mass of cephalopod arms. The mass began grabbing the people trying to run for their lives from the enormous horror that had stomped its way into their Wednesday afternoon, popping them in its slavering jaws like chicken nuggets.

Erin and Peter, still a hundred yards from southern exit and the massive monster blocking it, continued to cover their ears as they gaped in disbelief at the logic defying entity. Their continued muffling paid off a second later when the daikaiju split the air again with another intense roar, this one extending out seven seconds longer than the last. Erin wanted to scream but was too stunned to use her vocal cords. Peter's jaw was slack, a low groan escaping from his throat.

Erin was incredulous, unable to get over one thing in particular in her stunned frame of mind.

"Peter, why does it have four eyes?" She mumbled the almost rhetorical question, then looked at her beau. His blank stare was all the answer she received.

She was too far gone to care about his possible catatonia, so she looked back at the kaiju.

That's what they were called, right?

She thought so. She liked the one with the big gorilla fighting the legless lizards with skull faces and Samuel L. Jackson. Ms. Marvel and Dan Connor from that sitcom were in it, too. Erin's brain slapped her mentally and brought her back to focus on the kaiju guarding the southern exit.

It was just staring at them all now, where they sat gridlocked on the bridge. A pile of wreckage smoked behind it.

The massive creature stepped up and completely blocked the entire south entrance to the bridge. A multitude of the thing's dark green tentacles shot out and snared the sides of the bridge's viaduct, the beginning of the bridge that preceded the thick, iconic cables that made up the crossing's suspension system. To Erin, the tentacled monster attacking the bridge looked like an octopus latching onto a crustacean. She'd seen videos.

The kaiju began to pull at the viaduct with obvious strength -- even from where they sat on the bridge. Erin and Peter could feel the repercussive vibrations a few seconds before the bridge under their car started to twist, the vehicle tilting and shaking. After checking behind her, Erin was surprised to find a way out and immediately put the car in reverse and hit the gas.

The aging car lurched backward, throwing an unbuckled Peter forward. His face smashed into his forehead slammed hard into the glass. There was a crunch, and a spot of red marked the spiderweb fracture created when he had hit, as his body mashed limply against the dash. Peter was unconscious before they passed the second set of pylons while still in reverse.

Erin's backwards exodus was a hair-raising retreat through the throngs of vehicles blocking the bridge. She weaved erratically between cars, pulling off some insane maneuvers in the vehicular pandemonium. The poor woman squealed as she barely missed some damn fool running around the bridge like a headless chicken. Her Taurus scraped harshly against a truck before she spun the wheel back, taking the car away from the pickup. The vehicle bumped into the back end of a hatchback trying to get out of her way. Screeching metal was drowned out by another horrible roar from the monster as Erin reversed the wheel again. As the car moved away from the hatchback and its stunned occupants, the driver of the vehicle flipped her off.

Miraculously finding the room to turn around, Erin did so, expertly spinning the car 180 degrees like a stunt driver. The spin tossed Peter into his car door with a meaty thunk as his head hit the passenger side window. The sickening sound made her want to puke.

"Sorry, baby," Erin said through gritted teeth as she threw the car into drive and pushed the pedal to the floor. *I'll make it up to him later,* she thought with optimism.

The Taurus lurched forward again, and something in the transmission made an ugly *ka-chunk* as it forced itself into the next gear before accelerating once more. Cruising past another pylon and its steel licorice ropes, she stared down the other end of the bridge. Erin kept her eyes trained on what she hoped would be their escape from the horror roaring behind them. Pulling to the right and driving on the correct side of the bridge, she didn't dare look back at the thing in her mirror as she sped forward.

Far behind the distressed couple, where they had been stopped moments before turning around, the whole viaduct of the bridge started to angle sideways towards the Pacific. The trusses underneath screamed as they started to bend, and stationary vehicles began to slide towards the sea while the beast wrenched on the bridge. At this point, none of the motorists remained in their vehicles, most hoofing it north across the bridge.

Then the monster suddenly angled back in the other direction as it pulled towards the bay, the sudden move throwing abandoned vehicles viciously to the other side of the northbound lane like tossed stir fry. Cars and fleeing people both plummeted into the bay.

A few foolish people had tried to run past the creature through its legs, but only one man and his young son made it past the attentive kaiju. The remaining people were swiftly plucked from the bridge's surface, then crushed in the serrated grip of a green tentacle before being mechanically fed to the gigantic maw atop the beast's neck.

Erin weaved through the last dozen cars before they were finally off the bridge. She drove a quarter of a mile further before stopping on the side of the road where the elevated roadway came back onto solid ground. The frazzled woman put the car into park and unbuckled her seat belt.

She leaned over and checked Peter's pulse. Her heart jumped with joy when she found one. Erin climbed out of her car and began dialing 9-1-1 on her cellphone as other cars fleeing from the bridge sped past her. The line was busy and a recording saying so was the last thing she wanted to hear.

As far away as she was, Erin could clearly see the kaiju; the titanic monstrosity was extremely visible even over a mile and a half away. With a deafening roar, followed by a loud, painful, metallic squeal, the beast's tentacles finally tore the 'Cisco end of the bridge completely free from its moorings. The viaduct was lifted up by the creature's many tentacles and began to crumple and bend from gravity, terrible noises piercing the air as a result.

An angry cry exploded from the beast as it dropped the bridge. The end it had held crashed into the Fort Point building located underneath, while the rest of it fell into the bay with a tremendous crash. Frothy sea spray and clouds of dirt and dust filled the air from the impact, before quickly clearing. The bridge's first section had been destroyed all the way up to the set of pylons that marked the viaduct's northern end, where the main expanse over the bay really began. The remaining cars and unfortunate people plummeted as well as the bridge buckled and fell out from beneath them. Soon, a mass of vehicles and multiple bodies littered the shore and water like discarded refuse.

On the severed bridge end, people left their cars, running to the edge and gawking at the destructive force towering over them across the way before coming to their senses and fleeing the other way. Cracks spider-webbed through the cement pylons from the fallen section's attempts to take the towering pair of structures with it as it fell. Chunks fell from the pillars into the ocean, but the supports stood fast.

Nautilus Rex's jaws split wide open again, its booming exaltation a combination of the roars of a lion and an elephant, remixed with a revving chainsaw.

Erin's bladder finally let go as she heard the sanity-crippling roar yet again. Her bleeding, unconscious boyfriend forgotten, she did the only thing her smartphone-obsessed mind could do: she hit "stop" on her iPhone, ending the 17 seconds of death and destruction she had unconsciously filmed instead of continuing to attempt contacting emergency services. She selected "share" on the application's top menu bar and posted it to her social media wall. Erin was an Internet star within an hour. She had done all of this on mental autopilot.

Numbly, Erin looked back at the car.

"Peter!" she screamed, her grasp on reality returning.

She ran to his door and slowly pulled it open. Her paramour fell out into her arms. She caught him just as the ground beneath her shook violently, causing them both to spill clumsily to the asphalt. The ground shook again, then twice more, before the sun disappeared.

Erin looked up and screamed as a second kaiju stepped up and over hills of the Marin Headlands next to the roadway, clearing Fort Baker in the movement. Its huge, cat-like paws cleared the monument and came down gracefully but thunderous, denting the ground with each step.

The new kaiju sauntered up to the road like a hungry man to a buffet line. Erin continued to scream until her voice went hoarse and quit altogether. She couldn't see what it looked like very well, as it blocked the sun. However, it could be discerned that its head was shaped almost like a monstrous raven or crow, but the beak was tall and thick like one of those "terror birds" that she had seen at the La Brea Tar Pits. Her mind was barely able to process the comparison, but the memory managed to make it through her shock and awe.

The second kaiju bent down towards Erin, flicking back and forth as a bird does checking out its dinner before it tries to flee. Suddenly it opened its beak and squawked at her, but instead of an ear-rupturing shriek it was a gurgled *squorrk!* This was accompanied by bright gouts of a blue magma-like substance that melted the unfortunate young couple and their car where they stood.

The giant bipedal bird thing, satisfied with the charred mess its fire vomit had created, turned to look at its fellow daikaiju across the bay. Screams reached its ears, reminding it of its purpose. With a savage jerk of its furry, feline body, two leathery bat-like wings unfolded and snapped into flight mode. Stretching out to a wingspan of over 400 feet, the extra-long finger digits that comprised the wings' frames flexed at the tips, where they stuck out like spikes.

It flapped several times to stretch them out, as a long tail flicked back and forth like that of a surly housecat. The Terror Griffin flexed the muscles on its separate set of humanoid arms just because it could. Then it took to the air with another *squorrk*! A second deluge of blue napalm vomit exploded from its beak and drenched the hillside surrounding the road, as well as the road itself, igniting everything it covered.

As it flew over the bridge and bay entrance towards its partner in destruction, the Terror Griffin made eye contact for the briefest of seconds with the tentacled dinosaur. Nautilus Rex roared at the gigantic newcomer with recognition, then turned back to chasing down the few remaining people fleeing for their lives. Once it was satisfied prey were all devoured, it followed the flying monster toward the main part of the city, tearing through the bridge's toll gates like they was made during arts and crafts time at a nursing home.

***

The squadron of AH-64 Apache helicopters arrived on a scene out of a disaster movie. They were the main front of the Army's forces that had been recently stationed in the Bay area after the Duluth attack. Their main objective was to provide some anti-monster defenses to one of the country's major metropolitan areas. This bulk up of forces was beginning to happen all across the United States.

The rampaging monster on the ground had carved a wicked path through ruined buildings and landscape, straight through Presidio and the headquarters of a legendary sci-fi filmmaker's special FX company. The 15-acre expanse had been transformed into a smoldering pile of debris and wreckage, artificial and organic.

Laurel Heights had been the next stop on Nautilus Rex's tour, where its tennis-court-sized feet crushed the old Victorian and Edwardian houses lining the streets like little boxes. People ran everywhere, screaming ants attempting to escape the anteater. Some had tried to flee in their cars. Most were plucked from the road by the erratically snaking coils continuously striking out in all directions from the two-legged carnivore's horizontally aligned torso.

A white minivan was ripped up from the driveway it was trying to back out of and flung through the air. The poor people inside were treated for the scariest ride of their life as the van arced through the air and punched through an apartment complex in the Haight-Ashbury district three miles away. Miraculously, they all somehow survived with only some broken bones and a few minor injuries.

Automobiles of all makes and models were thrown, tossed, flung, and spiked into the asphalt by the writhing flurry of green, ropey, toothed squid arms. A Chevy Aveo tried speeding back towards the crowned kaiju terror, attempting to flee through its legs, a trick tried once before with little success.

With a growl, it shot a tendril-like arm out, wrapping around the small, bubbly hatchback. The arm came up quickly, rising just above the huge head of the monster, then hurtled the light green fuel-efficient car into the front picture window of a large Victorian house nearby. The car barreled through walls and people. The load-bearing supports destroyed, the second floor collapsed down on top of the car and the entirety of the first floor, only to be blown into sky-high bits as the gas line ignited. A huge fireball rose up into the sky, the flames reflecting off of the beast's black and green scales.

Vehicles, humans, and pieces of demolished buildings sailed through the air in every direction as the beast stomped on. It was heading towards the University of San Francisco to the south.

Rounding the west side of Lone Mountain and the USF's Lone Mountain campus that dominated its surface, Nautilus Rex tore through Beaumont Avenue and the neighborhood there. Several rows of houses that were crammed next to each other like sardines in a can went up in clouds of dust, smoke, and flames as the mighty beast trudged through them purposefully. Its giant redwood legs and clawed feet crushed and carved jagged gashes through the clustered condominiums and houses like a child with overlarge snow boots walking through fresh snow with an icy crust. Each step met a small amount of surface resistance before crashing through when as just enough weight was applied.

Here people had been slightly more successful at evacuating, as most were already at work or school. Those unfortunate enough to still be home were obliterated with little warning, their worlds caving in on them along with their houses.

***

Sondra Beverley had been one of the lucky ones. She had seen the chaos on the news, including the first images broadcast as Nautilus Rex had torn through Lucasland. She actually felt the tremors from the destruction ensuing mere miles away from her. Sondra had quickly called her fellow network of daycare ladies, organizing a mass evacuation from their separate homes within a six-block radius. Within minutes, eight women had rounded up their daily wards -- 39 children in all -- loaded them into their kiddie cargo vans and drove east. They would eventually rendezvous at Lafayette Park sometime later.

As Sondra drove away from her house of twenty years, she saw the monster approaching in her rearview mirror. She veered into the adjacent lane in a panic, and almost lost control of her Toyota Sequoia. This resulted in her sideswiping a parked Subaru and eliciting an outburst of frightened squeals from the already terrified children in the back seats. What Sondra had seen in her mirror had messed her up.

The green tentacles were thrusting themselves into every house surrounding each step the prehistoric thing took, retracting with tidbits about half the time. *My neighbors*, she thought grimly as her breath hitched twice in her chest.

"Don't look back kids… I mean it," she heard herself say, knowing full well it was a mistake.

In an obvious reaction to being told not to, all seven of her kids turned and looked back at the primeval terror stomping towards them even as Sondra sped away. Four of them screamed loudly, deafening her and causing a slight zig zag as she drove down Turk Street towards Cathedral Hill and Hwy. 101.

"Miss Sondra, there's a dinosaur chasing us!"

"Godzilla! He's gonna get us!"

"Kids, it's okay, we're getting away from the big, nasty dinosaur, and we're going somewhere safe, okay? Please try not to scream, it hurts Miss Sondra's ears and I need to pay attention to the road."

She tried to reason with them in her light, almost singsong, daycare voice. To her surprise, it worked. Whimpers and sniffling noses were still heard, but they sat and stared silently at the towering terror slowly getting smaller as it faded into the distance.

Tearing through the last of the residences in Sondra's neighborhood, the daikaiju's left foot slammed down into the parking lot of the University's soccer field. There had been a kid's game in progress when the monster came into view, but they had fled already, leaving sports equipment all over the field. Also left behind was a small army of coolers and personal bags in the stands where players and spectators alike had simply dropped everything and gotten the hell out.

Leaving a couple of its trademark footprints across the field, the beast trudged towards the XARTS Lab and the neighboring USF buildings to the east of it. As it raised its right foot to step on the arts and agriculture labs building, a volley of Hydra 70 rockets exploded as they pummeled the daikaiju's left flank. The first flight of Apaches had arrived.

***

With an anguished roar from its elongated, *acrocanthosaurus* head, the towering brute went down, toppling to its right before crashing down hard and sending up a plume of dust from the instant rubble created by the fall. The second flight of choppers flew over, peppering the bloody flank of the monster further with hundreds of rounds from the helicopters' 30mm M230 chain guns. A louder, higher-pitched roar was the downed beast's only retort, its wildly lashing tentacles unable to reach the flying mechanical enemies plaguing it.

Suddenly, it was back on its feet, the army of cephalopod arms pushing it up in an instant. Nautilus Rex spun around with amazing

84

speed and opened its maw at the third flight of choppers just as they were coming in for another attack. A jagged red bolt of what looked like lightning struck out from its throat and instantly connected with the three choppers closing in. For a split second, they seemed to freeze in midair as the bolt of unknown energy hit and surrounded them in its strange red glow. When it quickly dissipated a millisecond later, the choppers dropped like stones, all signs of electrical or mechanical activity absent.

As the three Apaches crashed into the side of Lone Mountain, crumpling into mangled versions of themselves and starting on fire, Nautilus Rex turned towards the fourth squad of Apaches heading its direction. This flight of four choppers unleashed a second barrage of Hydra 70s, thirteen rockets streaking towards their target like angry snakes. A red bolt of the strange lightning was there to greet ten of them, dropping them uselessly onto the lawn of the University campus, leaving furrows in their wake.

The other three rockets hit home, however. Already bloody, the beast's left side again blew apart, chunks of flesh and bone scattering all over the area, covering most everything in thick, maroon blood. With a resounding crash, the kaiju fell once more, this time landing on the Church of St. Ignatius. It did not get up again.

The rotund chest continued to slowly rise and fall, but at a quarter of its normal rate. The choppers flew over once more per flight, blasting the gaping wounds of the unconscious monster with a fresh volley of gunfire before flying towards the downtown area. There they had a date with the bipedal, prehistoric griffin that was destroying everything.

Unseen by the Apaches as they flew towards downtown, the edges of flesh around Nautilus Rex's ragged wounds on its left side began to take on a tarry, black appearance. The gooey coagulant slowly began to cover the mortal injuries. In the span of two minutes, thirty percent of the wounds had regenerated anew.

Unlike the original skin the beast had possessed, however, this new flesh was solid black. The epidermis had the sheen of an orca whale's skin fresh out of the ocean's depths. The black patches of skin also had some new features. Several eyes, gasping mouths, and dark tentacles of assorted sizes grew in its reformed flesh. The smaller tendrils writhed in the air for the first time like vines growing in time-lapse photography, as cat eyes blinked and human-like mouths gnashed crooked teeth and licked nasty lips with discolored green tongues.

The black flesh rippled with each breath the prone animal took, decreasing in intensity with each subsequent breath. Soon, it was still once more. The huge barrel chest stopped moving as well. For ten seconds, the monster was completely immobile.

All at once, its four original eyes snapped open, darting back and forth. It roared, blasting the tiny, human gawkers who had accumulated nearby in a wave of audible agony. The Nautilus Rex rose again, propelled to its feet by its nest of boneless appendages once more. It charged in the direction of downtown San Francisco and the puny flying metal insects that had hurt it so much.

As the monster decimated the campus buildings, the new mouths on its left flank began to wail and shriek. The ungodly sounds tore at the sanity of those unfortunate enough to hear it. In the aftermath of the San Francisco attack, many of these victims would later have their causes of death be determined as heart attacks, puzzling morticians city-wide. A local newspaper would boldly claim later:

CITIZENS DIE OF FRIGHT!

***

A group of seventeen Hydra rockets streaked towards the colossal form atop the "Tweezers Towers," or 345 California Center. It was the third largest building in San Francisco and was located in the financial district. The hotel/office building consisted of forty-eight floors, the top eleven having been built at forty-five-degree angles from the lower floors.

These two sections, originally designed for condos, had since become the Mandarin-Oriental Hotel. The nickname "Tweezer Towers" stemmed from the two spires reaching up to the sky from the middle of the 720foot-tall building. They stood side to side like the simple medical tool of the same name.

The Terror Griffin was perched on the roof like an oversized feline gargoyle. Its front legs were on one of the hotel towers and its rear legs on the other. Immense bat wings were folded back behind it, the pleated chiropteran flight appendages looking like a pair of leathery antlers or horns protruding from the furry, striped back. The Griffin's ugly bird head -- with its prehistoric raptorial beak -- pivoted back and forth as it studied the surroundings and mass chaos on the streets below.

It heard the Hydras seconds before they struck, suddenly standing straight up in the air like a human and turning sideways like some gigantic action hero. The missiles all shot past the Terror Griffin save for one, where they exploded as they hit the buildings behind the monster, causing massive collateral damage. The one successful rocket struck the beast in its rear, the exploding result making the bird beast cry out in pain and lurch forward. A ball of blue phlegm reflexively flew out of its mouth and sailed through the city before slamming into the Transamerica Pyramid's tower.

The dunce cap-like cone tip on the tallest building in the city was splattered by the burning vomit ball. Already on fire, the excess splatter hit the ground below seconds later, engulfing everything. The helplessly massive traffic jam of panicked commuters and tourists, already tangled in an accident-ridden gridlock, was now a burning disaster zone. People abandoned their burning vehicles and ran any way they could to escape the potential explosions that were anticipated from all the Hollywood movies the fleeing throngs had watched over the years. Several unlucky citizens and vehicles were hit by falling liquid instead and instantly self-immolated in a white-blue inferno.

Terror Griffin's rear end was already healing quickly, black ooze covering the wound before transforming into the same shiny black skin that the tentacled dinosaur hybrid had sported. A single mouth was the only extra part that formed on this injury, however, and it began to shriek like a banshee immediately upon completion.

Two nearby Apaches instantly crashed into the buildings on either side of the 345 building. The shriek tore at the pilots' minds the second it penetrated their headgear, causing them to lose control. A mushroom-like cloud of non-nuclear smoke and flame billowed up from the smaller office buildings as the Apache exploded. This set off a chain reaction as the cluster of buildings ignited and soon become completely consumed by the resulting fires.

The other Apache, however, slammed into the top floors of the major bank building nearby. The rotor blades sliced through the windows as it cut into the front of the structure at an awkward angle before pushing through into the building itself. Smoke poured out like an angry volcano caldera. Flames soon followed, racing up the sides of the high rise.

As the fires found the leaking fuel tank of the chopper, it caught fire and also exploded. The resulting blast expelled chunks of office building, helicopter scrap, and the white-collar workers that had been inside onto the street below and careening into the buildings across the street. This started more fires that grew and soon raged out of control.

The remaining flights of Apaches flew at the Griffin one more time, the first firing more Hydras at the creature. Unfurling its wings quickly with a snap of its body, the daikaiju took flight from the building at the last possible second. Its huge wings caused the billowing smoke from burning buildings to curl up into a large cloud. The smoke also concealed the mighty monster's escape into the plumes as the rockets hit the roof of the Mandarin-Oriental.

In a series of explosions -- each pronounced by a loud *whump!* -- the Hydras took off the entire top five floors of the hotel as the Tweezer Towers were blasted to bits. The staccato explosions were followed by the cracking and splitting, before both hotel towers suddenly collapsed inwards, crumbling down the sides of the building and taking out much of the lower structure's front façade on the way down.

What remained was a smoking, dusty ruin. Flames still burned in the exposed pockets that had been the building's uppermost floors. Charred furniture and decor was mixed with the structural debris on California Street. The gory remains of prematurely evicted hotel guests lay strewn about the fallen rubble like squashed insects.

Emergency services began to arrive in droves to the scene, pulling up as close as possible before attending to the scores of injured and the dead. Firefighters arrived as well, brandishing water and foam rack and reel trucks and many wheeled fire extinguishing units on large, inflated tires. They began trying to extinguish the burning blue-white flames, eventually finding success with the dry chemical-based wheeled units. The purple powder soon covered everything burning, smothering it and tamping down the smoldering flames quickly.

Suddenly the ground shook violently and everyone on the scene looked down California Street towards the noise's source. Buildings mere blocks away exploded, contributing to an expanding cloud of dust behind them as a tentacled horror burst through the obscuring dirt and debris. The giant dinosaur roared its grinding, predatory war cry.

This was now harmoniously accompanied by the newly grown mouths of sharp teeth that had sprouted from the obsidian-colored skin on its left flank. The pairs of tooth lips screamed in short bursts simultaneously with the longer predatory roar of the monster's head, the eerily human lips sometimes smiling cruelly in between shrieks.

Very few who heard this unholy cacophony maintained clean underwear as instant fear flooded even the strongest minds. The sanity of so many witnesses unraveled even further as the unfathomable cries penetrated a deeper, subconscious level of fear. It was a level of fright that most people do not realize they still possess that mind-crippling fear of the unknown, of things beyond the breadth of our knowledge and the scope of our imaginations. Fear that humanity's ancestors knew daily -- whether from ignorance of the way things worked or because the insane myths and legends were true. The sort of fear all who remained in the ruined, burning financial district were all too aware of.

Stupefied and crippled by this phobic phenomenon, many people were trampled as Nautilus Rex plowed over them like frozen blades of grass and ran straight into the side of the 345 building. The monster's down-turned, keratin crown of thorns and reinforced bone helmet of a skull punched through the already crumbling face of the ruined structure. The floors above the new impact point collapsed and fell apart with a tremendous noise as debris rained down on the daikaiju's head.

Withdrawing from the destroyed target before being buried in rubble, the Nautilus Rex swung its body around 180 degrees and slashed its thick, scaly tail through the smoldering remains of the building next door. One of the stunned choppers had crashed into it and continued on, slicing deep into the structure's west side before cutting through most of the center supports of the building's framework. This essentially severed its inanimate spine.

The beast finished its half-circle spin and faced the decimated structure once again, just in time to watch it pitch forward. In a flurry of motion, the stretching coils that were its arms whipped about in a thrashing fury, obliterating and batting away all rubble that threatened to fall on the thing's head. Chunks of concrete and steel were later found as far as five miles away from the defensive maneuver.

Even with the flailing of tentacles, the toppling building still managed to pummel the young kaiju into the ground. It hit the decimated street with an audible groan, like an old dog laying down on a hardwood floor. Then it laid there helplessly as crumbling floors of the building piled up on top of the monster. The dust cloud created in the collapsing mess soon cleared, revealing the kaiju's already rising form.

Its left side exploded again as three of the remaining five Apaches swooped in firing more Hydras. It cried out in agony, but when the smoke cleared, its smooth, new flesh remained unscathed. A few of the extra appendages had been blown apart, but instantly healed over with the shiny, regenerative tissue. Unharmed, the rockets had only pissed it off.

With a crackling boom, electromagnetic lightning erupted from its throat and instantly arced towards the fleeing vehicles. Only one managed to avoid it, banking to the left sharply and taking cover between two tall buildings. The electric streaks found windows and concrete instead. The other two choppers were hit directly, instantly losing power and bursting in flames as gravity ripped them out of the sky and pulled them down into two office buildings below. Explosions further ripped the buildings apart moments later as mangled remains sparked and burned. With a rapid-fire bellow almost like a laugh, the beast turned its head back to where it had last seen the one evading warbird.

Suddenly, the chopper shot past Nautilus' horned head, streaking through the air in a burning, smoking ball, and burying itself into one of the buildings already burning. The creature looked up in the direction the fastball had come from to see the Terror Griffin flapping its giant wings above the remnants of 345. Its beak opened wide as a cry of victory tore from its throat, followed by an ungodly wail from the newly formed, screaming orifice decorating its freshly healed patch of ass skin.

Roaring in response, the Nautilus Rex turned towards San Francisco Bay. Then it was off, charging in the bright sunlight down California Street until it ran into the huge hotel at the end. Momentum, tentacles, and brute strength spelled the end for the hotel as monster met building and the building lost, crumbling easily before the Hidora Neo creation continued on. The kaiju leapt up over the Ferry house building, taking its clock tower with it as the titanic creature splashed into the bay beyond.

Waves of displaced water doused the waterfronts on all sides of the bay like mini tsunamis, flash flooding the city streets nearest the shore. Then the beast was gone, concentric circles expanding out from where it entered the bay being the only evidence it had submerged.

Meanwhile, the Terror Griffin had flown up and up into the sky, disappearing into a giant cotton ball cloud that was threatening to block out the sun for a time. The remaining Apache began to give chase from its position in the sky but turned and flew back the way the destroyed squadron had originated from, returning to base with tactical info the brass was extremely interested in. This effectively spared the two pilots' lives, much to their unspoken delight.

The behemoths' rampage was over. The chaos, however, continued as the city began to pull itself back to its feet. And the unspoken question looming over everyone's minds was the obvious one.

When would they be back?

***

Deep under the Pacific, the last remaining scientist responsible for the creation of Nautilus Rex and the Terror Griffin watched her captor, Burke Riser, prepare for the beasts' return to their enclosures, impossibly hidden from prying eyes beneath the waves near Monterey. She was only a little scared of the man -- a man she mistakenly thought she had known all too well -- but was silently cheering mentally, regardless. In his haste to prepare the kaiju's habitats for them, Burke had missed her activating the distress beacon under the computer desk she was parked at.

It was obvious that her captor had no knowledge of the emergency alarm. He would not have put her so close to it if he had. Dr. Natasha Kutsenko, the last surviving scientist of Hidora Neo's Monterey Canyon facility known as Trench Town, would be patient. Hidora Neo would not let their West Coast facility fall without doing something about it.

Then Burke Riser, who was an asshole spy from Hidora Neo's government sanctioned rival, Bionautics, would truly see how screwed he was.

***

Far above the Earth, the rippling, light bending camouflage of the mechanized robot that Volk'narr had bonded with and piloted for almost as long as he could remember shimmered like quicksilver. It was barely noticeable in the orbit of the planet, with only the sun, moon, and stars to give away its presence. He had witnessed the entire San Francisco incident with his mechanized weapon's instruments and cameras -- devices that put a certain search engine's application to utter shame. Through each of his nine eyes, he watched the regeneration capabilities of the DNA train wrecks that destroyed the California town with piqued curiosity. How had the monkeys achieved such madness?

Convinced he knew the technology behind it, having seen the black, oozing flesh with its terrible add-ons before, Volk'narr used his mech's computers to search the globe for the life forces of the race he suspected. Immediately, the readout showed a major concentration of the Elder race's genetic makeup. The largest mass contained within the continent at the bottom of the Earth. There were also little specks of their essence all over the planet. Volk'narr hissed, his mandibles flexing back and forth rapidly in anger and frustration. He was going to have to work for this one. It wouldn't be an easy victory.

He entered another species into the database. Again, splotches here and there covered the Earth's surface, this time a series of medium size concentrations instead of one big one accompanied by many smaller readings. He frowned, as much as an invertebrate life form with a mouth of sharp teeth was able to.

This was going to fall into overtime pay.

A celestial invader *and* planar invader, both influencing the piteous dominant race into acts of extreme chaos?

He was surprised the planet's fail safes hadn't already risen. Surely the planet cleaners would awaken soon, if they hadn't already. Time was of the essence now.

Volk'narr's race had a great interest in the world of humans. They were the closest possibility for allies in the future wars that his people had known about for centuries, and their capacity for goodness made them a logical choice. The fact that so many of them were wastes of life -- those destroying the good in their world -- mattered not, as there were a considerable number of redeeming examples to choose from.

Compatible examples. He went back to the first search, looking for Elder signs. In the middle of one of the huge lakes on the apparent ruling continent, a major mark stood out among all the other minor readings. He decided to enter the atmosphere and head for that location first, assess the situation, and go from there. Volk'narr had absolutely no qualms about eradicating the Elder infestation there, but he had to at least check it out fully first. No need to reveal his presence until absolutely necessary.

He set his mech's computer for the approximate coordinates, and began to descend into the Earth's atmosphere, listening to a group of musical monkeys named Led Zeppelin sing something called "*Achilles Last Stand*". The building storm of the song got him excited, and he let himself dream a little about finally returning to his home world after the mission was done. He knew he was kidding himself, mech warriors never returned home, but he let his mind wander, regardless.

***

As the U.S. scrambled to figure out why their naval forces failed to intervene on the Californian city's behalf in spite of the close proximity of their destroyers, many of the world's top governments began preparing their forces. Top officials began considering realistic nuclear options (there weren't any yet that wouldn't decimate populations worse than the monsters) and scoping out possible places within their countries to send displaced citizens -- should one of their cities fall to the giant freaks of nature. Most countries with any sort of military set to work developing their own weapons to deal with the monsters, many with indirect prompting from the Bionautics' lobbyists. Prototypes in the works for years suddenly became a reality for multiple weapons divisions from various nations.

Very soon, the game would change again, hopefully in the human race's favor.

CHAPTER 8

Superior X Station
Lake Superior
North America

"Payback," by the metal band Slayer, roared out of the speaker system inside Doctor Emmett West's personal lab. To say he was pissed off was an understatement. The angry track from an album entitled *God Hates Us All* fed his rage like fuel to a fire.

He had been lied to and betrayed.

His beast, nicknamed Rampage, had been slotted for the next attack. Before that could happen, two kaiju had appeared in San Francisco, no doubt released from Trench Town. His glory had been stolen, West regrouped his thoughts after the initial fury and had convinced Brown and Brundle to help him prepare a slight addition to the Chicago lineup. It did not take much convincing on his behalf to get them to agree, which really hadn't surprised him. They were deceived as well, after all.

Shellshock, freshly augmented with several enhancements after Duluth, including size, was to be Rampage's right hand. In addition to the Devonian-headed monster snapping turtle, Brundle's own pet project was a mammalian-pterosaur hybrid he had nicknamed Conquer. The three beasts were being awakened from their suspended animation as he stood in front of the monitors for the enclosures these certain creations were housed in during their downtime in Superior X. Enclosures much larger and separate from the tank all three were birthed in. One by one, five sets of eyes opened, and their owners began writhing in their amniotic, fluid-filled tanks. West smiled.

At last, the fun could begin.

As he and his two colleagues monitored the monsters' vitals, preparing them for the attack, the three men discussed their plans for invasion, destruction, and hopefully impression. Sadako would realize the error of underestimating her Superior X geniuses. Then she would recognize the potential the three of them had in furthering the organization's ability to dominate the world with these creatures. Wasting time with hit and runs was acceptable for practice, but now it would be *their* turn to really start something.

After finding out about the San Francisco attack, the three of them had hashed things out in a drunken, ranting... *bitch-fest* really was the best word for it. West realized he could rely on B&B a lot more than he thought. He was not worried about their casually mentioned "surprise" at all, in fact, he couldn't wait to see what it was.

West switched to the album *Broken*, by Nine Inch Nails, then locked himself into an updated control setup. His body became linked into the three daikaiju who would ruin Chicago. His excitement was beginning to overthrow his rage at Trench Town's shenanigans, and he marveled over each of the giant wonders with teeth that the three of them had created as West's vision synced up with the kaijus'. He could see through their eyes either individually or all at once. All at the same time made him nauseous, but it was maintainable.

Upon first seeing through Conquer's eyes, his breath was taken away as she finally broke the surface of Lake Superior. She began flapping her huge pterosaur wings rapidly to expel the water from them before ascending impossibly into the dark skies, shaking her wet fur dry enough to not freeze before flying into the clouds above. West felt the exhilaration of flying through the new interface, minus the detrimental effects of being thousands of feet up in the sky. This new airborne sensation, coupled with the aquatic travels of Brown's shark-headed turtle and his own marine reptile powerhouse, West's mind overloaded for a split second before it abruptly snapped into a sort of synchronicity with the three monsters. Fortunately, this happened just as the submerged pair of giant beasts approached the first target. The ensuing attack would be an *un*fortunate case of wrong place, wrong time for the poor fools about to meet their doom.

***

Lake Superior's Surface
North of Michigan

At about 1:30 A.M., the bulk carrier ship, *Yearning Ways,* headed on course towards the Sault Ste. Marie, Michigan Soo Locks to the east and then onto Lake Huron. The vessel's final destination was Detroit. The giant, 304-meter vessel -- about 1,000 feet, total -- was carrying about 63,000 deadweight tons of food. This mostly consisted of grains, but the ship had been retrofitted with cold storage in the stern-most cargo hold that also contained a major shipment of beef and chicken bound for restaurants all over the U.S. Consisting of five immense storage lockers, with a small wheelhouse and crew quarters at the back end, she was a small example of her nautical class. The large crew of 30 were all excited for the week's extended stay in Detroit, giving them time for some much-needed rest and relaxation...and most likely raucous revelry. The four R's.

Miguel Hernandez and Fred McBride were hard at work smoking cigarettes and leaning on the starboard side rail nearer to the bow of the ship, standing above the second hold. With nothing breaking up the landscape of the deck save for the series of large, square hatch covers, each with an adjoining crane, there was a sharp breeze that blew constantly across the water at them, chilling the two men regardless of summer's fresh reign. Neither man cared, loving the fresh, unsalted air and small waves, relatively speaking. Lake breeze was such a change from the ocean wind, and they relished each breath between drags of their coffin nails.

Between bullshitting about sexual conquests past and present, and what they were going to do when they got to Detroit, neither noticed the enormous, round, shadowed object that slowly rose up and kept pace with the back end of the much larger ship. They definitely missed the long, serpentine neck and head sprouting up out of the water on the port side opposite from them. The silent shape rose up about a hundred feet or so, the water cascading off the head drowned out by the ship's engines. Atop the ropey, steel blue colored neck -- its girth that of a large grain silo -- sat the enlarged head of the Loch Ness monster. It was a visage ripped straight from a child's worst nightmare. The overlarge *Elasmosaurus* head was round at the braincase and tapered to a reptilian snout full of wicked, hook-like teeth that sprouted out all around both of its jaws like a hundred velociraptor talons. Cold, semi-intelligent eyes shone with a malevolent fury that was normally reserved for human beings.

It watched the oblivious primates on the other side. The monster's unseen form kept pace with the *Yearning Ways* without difficulty. Further out from the first head, an identical head and neck rose up slowly out of the water, craning almost comically around the original to peer at the two clueless deckhands. The two heads hissed loudly like aggravated crocodiles, with the sounds very audible over the ship's engines.

Miguel and Fred's heads snapped around, and they both issued the high-pitched scream of a child waking up from being devoured in a Loch Ness Monster nightmare. The heads both charged the ship before the unseen bulk of their submerged bodies latched onto the much larger carrier with enough force to noticeably push it to port fifty feet or so. Cliché Klaxon alarms immediately wailed throughout the ship. Soon men began to scramble on deck, most freezing in their tracks upon gazing up at the multi-headed horror now latched onto the *Yearning Ways*.

Fred got back to his feet first and picked Miguel up from the deck where they had both been knocked down from the impact. They looked on in dumbfounded horror as the two giant, prehistoric creatures rapidly plucked screaming men up, gnashed them to bits and gulped them down as if they were messy beef sticks. *Talking about snapping into a Slim Jim,* Fred thought as one of the guys he knew, James Mullins, was chewed up into pieces before his eyes. Fred's horrible internal monologue caused him to puke all over the place. He quickly wiped his mouth off on his sleeve, then ran towards the cargo hold stairs. Miguel followed quickly behind him, narrowly avoiding the puddle of upchuck.

Still unnoticed, the floating, shadowy object pacing on the port side of the ship began moving towards the now halted, commercial cargo vessel. Huge razor claws shot out of the water and punctured the top deck of the ship, locking into place. The flat, yet rounded face of Shellshock emerged from the lake, his opaque, blue-gray eyes focusing on the chaotic deck almost voyeuristically, like a peeping Tom. The beast enthusiastically snapped his bony choppers together rapidly, the agonizing sound sending the few remaining men to the wet, shiny deck. They held their hands to their ears while grimacing in pain, effectively incapacitated from the decibel attack. The monstrous *Elasmosaurs* on the starboard side snapped them up before they knew what hit them.

Shellshock's head dipped back into the ocean, tearing its claws back across the deck as it re-submerged. The enormous, curved turtle claws shredded the side of the gigantic bulk carrier, tearing a gaping hole into the side of it as they withdrew. Lake water rushed into the exposed fourth cargo hold, flooding the giant compartment full of grains. Seeking refuge there, Miguel and Fred became mixed in a deadly slurry of product, equipment, other hiding workers, and the cold Lake Superior waters.

As the cargo hold filled with water, the *Yearning Ways* began to sink, listing horribly to the port side as it was pulled down by the kaiju, who was using it like a pool toy. The ship's tonnage limit was becoming severely compromised by the additional weight of two giant monsters and a hell of a lot of water flooding the cargo holds.

Underneath the rapidly sinking vessel, Shellshock let go of the fourth hold and swam back to the fifth hold of the ship. The monster bored into the hull with its claws, tearing a jagged gash open just far enough to shove its greedy snout in. Gouts of frozen air and icy chunks violently bubbled and frothed out of the newly opened hole, chilling the monster's blood.

Practically inhaling a large amount of the frozen meat from the refrigerated cargo bay, the beast's clacking jaws thundered in the large meat locker, bits of its serrated jaw bones chipping off on the frozen nom noms. Even flooded, the large metal chamber amplified the sound to the point of being heard by the denizens of the Hiawatha National Forest, albeit it only a deep, bass thumping. The wilderness area was miles away on shore, in Michigan's upper peninsula, yet Shellshock's muffled, snapping jaws startled dozens of highly sensitive critters into flight, their exoduses taking them as far from the lake as possible.

The shelled monster's gorging had pulled the back 300 feet of the ship underwater, flooding most of the top deck even further. This was mainly the three-story wheelhouse at the very back of the ship's stern. With three cargo holds still intact, the remainder of the buoyancy left in the distressed carrier resided in them, the unbreeched cavities of air passively fighting the beasts' attempts to sink the *Yearning Ways.*

On the top starboard side, Rampage grabbed the rail of the ship and tried to climb up onto the deck. The twin *elasmosaur* heads hissed and their serpentine necks undulated as two massive claws reached up and dug into the deck. The taloned mitts grabbed the side like a person about to hoist themselves into a boat. The action pulled a huge bulky form out from the water, but also pulled the rising bow back down into the water as the additional weight leveled out the sinking ship. The center head emerged from the lake, its humongous mouth filled with large, conical teeth. The crocodilian jaws open wide, lake water and saliva pouring out of them as its large brown eyes were revealed, showing equal parts intelligence and mirth.

The top and bottom jaws flipped open and an excruciatingly loud roar blasted out from the *Tylosaurus* head's mouth. The victorious ululation drowned out all other sounds for its fifteen-second duration. No one aboard the cargo ship had heard the roar, as the crew were all dead, but many people on land called the roar into the authorities, thinking something had exploded.

Out of the night sky, a dark form streaked down and crashed through the middle of the ship, smashing the wheelhouse into oblivion before the deck split in two. Both bow and stern rose up into the air again as the cannonballing daikaiju plowed straight through the ship's midsection. The severed halves continued their dance with gravity as they were torn from each other, upending and quickly sinking as the remaining compartments flooded almost at the same time. Rampage and Shellshock let go of their ruined prizes and fled the vortices created by the ruined pieces of the nautical vessel.

The shadow monster from the air burst forth from the water, hastily shaking off its great, leathery wings. The furious action shook the excess water from off the kaiju's 500-foot wingspan and allowing it to propel itself back into the sky. Dripping fur rained into the lake below as the physics-defying creature ascended back into the air. The monster's cries pierced the night, the shrieking chatter elicited by the thing a mixture of squirrel and pterosaur vocalizations that reached crescendo as they harmonized. The shrill roar cut through the sky like thunder as the furry winged creature ascended into the night sky before vanishing once again.

Shellshock and Rampage submerged, leaving the bubbles, expanding waves, and swirling water from the sunken ship as the only remaining evidence that anything had been there at all. Minutes later, even this activity ceased, and Lake Superior was dark and quiet once more.

***

The Coast Guard arrived on scene about thirty minutes after the creatures had turned south towards the upper peninsula of Michigan. Captain Peretti of the *Sturgeon* radioed the wreckage in, as well as the blips disappearing off his radar right as he arrived on-scene in his Cutter.

"Coast Guard Station Duluth, this is U.S. Coast Guard Cutter *Sturgeon*, I have arrived at the coordinates of the mayday issued by the *Yearning Ways*. Upon arrival, my equipment displayed two unidentified targets... I'm pretty sure they were… ahem… *monsters*

-- given the size and path they took. They were headed south towards the Hiawatha National Forest, at about twenty knots. Please respond, over," he said into the old, outdated radio mouthpiece.

"Copy that, *Sturgeon,* Duluth Air National Guard is scrambling F-16 Falcons as we speak, E.T.A. thirty minutes. Maintain location and wait for further instructions, over," the fuzzy response barked out of the speaker next to him.

"Copy that, Duluth. Over and out."

Minutes later, the deafening scream of three fighter jets drowned out everything else, prying hopeful smiles from Capt. Peretti and his small crew of three on the bridge. Their thoughts and prayers were with the Fighting Falcons as they sped towards their foes. Duluth A.N.G. had immediately contacted Scott AFB in Belleville, Illinois. They were sending a squadron of A-10 Thunderbolt II's to Michigan as well. E.T.A. was 45 minutes.

***

The three jets flew over the vast Hiawatha National Forest, directly over the devastated remains of several miles of coniferous and deciduous wilderness, lain to waste in the wake of the two -- so far elusive -- kaiju. Then they were painfully obvious, the darkness of the cloudy night seeming to reveal them from its black folds, even with the night vision equipped aircraft.

The first monster to come into view was the turtle from the Duluth attack... but much bigger. The tower points of its shell scutes stuck up almost like the spikes of an inflated blowfish. The fifty-foot-plus long, spiky tail whipped randomly back and forth, simply trailing behind it, kicking trees and chunks of earth up into the air like some berserk weed whacker.

Its turtle legs were longer than before, looking more like the legs of a rhino or elephant, but were in reality borrowed from a *Triceratops.* The clawed, hand-like feet were very much still those of an alligator snapping turtle. The combination of quadruped legs and reptilian claws made its gait as it charged over the wilderness almost comical. Almost.

The razor talons punched and tore up the ground as Shellshock thundered behind its apparent leader. The thick, rounded block of a *Dunkleosteus* head flinched and glanced back at the approaching airmen and their noisy metal steeds. The glowing blue irises shone in the scarce moonlight as it clacked its jaws at the F-16's in defiance.

The daikaiju leading Shellshock was an even more incredible sight to behold, and then some.

It stood 275 feet at the shoulder, with its two long-necked heads towering even farther above, likely 400 feet. Two parallel rows of flat, armored plates stuck up vertically from the vertebrae of its spine and branching double tails, the flat sides facing the right and left flanks in alternating positions along its back. Each tail ended with a different weapon that some of the pilots recognized from the dinosaur books they loved as kids. One a *Stegosaurus'* thagomizer, one the club of an A*nkylosaurus.*

The monster was broad-hipped, with shorter back legs than the front, almost like a giraffe...or even a gorilla running on its fists. Its longer front legs transitioned to a broad chest that ended in not one, but three heads. On either side, by each shoulder, were long, twisting necks, both similar to a snake or an eel, and ending in almost dragon-like heads that were decorated with curved hooks for teeth. The middle, no-necked head between them had huge jaws on a big, thick skull --almost like a hybrid of a whale and a monitor lizard.

Rampage roared at the planes in annoyance, all three heads emitting a simultaneous cry. The daikaiju were both charging over the forests and fields that made up Hiawatha Forest. At a speed of about 25 mph, but in supersize format, they were over halfway to Lake Michigan already.

"Falcon 1 to base, we have a visual," the lead F-16 pilot said into his headpiece. "Permission to engage."

"Permission granted, Falcon 1."

Something slammed into Falcon 1, coating it in a burning, napalm-like substance that crawled and roiled with a *colour* like nothing the pilot of Falcon 2 had ever seen. The surprise attack instantly set the jet ablaze, rapidly eating through the fighter jet's metal hide and electronic innards until eventually reaching the fuel tank, causing the plane to explode. It took all of three seconds.

Just long enough for the pilot to scream.

Falcon 2 was likewise coated in the incinerating ooze. He lost control of everything, the jet, his bladder, and finally his mind. The hypnotic, flaming *colour* chewed through the hull of the F-16 in mere seconds, filling up the cockpit and consuming its occupant, whose shrieks of agony were abruptly cut off as Falcon 2 burst into flames.

Falcon 3 veered sharply to the west and flew up. The pilot frantically tried to locate the source of the vile napalm bursts. Not seeing anything on the scope or through the windshield, he leveled out and then nosed down directly at the two earthbound monsters that were rapidly crossing the peninsula, getting closer to their destination on the southern shore.

The pilot's eyes registered something above and in front of him, and they flicked up to look...just in time to see a massive, scaled beak burst from the darkness and slam into the nose cone and fuselage. Giant, rodent-like incisors punched through the cockpit glass as well as his legs and kept going straight through, severing the front of the plane clean off.

His body a pin cushion of broken glass, Falcon 3 watched in stunned agony as his legs and the nose of his F-16 spun away from him. His soon lifeless head flopped limply back and forth behind the still attached seat belts, as the rest of the plane fell to earth in a mangled heap before combusting into a cloud of flame five minutes later.

On the ground, Rampage looked back with both *Elasmosaur* heads at the burning pockmarks dug into the earth where the burning jet debris had hit the ground. The constantly changing, molten *colour* oozed onto everything it touched as it covered the ground, igniting the vegetation like paper. Soon the forest was an inferno of the strange colored flame.

Neither Rampage or Shellshock stopped moving towards their destination, not even when the A-10 Thunderbolts arrived, belching machine guns and rockets. Most of these hit home, smothering both monsters in flame and smoke. The A-10s circled back around just in time to see both gargantuans burst forth from the smoke, unscathed and undeterred. Like charging bulls, they ignored everything the planes spewed at them – even when the A-10s started dropping bombs. The dropped ordinance only aided the daikaiju in leveling the area even further, as countless trees went up in flames.

Ten minutes of futile firepower later, the monsters still loomed over the shores of Lake Michigan as the Thunderbolts continued to bombard them with cluster bombs that did nothing but destroy wilderness and the few unlucky Yoopers living in that part of the Upper Peninsula. Both daikaiju stopped when they came to the northern shore of Lake Michigan.

Rampage turned and reared up on its hind legs, putting the beast up around 450 feet tall, not including the long-necked heads. The middle head and its huge jaws with wicked, conical teeth opened wide, as a cloud of oily black smoke billowed from the open maw in a ragged, twisting cone. The unusual breath weapon shot directly at the closest A-10, still hundreds of yards away and incoming. The A-10 rusted up instantly and dropped from the sky. Before crashing to Earth, the rusting spew reached the pilot, where it melted the flesh off his bones into an ashy tar. The pilot was reduced to a screaming skeleton wearing a soggy jumpsuit in a flash of searing, necrotic agony.

The four remaining Thunderbolts shot back up into the sky above the clouds. Conquer was there waiting for them. The pterosaur-mammalian crossover could fly like a bat and glide like a pro. Dive-bombing the fleeing planes in their tight formation, she unfurled her wings right before impact and revealed the gray, furry, four-legged body underneath. The muscular arms it possessed each had hands with opposable thumbs. Each paw was also clawed - sharp, curved nails made for climbing and gripping, but just as useful for mutilation.

With these, it snatched two of the planes out of the air like they were nothing but floating feathers. The third Thunderbolt was skewered by the beak full of gnawing choppers in a quick flick of the crested beast's head. The fourth Thunderbolt barely dodged the huge right wing, pulling up and soaring over it before flying back down through the night's black clouds towards the ground.

Conquer's giant, fluffy tail shot up behind her back and smacked the last plane like a flail, tearing off a wing and sending the rest arcing through the air like a frisbee, spinning in circles rapidly. The pilot managed to eject, propelling his chair from its cockpit moorings. He ditched his seat after opening his chute and drifted slowly down once his parachute was deployed. Miraculously, he escaped notice and landed in the woods far away from the stampeding monsters.

Rampage slammed back down to Earth, registering Richter's on seismographs within several nearby states and Canada. The kaiju roared in triumph at the night sky. Shellshock clacked its teeth in response and clucked shrilly like a parrot. Far above, a squawking chatter of a retort made its way down to them from the squirrel abomination in the sky. Both grounded kaiju splashed into Lake Michigan, swimming down to the deepest spots to hide and make their way south as Conquer flew through the clouds on a parallel flight path.

***

The U.S. Military responded by sending troops to Milwaukee and Chicago, as well as a few other cities along the shores of Lake Michigan, where they would begin setting up perimeters on the waterfronts of both Midwest cities. The hope that the creatures would stay submerged long enough to accomplish this was present everywhere.

Eventually, the news was broken to the public, and a voluntary evacuation began. Once the beasts were sighted, it would become mandatory for people to evacuate, depending on their locations. Mass numbers of people fled most of the shoreline cities, moving away from the lake. Madison, Wisconsin and Rockford, Illinois were flooded with fleeing refugees, as were the surrounding small towns in between.

The military vehicles rolled into each of the two cities en masse and set up shop by one o'clock in the afternoon the following day, a little less than twelve hours after Rampage first attacked the *Yearning Ways*. Everything from armored personnel carriers to tanks to helicopters patrolling the skies above was used to prepare for the worst. National Guard and Army Reserves were everywhere. Soldiers and vehicles were stationed all along the shore, as well as at strategic points across each city.

Colonel Timothy Giossi oversaw the Chicago-based military covering the city and her Lake Michigan waterline. A recently assembled brigade of National Guard, Army, and Marines plus several scores of land, sea, and aircraft were all on guard. Giossi hoped it was enough.

Immediately after the incident in Duluth, the Coast Guard sent a little more than a dozen ships south, where they were currently patrolling Lake Michigan on full alert and armed to the teeth. Several vessels were on the way from the Navy as well but were delayed by paperwork and politics. Now, positioned in a small fortress set up on top of the Hilton Chicago, Giossi could do nothing but wait. His communications officer kept informing him of multiple sources of seismic activity being reported by geologists in the states and provinces around Lake Michigan, all sources moving towards the Windy City. There were disagreements on how many bogies there were, seven being the most, three the least. Regardless of the numbers, they *were* coming.

The city was in the process of being completely evacuated, and angry citizens were not cooperating well. Riots and looting broke out across the city and forced removal in certain sections of the city became necessary to clear people out before the monsters came ashore. The already oppressed masses were treated like cattle in the attempts to empty the most likely areas of emergence of the potential human collateral damage. Sadly, over a dozen people died or were injured in the poorly executed process, on both sides of the badge.

The few citizens who remained after evading the evacuation were the stubborn people hiding in the city's many nooks and crannies. These refugees would be left to their own devices after the evacuation crews had pulled out an hour prior. It was down to Giossi and his battalion now, hopefully receiving back-up in a few hours from the Navy's newly formed lake patrol, made up mostly of Coast Guard vessels. Sweat started to break out on Col. Giossi's paling face as he comprehended the magnitude of what his forces were about to face.

The war room he was in bustled with activity. Military strategists and scientists, armed grunts, and a handful of city and state officials worked in rapid fashion to prepare the defenses, exit strategies, evacuation plans, and last resort contingencies of the coming invasion of the giant monsters.

As laughable as that last statement was, it *was* true. Giant monsters were invading America, apparently seeking out the board executives from the global powerhouse, Bionautics. The unofficial theory was that Sadako Sōzō, the Japanese madwoman who had inherited the rogue organization Hidora Neo, had somehow created these nightmares that had assassinated six of the top corporate fat cats behind the number one genetic engineering laboratory in the world.

And she was far from finished.

Many scoffed at the possibilities of this, but Giossi had heard so many rumors about this "New Hydra" company run by Sōzō, he believed them all to a point. It was almost dangerous *not* to, given the copious amounts of evidence. As such, Sadako Sōzō was very much a wanted woman, the United States' best informants placing her last known location on a ship bound for Antarctic waters 36 hours previous. A greeting party was attempting to intercept her.

Of course, the hows of the continental attack on America were still unanswered. It was believed there was a Hidora Neo base somewhere in the Great Lakes region, most likely in or around Lake Superior, but so far there had been no success in finding one. The genetic prospect was mind-boggling.

How the hell did she make a bunch of Godzillas?

Kaiju, or daikaiju more appropriately, were the preferred terms used, phrases made popular by the Japanese monster star's movies, as well as movies like *Pacific Rim,* a special effects-driven film depicting otherworldly behemoths fighting against humanity's giant army of robots made to stop them, as well as a resurgence of Godzilla movies at the end of the last decade.

Unfortunately, giant robots weren't realistically possible. The dynamics of creating the automatons, coupled with the unachievable task of powering the things made them fantasies to be wistfully dreamed about by every branch of the government as they tried to figure out just what the hell they could do to deal with this new threat and still suffer as little collateral damage as possible, structural or living.

Nukes were out of the question, the last resort.

Then there was Bionautics.

The target of the monsters' wrath was right now working on what they claimed was a prototype kaiju of their own, a new piece of biotech they successfully created and grew out of cells from the hideous turtle creature that had torched poor little Duluth, Minnesota. It had barely been a week since the attack, which led Col. Giossi to wonder... how had they created a giant monster so quickly, having no idea prior how to do so? Could they really reverse engineer a monster that fast? When it really came down to it, Bionautics scared him a little more than Hidora Neo -- they were officially sanctioned by the governments of the world, after all.

"Colonel!" A pale-faced kid from communications called out to him, pulling Giossi from his thoughts. He tore himself from his zone-out and hurried over to the computer the soldier occupied. The satellite GPS program on the screen was tracking the seismic sources through the USGS' servers, identifying them by different colored Richter scale ratings.

The beasts were all close. *Very* close.

"I want all units locked and loaded, and on high alert. Wait for my signal to fire," he said in a calm voice that belied the shaking hands at his sides. He had never felt this close to staring death in the face in all his 40 years. He prayed to God silently to see him through the impending doom making its way to Chicago's doorstep.

***

"Dr. Brown, does West have any idea what cards you and I have up our sleeves?"

"No, Dr. Brundle, he has no clue," Seth Brown said to his younger colleague with a sly, toothy grin that barely showed off his dentures. "I'm fairly certain he's actually *trusting* in us, as a matter of fact!"

"Wow. I guess our little trio has come a long way, eh?" Herbert Brundle said to his elder conspirator. They sat at the consoles in Superior X's control room. More efficient than the original computer stations they had used for Shellshock's first strike, each of these consoles was like the old school sit-in cabinet arcade games, like *Afterburner*, *Star Wars*, or any of the countless racing arcade games that populated arcades in the 1980s.

Each consisted of a rhombic frame of metal and fiberglass, with a cushy seat, user interface, and display that was housed in the front part of the unit. A scientist would climb into either of the open sides and sit down into the chair opposite the console. They would then strap into their chairs, pulling the interface towards them until the sidebars found their corresponding latches on the back end of the fame. Once lined up properly, the frame would naturally lock into place.

From there, the controller would don a headpiece consisting of a multitude of wires, sensors, and a monocle that rotated down across the user's left eye. This would keep one in contact with the other controllers and their respective avatar monsters through a series of neural implants and optical cameras surgically installed into each of the beasts using robots created by Ripley Station's top tech guys, Donovan and Beane.

While the users could influence and command the beasts - who possessed genetically modified, canine-like comprehension - they did not directly control their movements. The sit-in control consoles had been recently finished by the two men using them now, each desiring a more direct contact than the hypnotic suggestion chips they had installed in all the other beasts that had come before the newest monstrosities.

Capable of adding new instructions and directives to their creations'... *programming* -- for lack of a better term, the new interfaces were tied directly to each controller, making them more simpatico with the monsters they unleashed through new brainwave technology Brown had perfected several months ago.

The two began waking up the consoles, syncing them to their surprise projects, who were still tunneling under Lake Michigan. The new kaiju were setting off every seismic monitoring device for thousands of miles, but hopefully were still fooling the military's tracking devices.

"Sadako certainly threw us to the wayside with the San Francisco attack, didn't she?" Brundle asked.

"Like discarded refuse, my dear boy," Brown returned. "Believe me when I say she will regret it. If West's unannounced visit to the Upper Peninsula and dip into Lake Michigan hasn't made her do so already. What kind of structure do we have if any scientist or Johnny-come-latelies can just throw a couple of hastily developed chimera together and just storm a major U.S. city without any sort of plan? Did you see the footage of the regenerative skin? My ass that's one percent or less of the alien DNA! Those screaming, tentacled mouths are like some bad Lovecraft story. What will happen when those beasts suffer all over damage? Will they become nothing but screaming amorphous blobs?" Brown took a breath and continued. "Shoddy science, my friend, and piss-poor technique."

"It almost seemed to me like someone let them loose on accident, the way they just appeared at the bridge as they did. That's a horrible introduction point, in my opinion," Brundle replied. "I'm wondering if something bad happened in Trench Town."

"Possibly, Herb, but the simple fact that we've heard nothing from our leader before she ran down to Antarctica worries me more. A simple, five-minute phone call or a text message, for Christ's sake? How hard is that? 'Sorry our West Coast associates bungled your approved operation, gentlemen, I assure you the transgressors will be seen to. Please commence with the planned festivities as soon as you are ready. Handsome bonuses are being transferred to your accounts as we speak!'"

Brundle laughed loudly. "That would be the day, Seth! I'm all set here, by the way. Mario Le Pew and Luigi El Diablo are programmed for destruction and following shortly behind your two diggers. Estimated time of arrival: two hours from now."

"Copy that, Dr. Brundle. Digger and Dugger are an hour and a half out but will wait for your boys to catch up before we commence.

113

West's trio will be in position approximately the same time as them, so things should align nicely. We will give him the benefit of the reveal. The shock of seeing Rampage alone will release the bladders and bowels of many of the soldiers patrolling Chicago. Once they regain their composure and try to strike back, our critter crew will make their appearance," Brown said with a smile that stretched from ear to ear. He was so happy he could sing.

"I need some music, my dear boy," he said.

He opened his console's music program up in a new window and selected "Figaro's Aria" from *The Barber of Seville.* Orchestral music blared from the Onkyo speakers decorating the room. Much to Brundle's dismay, the white-haired mad scientist began belting out the operatic verses, like a seasoned veteran, in sync with the recording. Herbert did have to admit that classical music did always make destruction seem more civilized, and Brown's singing wasn't really all that bad. The younger scientist began humming quietly along with the piece as their monstrous creations neared the city of Chicago, Illinois.

CHAPTER 9

Antarctic Ocean
Three days after breaching Pandora's Room

Ominously silent, the black ship swiftly cut through the choppy waves, kicking up salty spray as it powered through the angry Antarctic seas. The retractable deck shields were extended and dutifully channeling the ocean away from the speeding ship's bow as it climbed each wave before slicing through and crashing down again on the other side. *The Manticore* was a former Japanese whaling vessel Hidora Neo had turned into a private research craft — with covert military tendencies. Had the seas been rougher, the going would have been much slower, but until the dark storm clouds behind them finally caught up, the crew of mysterious craft was still ahead of the front.

On the ship's bridge, Hodder and Sadako stood next to the ship's captain. His name was Wesley Englund III, and he was a former Marine and one of Hodder's old chums. Ahead of the captain stood the Officer of the Watch and the two pilots manning the navigational equipment, all three men busy keeping them on course. They were also staying vigilant to keep their heading away from major shipping and travel lanes. Not that discovery was a worry in the weather they were foolishly traveling in, given the specialized Hidora Neo enhancements that the one-of-a-kind-ship possessed. However, it was really the suicidal nature of their ship's captain that made it possible for them to make it to Antarctica, let alone Ripley Station, in such record time.

In June. During the continent's winter.

A season of darkness and unpredictability. If they were not so familiar with the route and the seasonal weather, the trip would have been impossible.

***

Sadako's eyes shot icicles at Hodder, freezing his blood. "I still do not understand how Sgt. Bottin and his men did not notice our disobedient engineers' absence. Do they not keep watch, Captain?"

Hodder had known this woman since the day of her birth, and the calmly contained fury she possessed had always unnerved him to his core. Bruce Hodder, the man who had killed more people in cold-blooded murder for two out of the three Sōzōs and all their enterprises. Without question, he feared this little woman. Not only was she ruthless… but, man, could she fight!

He had trained her well.

"I will find out, Sadako, and the weak link will be strengthened. You have my word," Hodder said through gritted teeth. "Have your techs been able to retrieve the security footage from the alien ship?"

"They have, but it suffered major interference as soon as the unidentified life form made its first appearance. They are cleaning it up as we speak, in the communications room below us."

Sadako turned and looked up into Hodder's eyes again as she said that. To his relief, the venom in them had subsided, at least temporarily, to be replaced by an uncommon look of concern.

"We have no estimate on the number of hostiles still in the unexplored area, though we knew there was something in there. But with the discovery of the Pangea machines, further exploration was deemed unimportant. Why open Pandora's box when we already had such an incredible source of power? Let sleeping dogs lie. That's why we left it sealed for years, installing motion detectors early on, devices Beane and Donovan obviously were unaware of. We will have to open up the rest of the ship now, I suppose. Do you have enough men with you, Captain?"

117

"Forty onboard, which includes as many of my elite as we could spare," Hodder said before he raised an eyebrow. "Keeping tabs on the remaining board members has become difficult after San Francisco. That task has required my people's full attention. The Bionautics' bodyguards are some of the finest in the business, so competence is vital. Otherwise, we'd have more of them with us. There are nearly three dozen orphans onboard, however, so I think we will be alright."

"Understood. We must get to the bottom of the events in California. I'm sure those boys in Superior X are rather incensed at what they must surely take as an act of betrayal." Sadako then changed the subject without missing a beat. "Now, on to the situation ahead of us. What do we know about the revived life forms so far?"

Hodder unlocked his gigantic smartphone's home screen and brought up the photos folder. He opened one of them and handed the device to her. Sadako looked at the mostly blurry images of the deceased, brutish creature. They were not fantastic, but they were adequate enough to get the gist of the alien's appearance, but not of a quality to fully comprehend the thing's strange head. Sadako pursed her lips and handed the phone back.

"I trust the body is secure?"

"Of course, Sadako. It was the first order I gave when I contacted Miner. He had a helluva time getting it to our facility, but he got it done."

"That's what I like to hear. Miner has always been an exemplary member of your team. Give him a reward. I apologize for choosing Bottin over him to lead the Antarctic crew. I remember that Miner was your first choice. Bottin's handling of the Vietnam incident we had in the early '90s was clearly a poor example of the man's worth. If he wouldn't have had his head crushed by this creature, I would have used him for spare parts for beating one of my family as he did." Sadako chuckled a little, then sighed longingly before continuing.

"It's been awhile since I've seen blood for myself. I miss it sometimes," she said as she gazed out at the dark sea vacantly, memories playing back in her head. Hodder cracked a smile. Ishiro's daughter was a spitting image of her old man.

***

24 hours later
Entrance to Ripley Station
Antarctica

As America and the rest of the world reeled in shock from the two attacks on U.S. soil by actual *monsters*, Sadako and her people arrived at the Antarctic complex in a pride of souped-up Sno Cats. The Hum-Vee-like vehicles were customized like all their rides, and normally stored in a private garage at McMurdo station -- the securing of which was a feat of palm-greasing Sadako would be forever proud of.

Christened Ripley Station, the underground cavern that led to the Antarctic headquarters built around the buried spacecraft was concealed by a hidden entrance. The rock with Sadako's name painted on it had been replaced with an artificial version. It looked like a real hill of rock, ice, and snow. Prompted by a button push from Hodder, the jumble of rocks suddenly sprouted an opening as two concealed doors slid back into it, revealing a tunnel descending into the earth.

The procession of treaded vehicles descended the man-made tunnel at a 45-degree angle on the reinforced rock and steel road. Seven rows of LED lights ran along the length of each wall, with two rows traveling along the ceiling. Driving the lead Sno Cat, Hodder kept the headlights on, illuminating every nook and cranny on the way down to the cavern below.

Sitting next to him in the front passenger's seat, Sadako was audibly grinding her teeth. The anticipation of the situation they were about to enter was grating on her nerves as well as her patience. She turned to a younger woman in the back seat of the vehicle. The twentysomething sitting on the rear driver's side was a Caucasian woman with wavy auburn hair tumbling down her shoulders.

"Has there been any progress on contacting Trench Town, Elizabeth?"

The woman looked up from staring out the window at the tunnel lights as they drove. "Not yet, Sadako. The comms seem to be completely down. I've pulled Mackenzie from her vacation. She and her team will be checking it out in a sub. They deployed from *Carcharodon* about three hours ago. I should have an update within the hour."

Sadako nodded in affirmation. "Very good, my child. I wish to know the status of our kaiju from San Francisco. Finding out why we suddenly lost contact with the facility is also of major importance. I smell a Bionautics rat."

She then looked to the man next to Elizabeth, a tall, thick block of a man. "Are your men ready, Gatimu?"

Gatimu Omondi was a Kenyan born 30-year-old, adopted by Sadako after she continued Ishiro's Orphan program. Omondi's combat prowess and aptitude for just about any type of weapon made him a valuable member of Hidora Neo's security force. He was well on his way to becoming the elderly Hodder's successor.

He grinned at her, flashing a mouth full of bright, white teeth.

"Yes, Mother, we only need to stop by the armory before entering the craft," Gatimu said in near perfect English, only a hint of Kenyan accent present. "I do not know about Hadeon's team, however."

Hadeon Voloshyn was an Orphan from Ukraine. The second team's leader for five years, the 39-year-old was a brutal man, very rarely leaving any witnesses or loose ends during missions, and often torturing victims purely for fun. His team was almost as savage as their leader. They were never dispatched for any mission where targets were not considered expendable. Sadako was impressed by their cold-blooded tactics, but in her eyes, there was a time and place for mass murder. In this situation, there was no hesitation in bringing Hadeon and his crew along.

"I'm sure that your psychotic brothers have prepared as you have, but we will all be visiting the armory before entering the ship, Gatimu," she said. "I will be coming with you."

The tall man grinned. "Of course, Mother! That is fantastic news, I've not had the honor to fight beside you yet. I very much look forward to it!"

"Kissass," Elizabeth muttered quietly into the glass of her window.

Hodder chuckled in the driver's seat, having barely caught her whisper.

Sadako glanced at the young Orphan woman for a split second, before looking back at Gatimu. "Let us see how rusty your *okaasan* is at using a gun."

Gatimu looked over at his backseat companion. "Better than Ellie, I'm sure. *Bitch.*" He whispered the last word to the woman seated next to him, though fully aware it was heard by everyone in the cab.

Ellie burst out laughing and flipped him the bird. "Right here, Gat," she said. "I'll carve you up like a turkey, and your stupid guns won't save you."

"Enough!" Sadako shouted to the pair. "Your mother has a headache. Save your bickering for later. We have a serious task at hand, and I need you both to keep your focus on the situation at hand."

"Yes, Mother," both Orphans replied without skipping a beat.

Nothing more was said the rest of the descent into Ripley's Station.

***

Ten minutes later, the seven vehicles sat parked in front of a three-story building. Behind it, the massive saucer loomed, fused into the frozen rock of the immense cavern's wall. The assemblage of Hidora Neo teams had only just entered the lobby of the building's first floor when three people came downstairs to meet them.

"Miner, give me a sitrep," Hodder said to the man in front.

All three men were dressed in black armor with forest green stripes running down the sides. Miner, the wider of the three soldiers, stepped up to Hodder and removed his tactical mask and headgear. Then he saluted.

"Yes, sir. Monday, at approximately 15:00 hours, New Zealand Standard Time, engineers Jean-Paul Beane and Louis Peter Donovan broke through the lock and seal on the door located just past the Pangea machine chamber. Shortly after, at 15:15, the two men encountered members of what is presumed to be the spacecraft's crew." Miner swallowed and ran his fingers through his sweaty, dark hair.

"A firefight ensued, resulting in the assumed death of one of the alien creatures. Our security team arrived in time to save the two engineers from an ambushing attacker. Beane had supposedly slain another one of the creatures just inside the room. Three of my team were killed, and after dropping the creature, Sgt. Bottin had me take Donovan to the infirmary and rally the remainder of the Ripley Station team. I left him and Beane in the Pangea room and brought Donovan to the infirmary, where Doctor Saxon started administering first aid.

"Approximately ten minutes after Bottin radioed me to return to the ship, I tried to raise him again with no success. As I returned to the spaceship, I ran into Beane, who had fresh wounds since I had last seen him. He told me of Bottin's contempt and hatred of the Orphans and his beating at the sergeant's hands. I let him return to the complex and moved into the ship's interior." Miner adjusted uncomfortably in his cheap chair. "When I arrived on the scene, Bottin's head lay crushed in the giant, elder thing's palm."

"Elder thing?" Hodder inquired with a suspicious look. "As in Lovecraft?"

"Yes, sir. Given where we are, and the starfish head, I immediately thought of *At the Mountains of Madness* by H.P. Lovecraft," said Miner, immediately earning strange looks from Hodder and Sadako. He smiled, his grey eyes reflecting some of the facial expression. "I'm not just a badass. I read a lot, too. Elder things are big, barrel-shaped aliens with wings and weird arms halfway down their bodies, with tentacles for legs. These were huge hulking versions, with massive legs and arms, and they have a lot more eyes."

"Yes, I know that story, I read it the first week I stayed here," Sadako said. "It is very appropriate. This makes me wonder about the alien DNA we use for our creations. From the footage we've seen of San Francisco -- the dark, regenerated skin that grew over the kaijus' wounds and sprouted tentacles and orifices -- I actually thought of the Shoggoths from that story. The black, amorphous blob monsters with similar random parts in their oozing masses. They were the Elder Things' created servants and slaves who eventually rebelled and started a war, if I recall correctly."

Miner looked dumbfounded. "We are making Shoggoths?"

"Hardly," Sadako laughed. "Our kaiju have less than one percent of the alien DNA. I am pleased with your handling of this situation, Owen Miner, and you will be rewarded."

"Thank you, Sadako. I live to better serve you," the humbled soldier bowed, keeping eye contact with his employer throughout the entire gesture.

"Well done, Miner. Now, go catch up on some sleep, some food, and a shower. Check back in with me in 8 hours but keep your headset active."

"Yes, sir! Thank you, sir!" Miner grinned, turned, and headed up the main lobby's front stairs to the second floor and the individual sleeping quarters.

Sadako passed the stairs Miner had ascended seconds prior and opened the double doors at the back of the room. Stepping into the hallway beyond, she turned right and walked down the relatively short corridor to a large, vault-like door. She leaned down to a round glass eye in the door's console. A green light flashed across her face, zooming in on her eyes. The panel beeped in an ascending tone three times, and a blue light above the scanner lit up. With a rush of air and a loud noise, the thick door to the armory opened. The small army filed in behind her as they entered.

Inside the loaded storeroom, rack upon rack of guns filled the first third of the huge space. There was everything from pistols and revolvers to machine guns -- even a few LAWs and RPG launchers. The three teams and their leader gathered at the back, where a series of monitors with a scattering of tables and furniture made up the "war room." It was already becoming hot in the gathered crowd of Orphans and Hodder's men.

Sadako stepped up onto the elevated area where the wall of monitors hung. She positioned herself in front of a screen that showed the blood-covered floor where the dead Starhead had killed Miner's team. Then she spoke out to her family of soldiers and miscreants.

"Inside the doors on the monitor behind me are members of an extraterrestrial race. Aggressive and strong, the species encountered by our resident engineers stands approximately five to seven meters tall, which is about fifteen to twenty feet. Depending on the individual, of course, and we *are* hypothesizing. This is what it looks like."

Sadako then opened the image of the dead monster they had in their morgue on the laptop to her right.

She brought the pictures up on the screen behind the laptop monitor, showing everyone in the room the body of something none of them had ever seen before. Also pictured were the corpses of several men. All dead, by inhuman hands. One of them had his head literally *squeezed* off. Gasps and expletives were audible as everyone gazed at the star-headed thing lying on the tiled floor next to a stainless-steel examining table, surrounded by Hodder's expired soldiers. It was easily twice as long as the examination table.

Sadako paced slowly back and forth in front of the monitors as she spoke. "Now, we can kill them, and apparently the shielded faceplate guards the thing's brain. Sgt. Bottin died finding this out, however, firing at least 25 shots from his M16 rifle point blank, and even then he only penetrated the face plate because of the concentrated fire.

"One of the engineers used a flamethrower on a creature's face with effective, but non-lethal, results. That creature is still alive and has since closed the door to what we are calling 'Pandora's Room'. It is likely to be extremely pissed off, having lost most of the secondary eyes between its five central eye stalks.

"Hadeon's team shall go in first and do a sweep of the immediate area. Once they give the all-clear, Gatimu and his team will enter and set up a temporary perimeter, including but not limited to the motion activated .50 cals leaning against the wall to my right."

The boss lady pointed to six cylindrical monsters attached to heavy duty racking in the direction mentioned as she mentioned that. There were oohs and ahhs, and even a few whistles and catcalls. Sadako smiled at this and continued.

"Once a perimeter has been established, I will be following Captain Hodder and his team in to provide support. Meanwhile, the first two teams are to explore the room beyond, mapping it with a drone Engineering developed."

Sadako picked a handheld device up from the table in front of her. It looked much like an overlarge video game controller with a five-inch, 4K high-definition screen in the middle. She activated the device, and the myriad of buttons on the remote lit up in differing hues.

Slowly squeezing the right trigger on the underside handgrip, she activated the drone. The sudden noise behind them made the back rows of minions jump as the two-foot-long object lifted into the air on spinning rotor blades.

Resembling a skeletal version of a jet fighter, the thin machine had two propulsion fans situated before the tail of the tiny aircraft. These pushed it forward towards the group as Sadako moved the rubber-padded joystick similarly on the large controller in her hand. It dipped forward like a helicopter as it advanced over their heads, hovering in place when it stopped just above the boss lady. She turned it around 180 degrees, until it faced her audience.

Sadako pushed in the yellow button on the top left of the controller, and a bright light flared to life underneath the front nose cone. Squinting at the intense spotlight, the collective watched as the light rotated around a full circle on its swivel mount connecting it to the undercarriage. Everything the brightness touched was illuminated brilliantly as the sweeping bulb spun around on its axis.

"Ladies and Gentlemen, meet the AMRD1, or Aerial Mapping and Reconnaissance Drone," Sadako said with a pleased smile on her face. "This machine can use ultrasound and sonar technology for mapping large areas, as well as take high-definition surveillance pictures and video. It can fire slow burning flares as well."

She then pulled back on the left trigger before banking the AMRD1 to the right with the joystick, which caused the sophisticated drone to descend. It eventually landed next to the laptop sitting on the desk.

"This will be used to scout the area, mapping it and transmitting the data to our computers while Hadeon's team follows it in."

Sadako walked back to the middle of the monitor display where she turned and faced her crew with her arms crossed.

"Now I will turn the floor over to Captain Hodder, who will go over the other armaments available to you. We will move at dawn, approximately 0700 hours. That gives you all about four hours to get a few winks in. Use it wisely, *mikatas*. I will see you then. I must deal with our San Francisco activity. Someone has released kaiju into San Francisco unauthorized, and I fear sabotage."

Sadako ignored the mumbles and gasps as she quickly walked out of the armory and followed the stairs to the third-floor communications room.

Hodder waited until she left to begin. "Alright, ladies and gentlemen. You heard the lady. Now hear me. I'm going to tell you how not to get killed by these things. So, listen up, because I'm not your fucking babysitter, and I don't want to be dragging your bloody corpses out of here!"

***

Sadako entered the cramped communications room at the top of the final flight of stairs. Computer stations and their wired connections overloaded the small room, each linked to a branch of Hidora Neo. Ming-Huá Chen was the only other person in the hot, electricity-scented office. The 26-year old's fingers flew on the keyboard as she worked, flipping through screen after screen of HN CCTV camera footage. Ming was selecting and dragging certain feeds to the secondary screen sitting to the left of the main monitor.

A plump little woman, Ming almost seemed to be a physical part of the computer nerd's dream chair she rotated back and forth in. Perspiration ran down her face occasionally, causing one wet wisp of her bangs to keep falling back over her thick, unisex glasses' left eye. As she brushed it back behind her ear for the umpteenth time, she noticed her adopted mother standing there. Ming jumped, a little squeak of fright escaping her like a vocal fart.

"Mother! You scared me," Ming said quickly in heavily accented English. "I was just finishing the sort of video feeds you asked for." She smiled up at Sadako, her pudgy cheeks giving up a pair of dimples that her mother loved to see on this daughter, in particular of all of them. She received a smile from Sadako for her efforts.

"Sorry for startling you, Ming-Huá. I'm pleased you have made progress. Anything to report from what you have seen?"

"Well, yes, ma'am. It's become very clear to me that the black, regenerative tissue is most definitely the foreign DNA... uh, shoggoth?" She looked at Sadako hesitantly, unsure of her usage of the fictional Lovecraft creature's name. Sadako frowned a little.

"Yes, that will do for now, even though I don't much care for it. Bring up any feeds you have that show me the effects of one of the scar tissue orifices screaming. I've been told it drives people insane." Sadako said that with noticeable gravity in her voice. "That could make control a problem."

"*Hai*," Ming said before she dragged several windows around, bringing up five in total -- all footage from stoplight cameras on the streets of San Francisco. The tentacled carnosaur Nautilus Rex occupied all five screens. "If I play the videos with sound, we could both have seizures. Gunther had one when we first found these. He's down in the infirmary right now."

Sadako raised an eyebrow. "Even through video filters?"

"Yes, Mother. I don't know why I did not have any, but I've not taken any chances. Earplugs do seem to dampen the seizure-inducing effects, but I can still feel it pushing through." She made eye contact with the older woman, fear reflecting in them plainly. "I didn't want to go crazy. Gunther was foaming at the mouth. It was pink foam."

Concern flashed through her mother's steel blue eyes. "You have done well, Ming. I hope your German brother will recover. I am sorry you both had to experience this. We had no idea the... *shoggoth*... DNA would respond in this manner. Dr. Brown is working diligently to correct the matter." She had not been in contact with Dr. Brown since leaving for Antarctica, but Ming did not need to know that.

Sadako placed her right hand on her adopted daughter's left shoulder, squeezing it in a very caring way. "I want you to take the rest of the night to wind down, my dear. Get some food and some sleep. Report back in the morning, at 0700. Okay?" She smiled down at Ming, who nodded quickly up and down.

"Yes, Mother. Thank you."

With that said, the overweight young woman stood up from her chair, the office furniture groaning from the sudden absence of the weight that had been pushing down on it for hours. She bowed to her mother and left the room for the stairs down to the small cafeteria, walking funny as her legs and hind quarters woke back up.

Sadako sat down at the warm computer chair and looked at all the feeds from San Francisco. She hoped her daughter Mackenzie would get to the bottom of that disaster. No doubt Superior X had a superior anger problem after the events in California, pun intended. She knew that Emmett West had to be absolutely furious.

She *felt* the anger flowing through him, one with his blood, even from half a world away. Maybe it was all in her head, but she still knew his rage to be a reality with every second she watched the Nautilus Rex and Terror Griffin attack San Francisco. They were clearly unsupervised, yet the duo of monsters had still managed to take out a couple of Bionautics assholes.

Sadako laughed at that because she had a sneaking suspicion the San Francisco incident was the result of a traitor's actions. And she had a good idea who that was… the one man she never trusted working in Trench Town.

Burke Reiser.

Destroy him, Mackenzie, make him gone.

CHAPTER 10

Chicago, Illinois
North America

Storm clouds roiled angrily above Lake Michigan. Below, in Chicago Harbor, a small pod of Coast Guard response vessels patrolled the main bay and its outside perimeter. The looming skyscrapers of the city blocked a lot of the setting sun's light and their shadows blackened the waters of Lake Michigan like shadowy teeth, the sun completely removed from the water's surface.

A coast guard RBM scanned the rapidly darkening waters with searchlights, as well as nautical detection apparatus aplenty. The medium size boat skirted the opening to Chicago's ports and docks and city proper sixty yards out from the Chicago Harbor Lighthouse. The lighted spire was the lonely guard of the harbor's entrance. The house's beam was lit, ready to illuminate the giant beasts, if they should appear.

The all-aluminum vessel had two twin diesel engines with water jet propulsion instead of propellers, a deep-v hull for speed and balance retention, and a machine gun mounted on each end of the watercraft. The already damaging M240 rifle was removed and replaced with a monster M2 machine gun, a giant ammo box attached to the side. Another M240 protected the stern.

The first M boat hailed out of Milwaukee, Wisconsin, while the other nearby M boat and her crew were on loan from the state of Ohio. Both had arrived that morning and relentlessly patrolled the breakwater walls surrounding the harbor. The smaller "Charlie" boats that flanked the two RBM's patrols, similar spotlights blazing, were each equipped with two of the M240s and a .50 caliber machine gun on the front end.

To compensate for the better armed C class vessels, the two RBM boats had some extra men carrying what they were calling "special circumstances." FGM-148 Javelin Missile launchers, with their infrared "fire and forget" heat-seeking technology, were on loan from the military forces on shore. The military was kind enough to loan them the soldiers to fire them, as well. Simplistically deadly, all one had to do was lock onto a monster and pull the trigger. The heat-seeking missile would more often than not do the rest.

These incendiary projectile launchers were dangerous in up-close situations, however. That is why the men entrusted with them on each M boat had been hand-picked specifically for their testicular fortitude in the heat of battle.

For the up-close encounters, the servicemen and women were also armed with M32A1 grenade launchers and AA12 shotguns full of FRAG-12 ammo. It was the best the forces on shore were able to provide, managing to come up with HEAT grenades for the launchers just before they had left the docks.

These armed response additions to the less aggressive members of the country's protectors did little to assuage the fears of the soldiers manning them. Monsters were coming. Actual living, breathing, gargantuan abominations intent on destruction. The governments of the world had no doubt they were controlled by treacherous renegades of the human race. Hidora Neo was a name that two out of three servicepeople in the Chicago metro area had already heard a whisper or two about.

As the nervous crew of each boat stayed vigilant, multiple helicopters circled the city and shoreline. The pre-determined route-takers were obviously military aircraft, whereas the non-sensical, erratic flight paths marked the various media, their copters buzzing around like a swarm of gnats at a summer barbeque.

***

The target audience of the news copters had already fled. In the massive exodus, many had evacuated to parts west or to the south, but mainly just *away* from the lake. For the most part, it was largely successful in a calm and orderly sense. Mostly.

The remaining citizens were unfortunately many of the lower classes, unable to afford the means to escape the city without losing everything they had in the world. The people in these neighborhoods refused to evacuate, to surrender their hard-fought earnings to violence, looting, or even burning. Never mind the possibility of destruction by strange beasts.

Soon, with time not on their side, the police and military lost patience and began subduing the already oppressed people with whatever force necessary. Clouds of tear gas could be seen billowing up out of some of the poorest neighborhoods. Sirens and screams filled the air where police in riot gear herded masses of people away from the shoreline neighborhoods and districts towards the armada of buses that were continuously shuttling people away from the city. With the newly arrived military assistance, any resistance had been quelled with a quick efficiency as the powers that be struggled to clear as many citizens as possible -- legal or illegal -- from the city as soon as possible before the impending doom swimming towards them all struck.

Hours later, downtown Chicago had been reduced to a mass of armed men and their vehicles of destruction, the military units spreading out across the city as angry rain clouds moved in overhead. The assortment of land-based response varied. From machine gun topped Humvees to missile launching trucks hosting dual arrays of explosive payloads, to tanks of several varieties. The city's ground forces were in hurry-up-and-wait mode. In the obscured light of the fading sun, the approaching darkness made the ominous body of dark water appear pitch black.

131

***

Out by the lighthouse, the sonar on both M boats suddenly came to life, revealing two giant masses streaking directly towards them from the deepest parts of Lake Michigan. With a massive splash, Shellshock burst forth from the lake, spewing his trademark blowtorch and frying one of the small boats instantly. Its resident M32 grenadier's last act before being barbequed was to launch three grenades at the Devonian-headed horror.

Poom! Poom! Poom!

All three hit their target and exploded, spraying kaiju blood everywhere. The resultant blinding smoke destroyed line of sight for the remaining sailors on the other vessels. The chelonian terror surged up out of the waters, the displaced air currents parting the billowing cloud like curtains. Shellshock straight flattened a second Charlie boat as it belly-flopped back down into the lake.

The black clouds began to weep their rains as if in response. The precipitation transitioned into a giant *Alice in Wonderland*-sized cry within minutes. Fat, pounding droplets decreased visibility by ninety percent, making it hard to aim the Javelins. A soldier on the M boat from Ohio had no problems, as Shellshock rose up again with the same strategy in his primitive mind.

The missile shot out from the launcher with a *pop!* and immediately rushed up to meet the shelled kaiju in the chest plate, exploding harmlessly but irritating the beast all the same, flames curling around his shell. The monster slammed down on top of the Ohio M boat just inside the bay, spraying the entirety of the remaining response boats with freshwater, simultaneously smashing the Chicago Harbor lighthouse to pieces like it was made of toy building blocks. The monster's back half also crushed a good portion of the remaining breakwater wall that had, until very recently, ended at the harbor lighthouse.

Darkness had arrived with the beast, eating up the dusk from the lake. Shellshock ignored the remaining boats and swam towards the shore, directed by a very eager Emmett West from his post deep in

Superior X station. Projectiles of all varieties homed in on the daikaiju as he got closer to the city, plumes of flame blossoming all over the spiky armored shell, ignored by the owner.

The Coast Guard ship closest to shore opened fire upon Shellshock for a whole thirty seconds from the harbor before the water exploded again. The smaller vessel rose in the air, clenched in the grip of the *Elasmosaur* jaws of Rampage's left head. The shoreline ignited as ordinance from at least a dozen sources streaked out across the water and connected with the monster's head. Smoke and flame engulfed the blue-grey neck and its serpentine top, but when the fireworks dissipated, the nightmare maw was bloody but intact. The rain was pelted down furiously, quickly rinsing the blood away. The long-necked horror shot down to the surface of the lake and plucked an unlucky Coast Guardsman from the dark waters, gobbling him down like a toothy robin with an earthworm.

Suddenly a small group of jets streaked through the stormy skies, ignoring the gravity-fueled downpour as they raced towards the giants' positions in the harbor. An hour prior, the army of helicopters that had patrolled the city had traded places with the faster, more weather efficient aircraft. The daikaiju were now halfway to shore and each creature stood well out of the water, their mammoth strides displacing huge currents of water that slammed into Navy Pier. The waves rocked the huge pleasure boats and cruise ships docked there.

Maverick missiles shot out from under the wings of each jet and rocketed towards the monsters just before the jets reached their targets. The F-18's broke away and veered off in different directions as their missiles all slammed home. Four struck Shellshock and six impacted with Rampage. The brilliant light from the rhythmic explosions that followed was hypnotic, even with the thunderous booms that accompanied the massive balls of flame erupting from each crash. Both monsters cried out in pain from within their auras of smoke and fire.

As the missiles hit, a group of six Abrams tanks rolled forward onto the wet, grassy lawn of Gateway Park, just behind the entrance to Navy Pier. On a sunny day, the pier was an all-in-one tourist attraction. Now it was being drenched in torrents of rain and covered in soldiers firing heavy weaponry upon the two approaching beasts.

The tanks adjusted their aim. They opened fire, the huge 120mm rounds burying themselves into the hides of both daikaiju before either monster knew what had hit them. This proceeded to shock them further as the ordinance exploded, effectively punching them with concussive fire. Rampage roared in protest, the horrible chorus dwarfing everything else. Nightmare jaws capable of swallowing King Kong whole opened as wide as possible, exposing the rear teeth at the back of the mosasaur's throat. These teeth functioned like another set of jaws to grasp its prey with and lock them down. Like the Xenomorph from *Alien*, but without the reach.

Shellshock snapped his jaws together like a colossal set of wind-up teeth as he moved inland. The extreme, pinpointed decibels that the clacking produced sent many troops occupying the pier diving to the boardwalk. They held their heads, some screaming, all with their eyes clenched shut uselessly against the devastating noise.

The rain quickly extinguished the burning monsters' flesh. Before it finished, Rampage and Shellshock unleashed their own firepower. Four hideous mouths opened wide at once, the blue flame of Shellshock's blow torch now accompanied by the twin strikes and billowing death fog that were the unexplainable breath weapons possessed by each of Rampage's heads. Ice cold lightning arced from each *Elasmosaur* head, hitting the Ferris wheel on the pier and instantly freezing it. The science defying bolts were like vicious blasts of electrified liquid nitrogen. The flash frozen amusement ride rippled and crackled with resonant electricity.

The wheel hissed and groaned in agony before it finally snapped and crashed down onto the pier. The weight and gravity of the unfrozen metal above the ice-covered patches obliterated the fragile, crystalized base. The wheel shattered at the middle, the top half violently crashing to the ground in a cloud of dust, debris, and statically charged frozen shards.

At the same time, a black, smoky plume of fog billowed from the center head, engulfing a nearby stadium and theater. The deadly exhalation coated both structures in the oxidizing vapor pouring from the *Tylosaurus* head of Rampage. The desiccating fog corroded everything it touched, despite the falling rain that was beginning to lessen by the minute. The stench from the corrosion was overwhelming. The multitude of vapors from so many varied materials – not to mention *people* -- rusting away dominated the air, oppressively. Those who could ran for their lives.

Some of the fleeing soldiers jumped into the harbor waters and attempted to swim to shore. The bulk of the forces beat feet down the boardwalk toward shore. The remaining stragglers and dumbfounded remnants of the troops had yet to realize that a timely escape was in order. They stood gawking, as fires ignited in the chaos and destruction all along the pier. Almost like it had been coordinated, explosions ripped across the pier in rhythmic succession, as compressed gas and various chemicals accelerated the blaze. The lagging few were either erased on the spot or blasted into Lake Michigan.

Rampage sloshed through the shallowing waters of the harbor as it neared the Abrams tanks lining the shore. All three of its heads roared in unison, the different vocalizations mixing together until they became a horrible symphony. The harmonious sounds drowned out all else for a couple of seconds before the tanks opened fire.

Exploding rounds tore into Rampage, fiery blooms flaring up in several places along its flank. A lucky shot hit one of the *Elasmosaur* heads. The blast knocked the head silly, snapping it back on its long neck violently. It shrieked, the high pitch squeal of pain getting the hopes up for the military on shore. Without missing a beat, however, the right head bounced right back to its normal position, hooked fangs bared and dripping with saliva. A loud, sibilant hiss oozed out from the parted jaws, more crocodile than serpent in its pitch. Arcs of frost lightning zig zagged across the lake's surface in an instant, reaching several tanks and their human components on shore faster than anyone could react. Each vehicle was transformed into an electrified chunk of frozen metal and flesh, rippling with electricity.

The remaining Abrams backed up a considerable distance in response.

Just to the north of Navy Pier, the Jardine Water Purification Plant was a burning mess. Built on and into its own peninsula that ran parallel to the pier, it was the largest filtration plant in the world.

Regarding that fact, it was hard to imagine a facility that normally delivered one billion gallons of water a day to residents in the north and central parts of the city could be so flammable.

Black smoke curled up from in between the blindingly bright blue flames covering the entire roof of the plant, completely ignoring the dwindling rain. Shellshock had ignited the entirety of the building's exterior, the roof already collapsing as it burned to ashes. The levels of contamination in the plant and water supply had already reached levels that would take years and billions of dollars to clean up and fix.

Shellshock roared as tanks on shore unleashed barrage after barrage on the Devonian horror. Jaws clacked together between agonized cries, the monster's tongue coming dangerously close to friendly fire between the gnashing teeth. The kaiju took a deep breath and held it for a second, as more 105mm rounds blasted off his shell and flesh. Undeterred, the monster exhaled.

The daikaiju puked out a blue and white fireball that catapulted towards the offending tanks on shore. It spun through the air like a baseball, the revolutions per second throwing off wisps of blue flame as it sailed towards the Abrams. The tanks were in full retreat mode, backing up in a panic to evade the new weapon the shelled kaiju had just employed.

Shellshock grunted in satisfaction at the retreating ground forces, sounding almost like he was laughing.

***

Deep in Superior X, strapped into his control interface, Emmett West *was* laughing. Sweat poured down his face from the toll controlling three daikaiju put on his mind. What he had just witnessed also made that toll well worth it.

"Gentlemen, we have our first incidence of evolution in our boy, Shellshock," he said into his mic.

"Excellent, my friend!" Brown's excited voice said into his ear. "I told you our formula was superior to all others!"

"Kickass, West," Brundle added. "I can't wait to see how the others manifest!"

"Indeed, young Brundle, indeed," he said before focusing on Rampage and Shellshock once more. He was well aware of Conquer's anxiousness turning to annoyance where she waited impatiently up above the diminishing storm clouds. The kaiju's irritation at being on standby was like a nagging thought in the back of West's mind.

"Soon, pretty lady, soon," he cooed to the impatient monster.

***

The quadruped daikaiju pair charged towards the shore, skirting the conflagrations they had each started. Thick legs made for stampeding carried the mishmash creations into the evacuated Windy City. The rains had ceased. The clouds had passed through quicker than predicted and were now northeast of the city, out over Lake Michigan. The dark of night was lit by multicolored flames at the city's edge. Shadows danced madly across the two monsters, adding to their fear-inducing appearances. The ground forces had fallen back after the last failed fusillade from the Abrams, per Colonel Giossi's orders.

Goliath feet shook the earth as the two monsters stomped closer.

***

Behind the scenes, Giossi gave the order.

"Fire! Roast the fuckers where they stand!" he shouted into his mic.

Like psychotic fireflies, dozens of rockets shot through the air from points all over. The hiss of the streaking projectiles was accompanied by the chatter of machine guns echoing across the empty city. The tracer fire rounds lit up the night as well, adding a nice orange color to the lethal fireworks display. Ordinance peppered the two daikaiju, most of the explosives finding their targets. A few shots hit the already burning parts of the city, while some flew into the lake, exploding underwater.

The resultant blasts showered the burning pier and filtration plant with lake water. This did little to extinguish the flames but sent up mushroom shaped clouds of steam from the places doused by the displaced water plumes.

The demolitions that found their marks exploded with ruthless efficiency, and plumes of flames appeared all over the monsters in a staccato of deafening booms. Their angry cries filled the air between the pounding explosions. When the smoke cleared, however, the daikaiju yet again had only sustained minor injuries. A lot of blood, burnt skin, and several surface abrasions made up most of the visible damage.

Shellshock suddenly bull rushed from the water with gusto, his recently augmented, longer legs propelling him faster than the regular turtle legs he had possessed in Duluth. The turtle-like kaiju obliterated a medical office building on North Lake Shore Drive, the Devonian horror stomping through it like a dog through deep, fresh snow. He continued on, crashing into the high-rise across the street. The damage that the apartment-slash-office building received took out the diagonal shear walls of the structure with efficiency.

The top severed section of the sixty-story building toppled back behind the kaiju as he plowed through the structure, the falling debris landing on the ruins of the medical building, further obliterating it. An untouched, cathedral-looking spire at the west end of the med building buckled and crashed to the ground as the high rise's top half fell onto it. Without the smothering rain to quell it, a giant cloud of dust rose up into the air, making breathing difficult for the unlucky few inside the thick, particulate smog.

After giving the same treatment to a cluster of nearby high-rises -- a sizable portion falling on top of the bulky destroyer's impervious shell -- the seemingly happy kaiju suddenly hopped around like a four-legged jester in the recently clear-cut section of downtown Chicago. Flaming death erupted from his maw in a steady stream as he twirled around, igniting everything in the perimeter around him. Several tall buildings south of the monster soon blazed in blue infernos all the way to their roofs.

Apartment buildings and a large bank office high rise went up like cardboard models, the insanely hot flames instantly adhering to the outer walls, regardless of the material. The burning structures were abruptly wiped from the landscape as the turtle-shelled kaiju plowed through them one by one. Flaming rubble rained down, the smoldering debris starting more fires.

As he throttled and burned each building, Shellshock would occasionally look at Rampage to see if his superior was watching. Each time the larger monster was not, the shark-headed turtle would roar louder with every destructive act. Rampage either did not hear or did not care, metaphorically boiling the other monster's blood in ways it was not aware of. West was, however -- if the controlling scientist was able to, he would have made Rampage pay attention to the shelled wonder. Alas, if he did instruct it so, Rampage would have likely attacked poor Shelly, and West did not desire that outcome in the least. Daikaiju high fives were not in the programming yet.

West awarded Shellshock with endorphins instead, every time the kaiju looked up in hopes of recognition from his ripple-headed peer(s). Conquer, meanwhile, remained up in the clouds, circling like a vulture or buzzard waiting for the animal below to expire. West tried to ease her impatience with some endorphins as well.

It worked.

***

Rampage walked out of Lake Michigan where it met Grant Park. The creature crushed Buckingham Fountain. The front door of the city -- featured prominently at the beginning of the television show *Married... With Children,* as well as practically everything else ever filmed in Chicago -- was obliterated by the tricephalic horror's first steps onto land. In two seconds, the iconic water feature was reduced to a dirty, debris-laden puddle.

The monster then turned north, towards Shellshock, now touring Streeterville across the Chicago River. Rampage's broad-chested front end gave the dominant kaiju an overseeing look, as if the beast was looking out upon its kingdom. Soldiers and their machine gun mounted vehicles positioned nearest the park opened fire, some driving circles around it. Rampage was unimpressed by anything they spit at it, growls of annoyance echoing from all three of its throats at the circling machines. Tanks stationed further in the city

139

started closing in, but still remained out of the daikaiju's visual range. Multitudes of projectiles shot out from in between buildings, successfully striking the daikaiju's body but once again causing little damage.

Each step from Rampage's front legs revealed the knuckle-dragging primate hands it was really walking on instead of plain feet. The thick fingers were seemingly locked together in a fist that mimicked the foot of a massive elephant, sauropod, or ceratopsian. The false-herbivore feet ended with short and simple nubbins. These resembled toe-knuckles, barely jutting out from the thick, cylindrical legs at their base. Decoy toenails decorated each knuckle-toe as actual toenails would.

Rampage roared its center *Tylosaurus* head, while the *Elasmosaurus* heads shot freezing lightning at nearby structures, desiccating several buildings with the impossible energy, and causing most of them to fall. A blast from the left *Elasmosaur* head toppled an entire condo when the bottom three floors turned to electric ice before they splintered away to nothing. The building careened towards the street for two long seconds. Then the doomed condominium complex gave way, crumbling into a million pieces as it hit the ground.

The noise was tremendous, exacerbated by the shattering of the frozen section. A dominating roar stifled the building's destruction, as a group of fighter jets streaked by overhead. Rockets detached from under the trio's wings, shooting down and slamming into Rampage before the monster's senses -- or West's, for that matter -- could register the jets' existence. Rampage's center head reflexively let go of the vile weapon its gullet contained.

Pulling off a kaiju hit and run, the black, destructive spew coated the 340 on the Park building as Rampage rushed past it. The charging monstrosity then slammed into the building next door with an angry bellow and twin shrieks. It began crawling up and into the much taller building with its clawed feet, the action making the structure noticeably *lean* as it did so.

Rampage pulled back with its front feet -- rearing up almost like a horse or an elephant -- and then the front legs extended back behind its shoulders in an impossible way. The strange legs seemed to rotate in their sockets, realigning so they were positioned like arms, and flexed. Biceps bulged, triceps snapped taught, and extensors flexed for impact.

With a frenzied, choral roar, the tricephalic daikaiju revealed its front feet for the man-like fists they were. Rampage pummeled the building relentlessly, false nails that sprouted from the knuckles digging into the sides of the luxury carton of expensive apartments with each powerful blow. The broken mirror-sided structure finally folded under the thrashing monster's weight and its constant barrage of jagged knuckle sandwiches.

Rampage rode the pulverized remains as they crashed into the tall residential building to the north. The evacuated building with its liquid-inspired design gave in to the weight of the kaiju mounted structure slamming into it like a domino. The monster roared at the sky as it rode the buildings to the ground, only to be cut off with a loud boom from the impact. A muted cloud of dust rose up from the crash, lessened by the wet city.

Rampage scrambled off the fallen skyscrapers and into the adjoining park. It had not reverted to its original quadruped form. Instead, it was walking on all fours with its improvised arms like a gorilla.

Lake Shore East Park sat in the middle of several skyscrapers and high rises. Predominantly surrounded by structures, it resembled a castle courtyard, or a miniature Central Park. There were several groups of armed vehicles driving across the grass, most unlike either comparison. Treads and tires mercilessly ripped up the public space's living green carpet. A front line consisting of Bradleys -- tank-like fighting vehicles that also worked as personnel carriers -- tore up the lawn further as they sped across the park toward Rampage. Their 25mm Bushmaster artillery blazed at the monster's three heads. Piercing the kaiju's flesh but feeling like mosquito bites, the waste of time and ammunition only antagonized the beast. Rampage stood up and shook its fists like an enraged silverback challenging an opponent.

The *Tylosaurus* head roared at the encroaching machines, while both *Elasmosaurs* shot frozen lightning at the oncoming vehicles. Most of the Bradleys avoided the blasts from each twin maw, zig zagging away from the bolts with inches to spare. An unlucky trio of the vehicles were hit, instantly freezing and shattering from the forward momentum and gravity, as well as the men inside each one, who were electrocuted before freezing solid.

The line of tanks following the Bradleys into the park finally opened fire, countless shots tearing into monster flesh as they lit up the night. Blood sprayed from each wound, covering a substantial portion of everything around Rampage. The tri-headed monstrosity rotated its arms in their sockets once again, slipping back into position as quadruped legs before slamming into the ground with a massive impact. The force registered seismologically all over the U.S., the armed units still in the park shaken by the shockwave.

The Bradleys lost control, some flipping onto their sides. The few soldiers on their feet at least a mile from the park were thrown to the ground in the wake of the slam. Things fell off shelves and walls all over the city. Car alarms started a scattered chorus line of beeps, sirens, and wails. Animals left to their own devices when the city was evacuated sought better shelter, further away. Cats and dogs ran down the streets and alleys in exodus. Rats and flocks of pigeons migrated west, south, and north away from Lake Michigan. Fish in the lake swam away from Chicago, towards Michigan, Indiana, and Wisconsin.

The tanks that remained standing, however, were unfazed, blasting more holes into the giant creature. Fed up, Rampage charged, stomping all over the Bradleys as it bull-rushed the Abrams. The raging kaiju's front legs pumped up and down as it ran over the vehicles, tamping them into the earth as it stampeded over them.

The beast did circles over the field of military vehicles, running over them again and again. The metallic squeals and crunches echoed for blocks as Rampage repeatedly smashed each heavy-duty tank literally into the ground. The park was suddenly still, and the massive monster hovered for several seconds, making sure that nothing moved. Satisfied with its victory, the daikaiju moved on.

***

Shellshock, meanwhile, had turned and headed north, seemingly on a path to the John Hancock Center. The fourth tallest building in Chicago, the 1,500-foot-tall skyscraper loomed over its portion of the city like the boss. The structural expressionist style, X-braced exterior that made the building's height possible also protected it from extreme winds and earthquakes. It would do nothing against the titanic horror pounding its way. As the shelled terror carved a path through the buildings between him and his newly acquired target, the jets came roaring back.

The F18's fired their remaining sidewinders, eight of them finding their mark and brilliantly exploding against the armored carapace. Shellshock cried out in anguish as the searing flames and concussive explosions ravaged his body, blood flowing freely from charred flesh wounds. The other two missiles found the building in front of the Hancock Center. The Ritz-Carlton Hotel burst into a million pieces as the sidewinders pierced the sides and detonated. Chunks of cement, metal, and hotel furnishings showered the city for several square miles like a bag of exploded popcorn.

***

"Oh shit."

The whispered expletive had come from the pilot who had missed the monster as he and the other five Hornet pilots veered off and away from the fray. Cold sweat beaded across the man's jump suited body and his bowels clenched at the sudden realization of how much property damage he had just accrued.

A shit ton.

"You are screwed, Red 5," his superior officer stated simply into his earpiece. "I wouldn't want to be you when we get back to base!"

Red 5 was about to respond when he was plucked from the sky by a massive, furred talon. Mammalian food pads with rodent claws clenched down hard on the front end of the fuselage, ripping the flying craft from its flight path, and jolting the pilot of Red 5 harshly

143

and giving him instant whiplash. The furry mitts covered the cockpit, blocking out the light. Red 5 could hear the rough texture of the pads scraping across the thick glass, the nails-on-a-chalkboard noise sending waves of agony rippling throughout the trapped pilot's teeth. He began to scream right before the clawed foot crushed him into paste.

***

Tossing the first jet aside like refuse, Conquer dove back down towards the second Hornet, plucking it almost effortlessly from the air with impossible speed and finesse. As she made contact, she simultaneously blasted two of the other three jets veering away from the strike with her colorful breath. The visually hypnotic cloud consumed both F18's before either pilot could really grasp what was happening to them. The agony of being melted away to nothing lasted a mere three seconds.

The physics-defying daikaiju chased after the final jet as it streaked back across the sky towards home base. Flapping her *Pteranodon* wings impossibly fast so that they looked like a hummingbird's, Conquer accelerated after the tiny metal bug. The final pilot began to scream continuously as the prehistoric flying reptile and mammal combination caught up to him. She snatched the plane from the air in her maw, squirrel tongue wrapping around it and pulling it from the front of her beak and back into the monster's set of rodential jaws. There it was chopped into bits and swallowed, the metal and fuel-bearing no problem for the winged kaiju's throat or stomach. She belched soon after, flames curling out around Conquer's jaws like stench vapors.

Screeching repeatedly in a rapid-fire, chittering call, the half-reptile, half-mammal monster flew down into the city and landed on top of Willis Tower. Her front legs latched onto the twin spires rising out of the top of the main structure, while the back legs dug into each of the smaller, side towers. Conquer was perched almost like a squirrel on a tree trunk, the Pteranodon wings folded back and out of the way. An overlarge, kaiju-sized squirrel tail flicked back and forth in obvious annoyance, consistently returning to a position that made it look like a fluffy question mark.

The furry squirrel tail lent a comic appearance to the cone-headed, flying reptile hybrid as it whipped back and forth angrily. The monster's square black pupils shone with an intelligence that was aware of her surroundings. The kaiju scanned the city around her like a wildlife biologist or a hunter getting the lay of the land before making their move.

Instead of doing anything, however, Conquer just roared. The conical beak spewed an ear piercing, warbling shriek that practically deafened everyone still in the city within a five-mile radius of the tower. It was like a songbird possessed by a demon who mistakenly *thinks* that it can sing like a pop diva -- but is very, *very* wrong. The mind scrambling cry reduced many of the city's remaining defenders to gibbering fools crying for their mothers. Soldiers clutched their heads trying to lessen the hell being inflicted upon their senses of hearing, most ending up in the fetal position.

This was not intended as a weapon, however.

It was a summoning call.

The party had just started.

CHAPTER 11

Earth's Troposphere
56,000 Feet

Volk'narr entered the Earth's atmosphere undetected. Still cloaked, his mechanical fighter sped towards the deep lake known by the planet's denizens as Superior at a hypersonic speed. Going the equivalent of Mach 10, the manned robot from another world cut back to about 600 mph right before slipping beneath the surface in an amazingly quiet and nearly splash-less dive. Using his mech's utilities, he drilled into the lake bottom, the vibrative repercussions noticed by quite a few sensors within a large radius from his point of impact. Carving out a burrow into the lakebed like his den on the moon, Volk'narr rooted the giant mech like a trapdoor spider into the substrate.

Once situated, he re-calibrated his systems to account for the change in position, depth, water pressure, and temperature to ensure maximum environmental control. Upon completing these tasks, he began scanning the ravine a couple of miles to the southeast of his current position. He had located his mech near a human research center that was built up out of the water.

The structure was very similar to the platforms used by men to harvest crude oil from the ocean floor. This complex in particular was a purely scientific station. It was inhabited by thinkers, not workers. He would have to apply a lot of discretion and stealth making his way to the deep-water facility that was housing and releasing some of the monstrous aberrations that he had been awoken to destroy.

Several specimens had left the aquatic installation earlier. Volk'narr was still tracking their attack on the mostly empty metropolis at the far end of the lake south of Superior. Volk'narr's readouts confirmed Lake Superior to be the source of the creatures with the most refined cell structure – likely the biggest threats to the planet. Whoever resided in the contained underwater lab knew how to splice like a professional of Volk'narr's own race... or even the Elder Spawns, for that matter.

Volk'narr's wicked mouth twitched in anticipation. He felt alive and rejuvenated by the prospect of battle. The thrill of facing down a megalithic beast -- never mind dozens of them -- in his advanced death machine sent him into near euphoria. He loved the release of showing daikaiju who was boss and sometimes saving lesser species in the process. It made him feel like a champion, or a god. The importance of the Earth being restored to the natural order wasn't just because they were approaching an apocalypse that dwarfed the virus that had swept the globe a little over a year prior. It was also because his people could not lose this part of the galaxy to their multiple rivals -- the elders and their slaves, or the Dark Ones and their kin. The latter had been building their forces on other planets and planes of existence for centuries now, and the Elder Spawn had always been a threat to the rest of the galaxies.

Volk'narr's sense of duty and moral conviction won out over his adrenaline rushes, however. He remembered all the people on the planet experiencing pain, terror, loss, and death from the recent events, as well as his ability to help them. It was bad enough they had just gone through the worst viral outbreak in decades.

He was frustrated that he could not interact with the evolved ape rulers, show them how to fight the daikaiju. It had been determined that humans were not responsible enough to receive his species' weaponry. They had to earn it, or not have it at all, given their highly destructive, selfish nature.

So, he would wait in this watery hole. Volk'narr would wait until the activity on the research station protruding out of the lake was at its lowest. Then he would move into the deep ravine beyond and into striking distance of the hidden underwater base.

Volk'narr stood up from his over-large pilot's chair, stretching his four double-jointed legs, each knee popping in protest to being stationary for so long. He rubbed his brown, human-like front pairs of eyes gently, attempting to stimulate tears. The other five red eyes surrounding his scaly bald head kept a watch on the monitors in the cockpit even as he walked into the next room, which was a sort of tiny kitchenette and bathroom combination. There he relieved himself in one half and refueled on food and hydrates in the other.

Pleasantly satiated, he returned to his chair and the controls in front of it. He reminisced on the days long ago, where he climbed the giant, spiny plants that towered across the landscape of his home world with his brother and sister. He longed to see the spires of his home again one day, even if his siblings were dead a very long time now. He missed them, but the life of a mech soldier sometimes meant losing those you loved to the universe's continued existence. He had signed on for the job to protect the good in the universe, after experiencing so much of the evil.

Tapping into the local signals, he brought up a major merchandise distributor's music application. He had grown fond of the apes' sounds on the flight in from their planet's only orbiting moon. He was becoming adept at tapping into the very same application. Volk'narr found himself particularly liking the electricity-powered music from twenty to forty years earlier, sounds called hard rock and heavy metal.

The mech pilot found them perfectly appropriate to his vocation and delved into everything he could. His particular favorites were songs from the 1980s decade of human history. Two genres mostly, one referred to as "Hair Metal" and the other "Thrash Metal," as well as some harder stuff from the decade after. The latter sounded like the singer's vocal cords were shredding in his attempts to imitate a species of local wildlife called a bear.

He chose an album by a band called "Guns N' Roses." The name of the assemblage of sounds was *Appetite for Destruction.*

How fitting, the pilot thought.

Volk'narr selected the first song with his holographic selection tool and it lit up in front of him. The late 1980s hard rock blasted from the speakers that surrounded him, his brain's translator chip doing its best to translate the vocals. Subsequently, he was blasted with a rush of endorphins at the pleasure the guitars, drums, and vocals stirred up from within him.

As a result, thirteen tracks later, Volk'narr knew one thing for sure.

He liked Guns N' Roses.

CHAPTER 12

Trench Town
Monterey Canyon
Pacific Ocean

Burke Reiser raced to the control room from the mess hall, his feet clunking down the metal hallway as he ran full-bore. The blaring alarms hurt his ears, making him wince as he booked it down to the control room. It was a proximity alarm! The company was not supposed to send a crew for another twelve hours. This sent a shiver of cold apprehension down his sweaty back as he reached the entrance to the main room of Trench Town.

The Monterey Canyon equivalent of Superior X station, the Pacific Ocean based complex was the origin point of the tentacled nightmare, Nautilus Rex, and the winged Terror Griffin that had ravaged San Francisco. The two monsters in question had already returned and were sleeping, tucked away and sedated in their daikaiju-sized stable built into the canyon walls. Burke made sure of at least that normalcy even during his hostile takeover of this western U.S. Hidora Neo stronghold.

Ten hours prior, he had shot everyone else in the station in the head with a suppressed 9mm pistol... except for Natasha, of course. The blonde woman in the white lab coat was still cuffed to the conference room-sized, stainless steel table sitting in the middle of the space. He had zip-tied her wrists behind the rolling computer chair's backrest, threading them through the side trim bars that

151

encircled the tabletop's perimeter. This way, her chair constantly faced the monitors and viewports that made up the wall the cookie-cutter room shared with the first slumber chamber next door.

Footage of the 'Cisco attack was constantly looping on several of the monitors. *Burke Reiser's greatest hits,* he thought. The others were relaying footage of the current Chicago situation, an unaccounted-for fly-in-the-ointment (*more like a* jar *of flies*) in his company's plans. The kaijus destroying the Windy City were impressive to be sure, their lack of rapid regeneration compensated for by an imperviousness to conventional artillery.

Barely noticing the computer's tracking of four new monsters all making a beeline to Chicago, Burke was more concerned with the proximity alert that showed a small submersible approaching. He brought the alarm's details up on the computer screen he stood in front of.

Hidora Neo Orphans no doubt. His blood ran cold at this realization.

They were frightening people. The four orphans he had recently killed would have literally disassembled him had he not assassinated them without their knowledge. Natasha was the last one of them. But he had always *wanted* the tall Russian woman with the cold green eyes. So, he had kept her.

He shoved his devious intentions with Dr. Natasha Kutsenko aside, focusing on the killers' impending arrival in their sub. The display estimated he had fifteen minutes before they were at the airlock, a.k.a., inside the complex. He turned and fled the room, smiling at the swelled face of his blonde infatuation from where he had pistol-whipped her right cheek.

Then a plan formed in his mind. He could let the hit squad deal with the tank babies that they had been growing in the lab. Even though the creatures were not much older than newborns, the things were already extremely lethal. A few lab techs had become lunch less than a week ago.

Burke was disappointed that he needed to use the fledgling kaiju. He had hoped they could be of use to Dr. Strand, Keene and Curran's program... *but desperate times and all of that!* He would have to use them for fodder now.

Fifteen minutes till dock...

***

Mackenzie MacElroy and her team spread out from the interior airlock door in a sweeping formation, covering just enough ground to establish a point inside the base. One that was clear of any threats before they advanced, moving forward one at a time. Mackenzie and her MK16 SCAR rifle immediately took point down the long hallway first, then signaling for her second, Chuck Ray, once she had reached the first door on the way to the control room.

Chuck ran up steady and quick, his assault rifle leveled at average head height for a human being as he advanced to her location. His red hair and freckled face appeared once he reached his location, after which he lowered his weapon just long enough to make eye contact with Mackenzie, then signaling back to the third person that was waiting at their original entry point. Then Chuck's rifle was back up and pointed forward towards their destination.

Masao Kobayashi and his laser-pointed weapon followed suit, quickly traversing the hall and stopping before the corner left turn at the end, leaning against the wall and bringing his lasered MP5 up to his chest, the dot pointing at the ceiling just above his head. He nodded and signaled to the last Orphan back at the airlock door. He exchanged nods with both Mackenzie and Chuck, before looking back at the group's room clearer as she advanced.

Yao Juncai was a massive Chinese woman. Her armored girth filled the hallway. Standing at 7 feet, 6 inches, she was one of the biggest of all the Orphans. Her pounding footsteps sounded like someone beating the floor with a sledgehammer. Like the other three soldiers, Yao's broad head was helmeted, but hers was a custom piece. It was decorated with spikes, making her look like Pinhead from Clive Barker's *Hellraiser*.

Except Yao was huge.

Her beefy, broad-shouldered body moved with a purpose, each step she took emphasizing how mammoth she was, muscles and girth making up one hell of a force to be reckoned with. The M32 Grenade Launcher in her hands helped a little with that as well. So did the assault shotgun holstered on her back, the black composite stock sticking up above her left shoulder ten inches or so.

Before Yao reached her Japanese brother in front, Masao slid down the wall he rested against, bending at the knees and dropping straight down from his standing position. Taking one hand off his weapon, he reached in a side pocket and removed a small mirror, which he slowly edged out past the corner. The small view the mirror gave him revealed another corridor, ending in a door.

There were three other doors dotting the fifty-foot hallway. One on the left, and two on the right side. Trash littered this hallway, mostly food cartons. The smell of dirty human living quarters had reached Masao's nose about thirty seconds after he had taken a position at the corner, so this was not much of a surprise. He held up a hand to Yao when she had gotten within five feet of him, signaling her to wait to engage. He pointed at Mackenzie again, signaling her to advance.

The Irish American woman narrowed her eyes in curiosity at their situation as she moved forward and then around the corner after checking for hostiles. Chuck, Masao, and eventually Yao followed until all four had made the uneventful transition into the next hallway. Mackenzie took cover on the left in the one doorway on that side, while Masao and Chuck were crammed into the similar shallow doorways across the hall. Yao came around the corner just in time to hear the first impact against the huge double-wide door at the end of the hall.

BOOM!

She squinted at the door from within her spiked headgear, uncertainty driving her eye gestures. The impact by whatever it was had dented the door as well as jarred it from the frame.

Another blow hit the metal door.

BOOM!

And another.

BOOM!

The door hung slightly crooked from its frame now.

Yao moved back around the corner just as the door flew off the hinges with a final *BOOM!* It flew at her previous location so fast that she felt the air violently rush against her backside as it crashed into the wall at the end with a loud metallic crunch. She pivoted back around and waited behind the corner, hopefully unseen by whatever had almost crushed her with the door. The thought of *what*ever made her blood chill a little.

The front creature was a combination of what looked like a dinosaur of some kind, a juvenile *Tyrannosaurus*, or an *Allosaurus* maybe, but instead of a neck or reptilian head, its shoulders ended with a giant piranha's head. Huge, snapping jaws full of jagged, river monster teeth clicked and clacked at the Orphans as it stomped awkwardly down the hall. Its giant round eyes looked at them in a cold but very hungry way as it stalked toward them. Four arms sprouted obscenely from where the thing's neck should have been. The misplaced appendages sprouted out of its body like a collar of arms. Each one ended in a three-digit, scythe tipped claw, like a *Deinonychus* or *Utahraptor*. Marine-savvy, webbed spines protruded from the backside of each arm, as well as a vertical tailfin that looked capable of slicing through flesh.

Chuck opened fire on the creature the Trench Town scientists had named Pirahnex.

The kaiju ran at Chuck as soon as the bullets pierced its flesh. Instantaneously, black splotches surged forth and started covering the wounds. The beast was unfazed, surprising Chuck who was at the front of their formation. The collar of arms snatched the man up, crushing his arms against his sides, as his weapon fell to the floor.

Then it fed poor Chuck into its maw.

His screams were cut messily short, turning into a gurgle, as the huge piranha head shredded him to nothing in seconds. MacKenzie puked in a moment of weakness and sorrow before firing at the monster herself. Dozens of bullet holes decorated the beast's flank, every one of them soon covered by a regenerative layer of black, whale-like skin.

"Masao, fall back!" Kenzie cried as she followed her own orders, retreating to the previous hallway with him.

The second creature advanced past the still eating Pirahnex. This second creature was similar, possessing a thick, carnosaur body, complete with the same quartet of finned, three clawed arms protruding from around the neckless head, and an aquatic tail to match. This one, however, had the head of a razorback boar. Its deep grunts and oinks drove a small spike of fear into Masao as he and Mackenzie retreated.

Yao stepped around the corner and fired the M32 four times and immediately stepped back again, the first round hitting the Razorback Rex in the face, the other three sailing over and exploding amongst the thing's monster siblings. Instead of exploding like a typical grenade, the modified flashbangs exploded in a brilliant, stunning display of light and sound. But where a regular flashbang relied on its visually and audibly debilitating effects, the augmented ones Yao had fired also released a knockout gas. One that had been developed by Hidora Neo scientists to specifically affect their monstrosities. After the deafening and blinding flare, which generated cries from all the monsters pouring into the hallway, the smoky cloud left in the air was like chloroform, knocking the beasts to the ground.

As soon as Yao stepped around the corner brandishing her weapon, the rest of the team had fallen back to the airlock area. Here they donned the gas masks that each Orphan carried in their small backpacks. The ventilation system for the station acknowledged the invading vapors, and its safeties kicked in. Extremely efficient fans came to life within the walls of the complex. The system sucked the clouds up and away quickly, dispersing much of the effects along with the smoke within minutes. Regardless of the ventilation system, they still rounded the corner again with their masks on.

All the monsters were on the ground, unconscious and breathing slow and heavy. The grenades had worked. Everyone breathed a sigh of relief before quickly darting to the far door and their unfinished mission. MacKenzie, Masao, and Yao all looked upon the gory remains of their fallen brother and teammate as they passed, disgust and sadness put aside temporarily in lieu of the ongoing operation. Masao picked up Chuck's rifle as he passed and slung it over his shoulder. He also grabbed what ammo he could find from his fallen teammate's body, thanking him as he did so.

The other monsters they walked past all had the same formula; meat-eating dino body, raptor-like arms sprouting from an overlarge, neckless head that replaced the normal theropod head.

Each head was a different animal, however. Counting five creatures total, Kenzie and company cautiously made their way around the Razorback and the Piranha-headed kaiju, as well as a tiger shark, a Pacman Frog, and a Wels catfish -- its barbells twitching spasmodically as they passed.

Miraculously making it past the beasts unscathed, the three Orphans ran into the mess hall the broken door had belonged to. They ran quickly through the destroyed eating area to the next corridor. An incredible mess of food, broken dishes, and utensils covered the cafeteria's floor and tables. As Masao cautiously entered the opposite side hallway that led to their destination, a soft noise followed by a ricocheting impact struck the metal wall close to his head, followed by two more. Masao quickly shut the door.

"They are in the hallway and armed, I think with a suppressed pistol," he said.

"How many are there?" MacKenzie bit her lower lip.

"Not sure, but I think just the one," he returned.

"I've got this," Yao said.

She moved to the door, her teammates giving her a wide berth. Barely cracking the metal portal, she fired three grenades through the small gap at different heights -- high, medium, and low, then slammed the door shut again.

WHUMP!

WHUMP!

WHUMP!

Three muffled explosions still aggravated their already razed senses of hearing. They heard a man scream in pain behind the door, his cry fizzling out, quickly. After several minutes of hearing nothing, they warily tried the door again. The room had cleared of residuals, and the motionless form of a haggard, grey-haired man lay on the floor, He seemed to have fallen from his hiding place around the hall's final corner.

Yao giggled in a deep, creepy laugh that sent goosebumps rippling across MacKenzie's skin in a flash. It was one of the quirks she liked about the huge woman, even though she was creepy as hell sometimes. They pushed into the hallway, where the traitor was promptly bound and gagged. Yao also closed and secured the doorway, hopefully preventing the chimera from getting to them, should the creatures awaken.

Twenty minutes later -- after freeing Natasha -- who summarily enacted her wrath upon the man like she was the goddess of vengeance Nemesis herself -- they interrogated Burke Reiser, number three undercover operative for Bionautics, Inc.

Forty minutes later, the juvenile kaiju woke up.

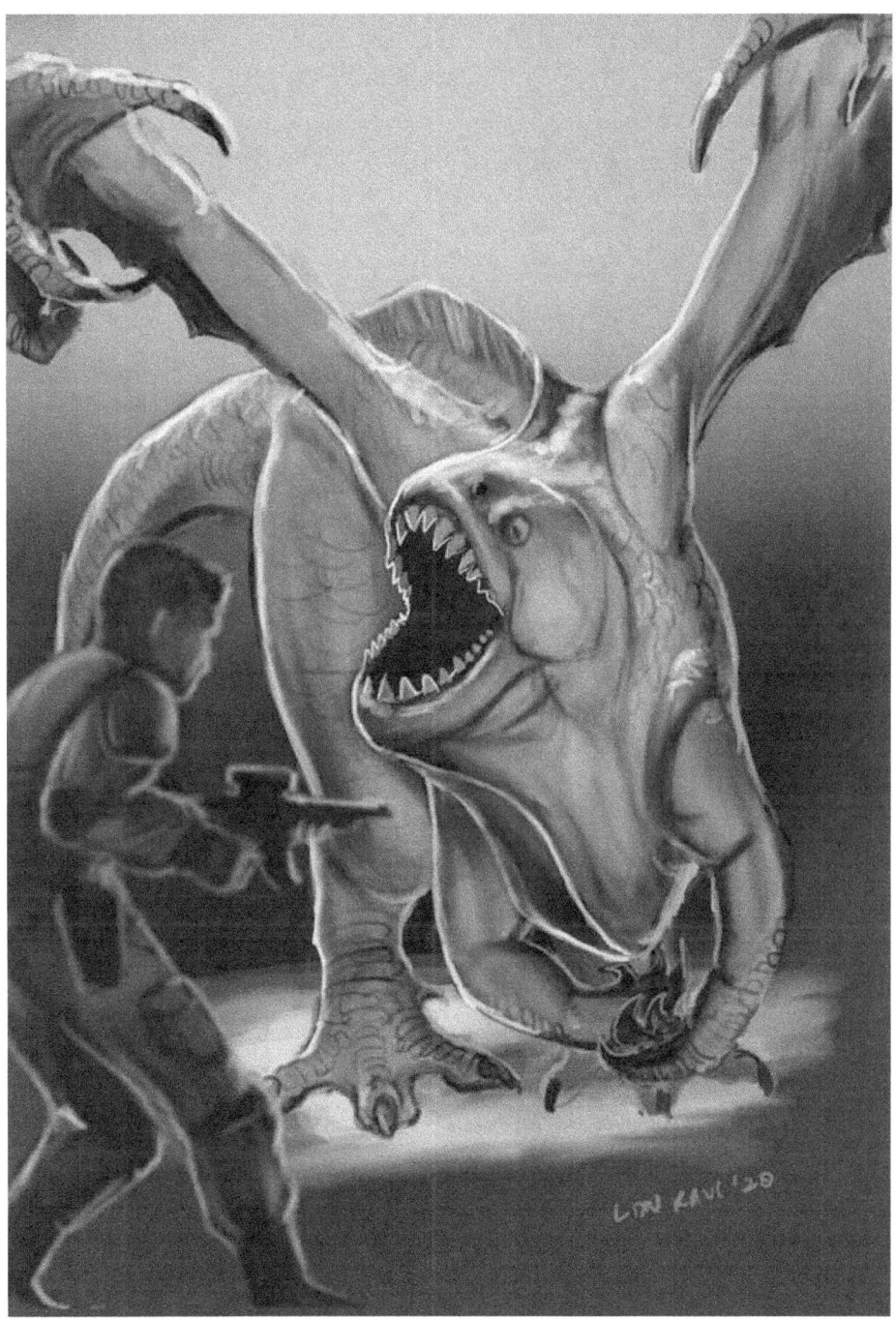

CHAPTER 13

Outside Pandora's Room
Antarctica
0800 hours

The next morning, the three teams of soldiers gathered near the Pangea machines, close to the spot where Bottin's team was decimated by one of the Starheads. The groups were all armed to the teeth with weapons from Hell. Hadeon's team, the Commiekazis, were prepping near the door they were about to breach, gearing up and testing out the AMRD1's controller. Gatimu's squad was close by, nearer to the first of the remaining Pangea machines, checking the portable barricades and motion-activated defenses they were hauling into the void beyond the door. Finally, Hodder and Sōzō geared up with their team inside the main creation chamber area, nearest the other machine. Little was said between them, everyone being too preoccupied with checking their ammunition, weapons, and body armor.

Hadeon's team consisted of seven men in pine forest camouflage armor, including himself. All were Orphans rescued in the late 1980s at the end of the Cold War by Sadako herself. All seven were from the countries that made up the former Soviet Union and were contemptuously nicknamed the Commiekazis by most of their adopted siblings, a nickname the group had actually become accustomed to.

Hadeon Voloshyn himself was a clean-shaven, handsome man. Long, stringy blonde hair poured off his head down just past his shoulders, clearly in need of a good wash. His light blue eyes shone his malevolent nature openly and most people avoided making eye contact with him for too long. A week's worth of beard poked out of his face like spikes on a hedgehog, adding several years to his appearance.

While loading magazines for his desert camo MK-16 SCAR-L assault rifle into the thigh pockets on his armored greaves, the bald-headed man next to him working the AMRD's controller asked him a question in Russian. Hadeon responded back in the same language and grabbed a handful of mags out of the bag sitting on the fold-out table in front of him. Then he handed them to the shorter but wider man, sneering as he made a sarcastic comment to him that elicited laughter from the rest of the men.

The bald man, Timur Dementyev, pocketed all the magazines except one, which he inserted into his Vityaz-SN submachine gun, locking the clip into the weapon with a sharp click. His scowl at the comment from Hadeon turned to a grin as he responded in a teasing, singsong voice and jabbed his thumb back over his shoulder in the direction of Gatimu's crew. Laughter erupted louder from the entire group.

Timur and Hadeon were also joined by Uladzimir Dashkevich, the demolitions man from Belarus; Viktor and Mykola Tereshchenko, fraternal twin brothers also from Ukraine - the near and far experts of the seven, respectively; Spiro Babayev, an assault rifle guru from Uzbekistan; and Sergei Zolotov, Russian tank and prototype tester.

Zolotov, a mountain of a man at seven foot even, was the biggest person in the room. His pale head was adorned with a gel hardened reverse Mohawk jutting out to both sides. Died neon Muppet green in homage to Keith Flint, of the electronic music group The Prodigy, it looked rather silly on the huge bear of a man that was Sergei. To critique him on his choice of hairstyles usually got the hell beat out of the critic, so it was a taboo subject among them all. Sergei's Fu Manchu style choice of facial hair earned him the nickname "Heihachi," a Generation X reference to a character from the arcade fighting game *Tekken,* who sported a similarly ridiculous hairstyle and facial hair.

Zolotov was sporting a thick and bulky armored vest, looking almost like a human roll cage, which was attached to a counterbalancing arm. The false appendage swung out from behind him and locked into place in the front. This Steadicam-like monstrosity made it possible for the man to wield a barrel-fed, German MG3 machine gun with little recoil. He finished up attaching his weapon to the bracket on the arm, locking him into the balancing aperture, and stood back to watch the others.

Viktor carried an FP6 shotgun, as well as a semi-automatic Benelli M4 Super 90 shotgun in an over-the-shoulder back holster. The ginger twin loved his shotguns and was extremely accurate from afar, as well as quick on the draw. Up close, not much stood a chance. He puffed on a cigarette as he waited for his team to be activated, leaning up against the archway entrance for the short hall leading to Pandora's Room. He tilted his head to the left, a loud series of cracks his reward. Viktor checked his pulled back hair and ponytail in its binder for any imperfections. Feeling satisfied, he stomped out his smoke, crossed his arms and continued to lean against the wall.

Mykola, Viktor's dark-haired brother, was checking the night vision scope's battery on his MK 11 Mod 0 sniper rifle, on "loan" from the USMC. It was his baby. He polished it constantly, to the point of annoyance among his teammates -- especially Spiro, the assault rifle freak. Naming the semi-auto SR-25 variant "Lulu", he would talk dirty to "her" after every shot.

Spiro, on the other hand, loved his M4A1 with grenade launcher attached. With the M4 in his hands, the dark-skinned Uzbek waited patiently for action, trying wholeheartedly not to look at Mykola polishing his Lulu again.

Uladzimir, or "Ul" to most, was filling up his demolitions case. The customized, armored backpack had many compartments inside, able to hold 25 grenades safely, 35 dangerously. There were five different compartments allowing for organization. The removable cases held everything from illumination flares to fragmentation grenades to chemical explosives. Ul was bringing a diverse selection this day, packing a little of everything. A pair of welding goggles skewed his sandy brown hair atop his head, the raised translucent welding lenses a dark shade of green. They helped diffuse the blinding flashes from the explosions he created, and he rarely went into the field without them. As he secured the lid on the illumination case and placed it back into the pack, he caught Hadeon's stare and flashed him a grin and a thumbs-up.

"Good to go, Boss," he said in Ukrainian to Hadeon. "Let's blow some shit up."

Hadeon smiled and turned to face the rest of the people in the creation chamber room the three groups of soldiers were gearing up in, his men following suit and watching the rest of the room as well.

Sadako noticed this and turned to Hodder. "The Commiekazis are ready, Captain," she said.

The giant, grey-haired Hodder raised one eyebrow at the motley crew staring them down. He grunted in satisfaction.

"They usually are," he said with a smirk. "That's why they go first."

Sadako laughed softly. Then she yelled at the top of her lungs to the entirety of her troops, "Ten minutes until show time, everyone!"

Gatimu and his team of seven other darkest blue armored Orphans stood ready with their three Can Am Commander C2 ATVs, each modified with larger cargo boxes on the rear of each vehicle, all capable of hauling 700 pounds apiece. On the back of each roll cage equipped four-wheeler was an automated .50 caliber mini gun sentry they would mount inside the room once the barricades were put up. An M2 machine gun was also mounted on top of each roll cage, with a small, cramped perch for a gunner to stand placed just before the storage box.

One of the vehicles was also hauling a small trailer stuffed with the barricade building supplies.

Gatimu and his second in command, a short but wide Mongolian man named Ganzorig, finished loading the last pieces of their front lines into the trailer. Ganzorig was built like a pro wrestler but packed into a 5'2" frame. With his dark hair pulled back in a short ponytail and Klingon-style facial hair covering his face, his appearance belied his mere 24 years.

"Once we get in there, I want you on the M2 perch in the C2 hauling the trailer," Gatimu said as they hoisted the final piece of barrier in. "I would prefer you and your halberd keeping our materials safe."

Ganzorig nodded once. "Yes, sir."

"Gatimu, we are loaded and ready, brother," Mashal shouted from the final vehicle of his group.

The 5'6" Afghani woman was Gatimu's own firebug. She carried a pistol grip twelve gauge and an electric-ignition blow torch "baton" as a side arm. She was also armed with fragmentation and incendiary grenades to reach out and touch someone with. She excelled at burning things. Her driver, Bekele, was a giant of an Ethiopian woman, and sat at the wheel grinning at Gatimu. Her obvious crush on him was apparent even though they were adopted siblings. The monster woman was adept at handling assault rifles and hand cannons. Her favorite weapon was a Colt Anaconda .44 Magnum, nicknamed "Barry."

"Very good, Mashal, but is your gunner ready?" Gatimu asked her this with a smirk on his face.

Bekele spun her head around and shouted at a Caucasian man sitting on the back of their C2. "Adam, get your Casper butt up on that perch, man! Time to go."

Adam looked up from his Kindle, closing out *TORMENT* by Jeremy Bishop.

"Alright," he said in a spoiled brat whine. He stood up and prepped the belt fed machinegun for action, loading it and positioning the cartridge feed across the roof of the customized ATV.

Adam was a former street urchin rescued from an orphanage in South Africa. The platinum blonde pretty boy loved his books and was always reading *something.* He also loved machineguns, as the intense look on his green-eyed face radiated as he readied the swiveling weapon.

Gatimu turned to his own mechanical mount, where his driver and M2 gunner were already sitting. Mani Nakufi was a tall Congolese man with a faded haircut, a tribute to his hero, the Fresh Prince of Bel-Air. His Gurkha prowess was unrivaled, but his skill at the M2 made him top choice for Gatimu's ride. His smile dimples made him popular with the ladies when he made it out to the clubs, which wasn't often lately.

Almost completely opposite of Mani, the Egyptian woman Hasina Gyasi was a plain looking example of her people. Her flat face and generic features gave her an androgynous look, except for her well-toned, modestly curvy figure. With a sharp sense of humor and a skill for driving just about anything on wheels, she had chauffeured Gatimu into the field on many occasions. He watched her expectant eyes as they darted around the room in her anticipation of the upcoming mission.

Kadeen Harrak, a big, beefy, Orphan originally from Morocco, was the driver of the middle C2 that hauled the supply cart. His black hair framed his head like a helmet and was connected to his chin by an over-groomed chinstrap that ended in a mossy patch of a goatee. Known for his abilities with all manner of firearms, Kadeen preferred a pair of Uzi 9mms over everything else. With years of practice and a muscular form to back it up, he had perfected the art of two Uzi firefighting.

Ganzorig jumped up into the M2 perch behind Kadeen without hesitation. The much shorter man slipped his double-edged halberd in-between the back roll cage bars for safekeeping. He nodded at Gatimu.

They were ready.

Gatimu's team turned to face the third and largest group, led by Hodder.

Hodder nodded and glanced at his own team -- made up of half killers, half scientists. The ones with weapons were already looking at him, ready and waiting. The scientists were also ready, but quietly chit-chatting about the creatures they were about to search for. Hodder caught the eyes of Miner and Coscarelli, his top two men, the looks on their faces pleading for commencement of the operation. The leader of the largest group grinned, his chapped lips cracking from the sudden stretching of such dry tissue. He turned to the other two teams as he loaded a round into the chamber of his assault rifle with surprising loudness. His voice boomed as he gave the command.

"Let's go and say hello to our gracious hosts! Open that damn door!"

***

The door to Pandora's Room elicited an unforgiving shriek as Sergei Zolotov and Hadeon Voloshyn finally ripped the massive hunk of dark metal open. The stench of burnt flesh and something else -- something not natural to the planet -- poured unseen from the darkness beyond. The smell of the antiquated flamethrower Jean-Paul Beane had used many hours earlier to save his fellow Orphan engineer Donovan was rife in the air as well. The two men stood back, as their teammates and their weapons moved closer, all constantly trained on the yawning, black portal before them. A series of low, gibbering voices were faintly audible to Viktor as soon as he entered but they quickly faded as Hadeon spoke softly next to him.

"Viktor, Spiro, move up once the drone drops the first flare," he said to them in a voice barely above a whisper.

The two mentioned men nodded once in unison. Then the AMRD1 drone flew over their heads, piloted by Timur. The Russian man stood back behind the rest of his team, but slightly to the left side of "Heihachi" so he could see past the man and his massive artillery support frame. The seven killers moved forward into the room's main area once they were all together.

Timur flipped on the rotational lights on the bottom of the small, rotor-powered aircraft. Brilliant white flared to life, making people in the other two teams squint even from the creation chamber room where they waited for their turn to enter. The almost scalding bright lights illuminated a wide walkway that stretched back for at least one hundred yards, divvied up by the equally spaced archways with the reflective spots. The trusses resembled a trailing ribcage.

The obsidian black material that comprised everything in the room seemed to eat up the light blazing from the AMRD's undercarriage. Each truss rib had three spots on it, one on each side and one on the ceiling part of each arch. These spots reflected their lights like beacons or signs of some kind, each one having some form of alien gibberish carved into each marker.

On the HD view screen above the joysticks on the drone's controller, Timur touched the option buttons on the small touch screen, bringing up a list of mapping filters. Choosing "Perimeter" from the list turned the view to an outline mode, using ultrasound technology to map the room's layout quickly, and without having to explore the whole thing lit up. It stopped registering at 300 feet, and it was not because of a wall.

"Hadeon, this room is enormous! The drone's mapping function hit its maximum range, but not the far side of this room," Timur said with a grin. "This is a catwalk we are on. The real bulk of the room is over that railing."

Timur spun the drone around until it illuminated the balcony-like railing starting after the fifteen feet of an entrance hallway that continued just inside the room. The railing was made of a reflective material like the spots on each rib truss that made up the long catwalk they stood on. It ran down the entire length of the balcony, turning at the far end to descend with a stairwell to the unseen floor below.

The men slowly stepped towards the rail, each still very much in defensive positions, except for Timur. Gun barrels with high-intensity flashlights pointed into the blackness in front of them, even though their beams were swallowed up almost immediately. The surprising heat and tension was making sweat cascade down each of the hardened mercenaries' spines. Their apprehension… no, *fear,* of the unknown lingered in the air like an unspoken truth nobody wanted to even mention.

The drone cruised over their heads, suddenly dropping down and circling around the room 150 yards out, recording the next section of their map in progress. The ceiling was nowhere to be seen above the tiny aircraft, only resolute blackness where its lights' reach ended above. They were able to see some of the floor below where they stood, however.

A multitude of misshapen crates, made of the absolute black metal, were stacked on top of each other four high. The metal boxes haphazardly filled the area below them, continuing past the edge of the drone's illumination. The perimeter map on the controller revealed the full numbers of the oddly arranged containers, or whatever they were. There was a literal maze of them, although it did not look to be an intentionally created one.

Mykola, Viktor's dark-haired twin, checked his night-vision scope. "I can't see shit, Hadeon," he said in Russian. "This scope will work from mere moonlight, and it's not showing anything. Something in the material this place is made of devours the light, I think."

"This place is definitely fucked up," Spiro, the Uzbek rifleman said between a suppressed chuckle. "But what else is new, eh?"

"Silence. Timur, fire some flares around this place, would you?" Hadeon asked with a patronizing tone. "I'm tired of being in the fucking dark."

The drone above their heads spit five times, five flares shooting out from chambers built into the front of the fuselage. The lights streaked throughout the room, each pre-programmed to land every sixty feet or so. The first four landed on top of the odd-shaped metal cartons, up to about three hundred yards away. The fifth, however, hit something else entirely. The last flare ignited, revealing its place on a second floor landing similar to the one on which the Commiekazis currently stood.

The landing across the way was *not* empty.

A dozen of the giant, starfish-headed brutes stood in wait -- motionless and seemingly at attention. As the flare slowly burned away, not one of the Starheads showed any sign of consciousness or even recognition of their team's illuminated drone and the burning flares that were only lighting a pitiful amount of the immense area. For three minutes they watched the things with their five-pointed heads. Five eyestalks stuck out around the creatures' heads in a rotational symmetry, starting with the main stalk jutting out from the center of each head. Every thick ocular stem ended with a fat eye at the end, all of which were closed beneath vertical, lashed eyelids. Even the fungal globs of secondary eyes between the five central eyes, filling in the space between the stalk bases, lay motionless and dark.

"That's it?" Sergei's voice boomed throughout the cavernous chamber. The big man laughed loudly, his hearty guffaw filling the air. "We'll have this wrapped up before lunch." He slapped Viktor on his shoulder as he said that, causing the man to stumble slightly before regaining his balance. "You're buying, right, Viktor?"

Viktor just smirked at the question.

Suddenly, the gelatinous looking mounds of stringy eyestalks filling in the gaps between each main eye writhed with motion, glowing faintly on the other side of the room. The much smaller optics wriggled and squirmed all over each other like maggots. Only Mykola noticed this through his rifle scope, however. Even then, he was barely able to see the dying light from the flares, given how far away they were from where the men stood.

"Shut up, Zolotov," he said simply. "You've woken them." "The smaller eyes look human," he added in disgust.

"Shit!" Uladzimir exclaimed.

Standing by Timur but behind everyone at the railing, he took off his backpack and quietly brought it down to the floor, untying the simple strings he preferred to noisy zippers or Velcro. Ul pulled out the top two boxes, both with a small diamond label on each lid. One had what was obviously an explosion in the middle. The other had a picture of the sun. These he placed on the ground and pulled out a box with a smoking green flame symbol on the front. A smile spread across his lips, his facial muscles creasing in a dozen places across his face, giving him the look of a man three times his age.

"Ahh, here we go! Trifluoroborane incendiary grenades, put your rebreather masks on, comrades," Ul announced in a harsh, excited whisper.

He pulled out a cylindrical tube and twisted it until he had the collapsible portions extended and locked into place. In seconds, Uladzimir had what looked like a t-shirt launching gun.

"Uladzimir, stop!" Hadeon commanded. "Do not fire yet. I'm contacting Hodder. All of you, stay silent," he hissed loudly to his entire crew.

His eyes were not on them, however. They were locked on the baker's dozen of Starheads across the football-fields long, warehouse-like room. So far, only the globs of maggot eyes had moved. They were languid now, their glow fading almost as if they were beginning to fall back asleep... or into torpor, suspended

169

animation, or whatever state they had been in before. Hadeon queued his headset.

"Captain Hodder," he said softly while pushing the button on his Bluetooth earpiece to open the channel.

Hodder's voice came back through the earpiece. "Go ahead, Hadeon. What's your sit-rep?"

"Thirteen hostiles visible on the opposite side of the room," Hadeon replied. "I trust you have seen our transmitted data of the layout already. They are on the identical balcony at the other end. Creatures are sleeping or in a listening mode or something." He then paused in thought for a second before continuing.

"Sound seems to rouse them, but Sergei's laugh only woke the smaller eyes between the Starheads' main eyestalks. No further movement observed." He paused before adding, "They seem to be going back to sleep. How do you want us to proceed?"

Hadeon looked at his men. "Stay down or out of sight until we receive instructions," he said sternly. "We don't want those ugly *duraks* seeing us just yet. I'm not convinced there aren't more down there." He pointed down through the floor, indicating the lower level.

"I know there are," Spiro whispered. "I can smell them." His face wrinkled in disgust.

"I can hear them rustling around," Mykola added. "Unless I'm hearing something else, then there's a lot of them." His lips formed a solemn line on his face.

"Why did none of the noise we made before Sergei laughed stir them?" Timur asked Hadeon in a sibilant whisper before he looked at each man in turn. "Opening the door, flying the drone, firing the flares. Even the flares themselves hiss. I think they are guards that are programmed for organic noises only. Mechanical and non-living noises aren't a threat."

"How does that make sense?" Viktor rasped harshly. "Are you just making this shit up as you go, Timur?"

"No, that makes sense in a way," Ul whispered. "Maybe they are just some kind of programmed sentinels. Whatever did the programming was unconcerned about other factors."

"If that is true," Sergei piped up, his whisper barely that. He leaned against an archway, his attached artillery-stabilizing gear resting with him, albeit awkwardly. "Then why are they not awake yet from all of your jibber-jabber? Did you want to discuss where they came from, what they eat, and how they screw as well? Shut your ugly faces."

"Hadeon," Hodder's voice filled the Ukrainian leader's ear. "Change of plans. My team is coming in next. Gatimu will wait until we've better assessed the threat level. I want you and your men to take up points along the walkway once we are in and cover us. We will provide you with invisi-shield camo. Give us five minutes."

"Copy that, Captain. We will meet you by the entryway."

"No, stay where you are. We will come to you."

"Copy that."

Hadeon looked back out at the things standing practically lifeless on the other side. The flares were starting to completely fizzle out, but he could sense no movement from them at all. The drone was still flying around a section of the room at a time, about fifty square yards, mapping each section and lighting it up, never revealing more than a stacked jumble of the odd-shaped boxes, or whatever they were.

"Timur, call the drone back until we know what we are doing here," he said to the man with the controls.

Timur obeyed, and soon the drone had turned and was heading back towards them. As it spun around to head back, a flicker of shadow between the weird crates under it caught Mykola's eye through his ever-scanning rifle scope. Then it was gone. He watched for the entire time they waited for Hodder's team but saw nothing else in the dwindling flare light that remained.

Why can't I see what I kept hearing? His frustrated thought bounced around in his head like it was a tricky riddle.

The lower floor sounded alive, as if snakes were slithering all over it. As far as he could tell, no one else seemed to hear it. He could see no sign of movement, save for the briefest of flickers when the drone turned. He reminded himself that the turn itself most likely produced the flicker with its spotlights, even though the reminder did little to change his mind. Warily, he backed away from the balcony rail, not trusting what might lie in wait below.

Hadeon noticed this.

"What is it, Mykola?"

"Things are moving down there, I'm telling you, *comrade*," the obviously concerned man replied.

"Everyone stay back until reinforcements arrive. I think I hear them, too," Hadeon said.

The men backed further away from the edge and took up what defensive stances they could on such a large, empty walkway. They all scanned the length of the railing, as well as the incredible volume of dimly lit space beyond their vision.

No one spoke. Apprehensive sweat continued to pour down their backs.

Movement in the light of the doorway they had entered through captured everyone but Mykola's attention. He had already heard them coming, anyway. Viktor liked to joke that back home on their childhood farm -- the one his whole team of Orphans grew up on -- his brother could hear the deer fart a kilometer away, and that's why he always brought home venison after hunting. Nobody ever argued.

Ducking low and moving quickly, Hodder's squad of six soldiers and three obvious eggheads made their way to Hadeon and company. Sadako was not with them. Hadeon was happy about that. His psycho bitch mother scared him. He had never met anyone in his life so impossible to read. He was very loyal to her and had what he thought was a crude semblance of some form of love for her, but the fear of his adoptive mother was so much greater.

He could never trust her.

Ever.

There used to be nine of the Commiekazis. Sadako had made them watch as she butchered Piotr and Nikolai in front of them, castrating the two men for a date rape incident during a mission in America. Rape was a grievous crime, one that was never tolerated within the ranks of Hidora Neo, or the Orphans.

Hodder reached them and stopped, the eggheads filling in around and behind his soldiers, so the armed warriors were between them and the dark, gaping expanse beyond the railing. Hodder's men, consisting of five of his most trusted soldiers, did not include any Orphans. All of them were ex-military -- SEALs, Marines, and even one ex-Delta Force. Besides Miner and Coscarelli, there was Reggie Scrimm, a giant of a man who rivaled Sergei in size, and the ability to use big guns. He was going light today, hauling around an M27 Automatic Rifle, a tad small for Scrimm, but fully loaded and complete with a grenade launcher.

Scrimm's usual partner in crime, Angus Bannister, was a submachinegun, pistol, and cigar aficionado. He stood right behind Scrimm, his eyes flitting around the room nervously but controlled. His weapon choice today was a vintage M3A1 "grease gun." The .45 caliber SMG was a World War Two classic adopted by Delta Force in their early years. With an extendable metal frame stock, the gun also had low muzzle velocity, which, combined with the .45 caliber rounds it fired, meant both control as well as excellent stopping power. This reduced the chances of friendly fire due to the bullet passing through the intended target and hitting those beyond.

The last man of the team, Quentin Roth, was the team's firebug and master of handheld firearms. A lover of revolvers and pistols alike, Roth was sporting a pair of machine pistols for the excursion into the ship, TEC-9's specifically.

"Oh, my god, there they are," said one of the scientists who had come in with Hodder's team.

His round, thin-framed glasses had a couple droplets of humidity hanging off them. His balding head was flanked on both sides and up the middle by wisps of receding brown hair. He wore outdated fatigues -- stuff from the '80s it looked like -- and no doubt wore a flak jacket underneath.

"Dr. Murphy, look at their eyestalks!" he said to another scientist.

"I see them, Trace. The one in the lab has obviously deteriorated rapidly," Dr. Kevin Murphy said to his colleague Dr. Trace Beaulieu. "I don't know about you, but I know Dr. Mallon agrees with me that a fresher specimen would be ideal!"

"Can we have one, Bru-- er, Captain Hodder?" Dr. Jim Mallon, the third scientist, was smiling like an eager child trying to convince his parents to let him open his presents early.

"Shut the hell up, Mallon," Hodder harshly whispered at the man. He looked at Beaulieu and Murphy. "That goes for all three of you. What part of 'don't use normal voices' do you not understand?"

All three men made facial expressions expressing regret for their moment of eagerness.

"Our apologies, Captain, it won't happen again, I assure you!" Mallon whispered very quietly now, even taking it easy on the sibilant sounds.

His co-workers nodded quickly in agreement.

Hodder turned back to his and Hadeon's men.

"Timur, I want that drone programmed to light up the area down on the floor below us with as wide a visible area as its lights will allow. Hadeon, take Ul and scope out a path down to the lower level. Bannister, Scrimm, and Roth, go with 'em. Secure a defensible area and radio me when you've done so."

The aging Captain stood up fully, prompting gasps from the scientists and a few of the soldiers.

"Coscarelli and Miner, take positions along the railing with Mykola and Sergei. I want your weapons trained on our friends over yonder. If they move, blast them."

Viktor giggled and put his hands up to his mouth. "Hey! Assholes!" he yelled at the top of his lungs. "Wake up so we can shoot you! I'm bored with this shit!"

Immediately after the twin Ukrainian issued his taunt, every eye on the giant aliens snapped open. Red eyeballs blinked rapidly as they adjusted to the AMRD1's lights directly over them. As one, they all turned towards the humans hundreds of yards across the room. The Starhead standing in front raised both arms towards them and shrieked like a body snatcher in a blender.

Suddenly the thirteen creatures were in motion, leaping from the upper-level catwalk opposite the teams down to the crate-laden floor. They ran full bore across the room, trilling in a bird-like, singsong way while weaving in between the long, odd-shaped boxes covering the lower level like discarded junk. Their glowing red eyes gave away each one's position as they charged through the dark towards the human intruders, coupled with the writhing fungal eyes and their swirling, maddening *colour*.

174

One thing was for sure: the Starheads would be on top of them in less than a minute.

"Viktor, you dumb commie bastard," said Coscarelli from next to Hodder and Miner. "If we live through this, I'm gonna tear you apart!"

"Gatimu, we need backup, now!" Hodder barked into his communications equipment before he looked at the men with him.

As they all took positions along the long railing and aimed towards the incredibly fast things racing towards them, Hodder uttered one last command.

"Open fire! Kill 'em all!"

CHAPTER 14

Bionautics Labs
Meditronia One Complex
Twin Cities Metro Area, Minnesota

Bionautics head of top-secret projects Ivan Strand made his way from the cafeteria on sublevel one to the elevator that would take him below to his lab and the most significant thing he had done in his life so far. He walked down the hall from the small cafeteria built in the sublevels underneath the Meditronia One corporate campus and headquarters, a slight swagger to the tall, aging man's step.

His mustache twitched a little as the verses of *Rapper's Delight* by the Sugar Hill Gang scrolled through his head, stuck there like a proper earworm. The lyrics were committed to his memory, his 21-year-old self having learned them back in 1980. He and his friends had even seen them play with Rick James back in 1981 at the Mecca Arena in Milwaukee, Wisconsin.

He had worked hard to pay for that concert, his butcher shop employer giving him as much overtime as they could pay him for. The job he had in addition to being in college on a full scholarship at the University of Minnesota. Briefly he reflected on the butcher shop job, one he had sought out specifically. He had wanted to get up close and personal with the violence of cutting things, learn how to deal with the blood, the gore, the *smell*. It had paved the road he had taken to become the cold, uncaring scientist he was today. As someone who had done terrible things to so many lives, not all of

176

them animal specimens, he had always done so with cruel detachment. Especially with the human subjects he had used over his years at Bionautics.

Miranda Shepperton had been one of those subjects, unknowingly. He had practically put the woman into a coma on several occasions over many months, stealing viable eggs from her body on his lab table. After stealing eight of her eggs, adding to his stash of pilfered, unfertilized embryos, a migraine headache caused him to slip with the instruments.

The damage to her reproductive system was permanent, and Miranda instantly sterilized. Shortly after she had recovered and realized she had missed a week of her life, she found his journal, which described the events in vivid detail, complete with astonishingly inhumane and incredibly sarcastic commentary. Fortunately for Ivan, when you do heinous things for a very private medical research corporation, it is hard to bring the law down on your coworkers.

Strand smiled at this, wondering when and where she might try to exact her revenge on him for his transgressions. Reaching the elevator at the end of the hall, he hit the down button. The elevator doors opened upon the car's arrival, and he stepped in, pressing the "S6" button as he turned around to face the open doors.

The doors closed, and the room soon filled with the smell of the dark coffee he had brought with him, the only leftovers from his bacon and eggs breakfast. The still warm liquid had given up most of its steam already, but Ivan didn't care. He would drink it cold. The bite of the coffee's bitter flavor and the caffeine it provided was what he wanted, not the heat. Today he would need the caffeine.

His creations were going for their first walk in the outside world. This brought an even bigger grin to his face, anxiously anticipating the insanity he would release upon the world and hopefully put an end to Sadako Sōzō and her maniacal cult organization. Bionautics would finally take over, and the world would bow to them instead, and Strand would become an indirect ruler of the world through his new creations. He would gain the alien technology Sōzō was keeping to herself, and then he would control Bionautics as well, removing the board of directors led by Neil Reibe and his old boys' club of withering, racist methuselahs.

He had already heard about Chicago and the monsters that were destroying it even as he rode the elevator down to the labs at the bottom sublevel. The Chicago kaiju were a mishmash of creatures -- chimeras, at best -- and although they were impressive, he thought they lacked imagination on the part of their creators.

His monstrosities were much more complex -- hybrids, not spliced combinations, and although still growing, the advances in technology he had recently... *acquired* from a certain secret source he had kept all for himself. Strand had finished *his* creation chamber and allowed for a more seamless hybridization of different traits and species. It made growing them bigger, as well as faster, a possibility as well. Currently, the four specimens were as large as the original turtle monster that had crawled from Lake Superior and attacked Duluth, which was around 200 feet long or so. That would soon change, their growth rates surpassing all his estimations.

The elevator reached its destination and the doors opened. Strand stepped out into an identical hallway from the one he had just left. Classic, hospital white walls and floors went down about fifty feet before ending in a thick, card-reader door with no window. Apparently, the life of a mad scientist meant working in boring, institutionalized spaces. After swiping his card and keying a combination of numbers, the big steel door popped open with a quick burst of air as the controlled climate within met the hall's mostly unfiltered air. The smell of vegetation, humidity, and several types of animal musk hit his nostrils, a smell he had grown a strange fondness for in the last week.

George Curran, Martin Keene, and Miranda Shepperton were at a conference table in the middle of the pole barn-sized underground room, looking at documents both physical and digital. Behind them he saw the bodyguards Robinson, Ellis, and Gilmour sitting at another table, playing Texas Hold 'Em. Their firearms were all lying next to their dwindling piles of chips, as casual as a cell phone or a drink. When the muscle saw Strand, they all stood and faced him in recognition of his presence.

"Sit down, you meatheads," he said with a minimum of condescension. "Miranda, where are we at with the growth rates of our friends in the next room?"

Miranda Shepperton looked up from her charts that were spread across the table in front of her.

"Right on schedule, Dr. Strand. The new DNA has expedited the process as we had expected, and it appears they will be the size of the kaiju in Chicago within days. However, our figures are also showing the growth rates may stop soon after they become bigger than the Chicago beasts. The cells have a limit to the amount of extra size they can give."

Strand smiled that trademark grin of his.

"Excellent. Are we on schedule for our test today?" He looked Miranda directly in the eyes, his penetrating gaze never breaking eye contact. Shepperton did not back down.

With hate radiating from her she said, "Yes, Dr. Strand. While I don't approve of your test site, they are indeed ready and waiting for us to release them."

"Wonderful! Let's get started then, shall we?" Strand said pleasantly.

After walking up the steps of a small dais, he glanced at Curran and Keene, each meeting his eyes and giving an almost imperceptible nod, both of which Shepperton missed. Strand walked over to the large steel shutters near a series of monitors and keyboards, each with its own touchpad. He typed a few commands into the middle of the five monitors and stood back up after pressing enter.

With a mechanical whir, the shutters retracted up into the ceiling, revealing the man-made cavern where his monsters were kept. He looked in the four occupied enclosures, the walls of each stretching to the ceiling of the fabricated, subterranean expanse.

If the people working in the Meditronia One building only knew what lies in wait underneath them.

Strand typed in some more commands, initiating the awakening procedure for his monsters. While Keene and Curran had helped with the inspiration, they were *his* monsters. He was the one who had found the silent -- and in a certain case, unwilling -- benefactors

179

who had provided the advanced technology that was allowing him to make his own life forms as easily as he had.

The stuff of comic books and science fiction, the machine worked similarly to a three-dimensional printer, only it made living, organic cell structures using genetic material provided by the scientists. For the most part, it was the contributions technology gleaned from their "sponsors." The results were then grown in a series of chambers of differing sizes until the specimen was large enough for the enclosures in front of Ivan Strand right now.

He nodded his approval at the sights before him, satisfied with their growth in such a short amount of time.

Strand turned from his new children and back to the six people looking up at him. He presented a genuine smile of joy, unnerving all those witness to it. Slowly walking down the stairs, he approached Keene where he was seated at the conference table. Keene raised an eyebrow at his boss, unsure of what the smile was for. Strand only continued to grin maliciously, as smiles were unnatural on his face.

"Martin, would you please release the hounds?"

Strand opened the small fridge located in the island cluster of a kitchenette that was close to the table where his three white-coated colleagues were seated. He came away with a bottle of beer, an India Pale Ale called Bitter Neighbor. A redneck in a trucker hat graced the black paper label; a sour, mean grimace stretched across his face. Ivan cracked the top with the bottle opener magnetically attracted to the fridge door. He raised the bottle up to the other occupants of the room.

"To my genius, our supporting benefactors, and all the challenging work we've put in these last few years," he said and proceeded to slam the bitter beer, upending it until it was empty, to the annoyed faces of those without.

"Ahhhh!" he announced with satisfaction and overemphasis, his mouth wide open and stretching to its limits.

With a wicked hook, Strand launched the bottle at Miranda's head, the bottle spinning through the air before striking her square in the face. The bottle bounced off her face and clattering noisily to the floor. Miranda flew back in her chair, holding her bleeding nose, tipping over once the center of balance was exceeded. Hitting the floor with another pained grunt, she clenched her eyes shut, oblivious to Robinson and Gilmour approaching her until they grabbed her and held her down.

"What the hell are you doing, you bastard?" She glared up at Strand, the man still smiling genuinely.

"Miranda, Miranda. Didn't you realize? We still need a controller! Oh, that's right, you *don't* know about that, *do* you?"

He began pacing around her and the two, strong, silent types that kept her pinned to the floor. The evil grin returned as he stopped and bent down, his face inches from her own.

"Now you shall have your precious children. I may be their father..." he said as he removed a capped syringe from his inside lab coat pocket.

He flicked the orange plastic cap off with his thumb, revealing the fine point of the needle beneath. Strand tilted the syringe upright, ejecting the air bubbles from the liquid within before he jabbed it immediately into her neck, pressing the plunger down and releasing its contents into her bloodstream. The sedative's effects began to darken her vision and hearing almost immediately. Before she fell unconscious, Strand finished his sentence:

"... but *you* shall be their mother."

***

Miranda awoke freezing, wet, and in extreme pain. She tried to scream but could not draw in a proper breath from the intense cold racking her body. Instead, she whimpered and sucked in quick, short breaths and flailing about in the chilling water she was immersed in. Her thrashing feet hit bottom, telling her the depth of her prison pool was maybe three feet.

As her panic slowly started subsiding, Miranda Shepperton's mind and breathing calmed, although she could remember nothing before waking in her cold isolation bath. She was in a round cell of some sort, ovoid in shape. The only light came from three lights set into the underwater walls of her tank. The top half of the tiny space was pitch black, save for the wavering light reflections from the moving water below.

Then she noticed the wires. Thousands of them. Embedded all throughout her appendages and running from her body into various ports in the floor of the pool underneath her. They were the cause of the pain. Each foreign cable, wire, and tube was suddenly apparent to her, their foreign material digging wretchedly into her flesh. She screamed out, not in fear, but rage. Someone she knew did this to her, she had no doubt. Someone she loathed like no other. Miranda had absolutely no idea who, an amnestic side effect to the sedative she had been given. She was aware enough, however, to be confident that her memory would return in time.

Suddenly, the wall in front of her flared to life with light. Miranda's eyes were assaulted by the sudden brightness before they adjusted. She was looking through four different sets of eyes as four separate views filled the round wall of the enclosure. Each was a different view of the large room where the monsters were being held.

She was seeing what they saw. Heard their distressed bellows and wails. She felt them too. They were aggressive... and hungry. Longing for release, the four kaiju knew she was part of them now, their wordless emotions boiling up inside her, making *her* long for their escape. The side of Miranda Shepperton that still claimed to be a part of humanity died and a new being surfaced as she called to her new children.

"Soon, my lovelies," she cooed to them as a strange, motherly sense of responsibility for their happiness emerged.

Her children simply wanted to eat lunch and then go play. What kind of mother would refuse?

All at once, four overhead doors opened, one above each creature's terrarium, the daylight beaming in from the top of each shaft a few hundred feet above. Wasting no time, the newly freed beasts began ascending the easily scalable paths to their freedom, harsh roars and cries echoing triumph instead of captive sorrow. Miranda smiled amidst her pain and captivity, feeling her new children's excitement at being unleashed upon the world above.

***

Jason Hill and his Australian Shepherd, Tobe, were driving west in his white Honda Civic on Interstate 694, passing the Meditronia One headquarters in Mounds View. In Jason's opinion, each of the buildings was ugly as hell. The center building was circular, while the other four were rectangular structures. A large grassy field to the west lay between the corporate sprawl and a daycare facility with an overlarge parking lot. The daycare was empty now, a publicized embezzling lawsuit forcing its closure a month prior.

Just as he had passed Meditronia One, his ears were assaulted by an explosion of sounds. It was a metallic sounding animal cry -- rusty metal hinges merged with an angry, screeching monkey. He swerved from the painful distraction, clipping the back end of a black truck in the left lane. The truck swerved and cut into his lane. Jason quickly traded lanes with the wobbling pickup, but the Chevy Silverado suddenly cut sharply to the right and flipped from the driver's erratic attempts to maintain control. It rolled it over and over lengthwise before it smashed into the cars behind it.

His ears still under merciless attack from the ear-shredding roar, Jason veered to the right, gunning it toward the exit for University Avenue. He pulled over on the exit ramp. Covering his ears, Jason looked back behind him at the medical science complex and what was emerging from the ground. Tobe was losing his mind, scrambling all over the back seat and barking and whimpering.

A huge form... no, *forms,* blocked his view of the Meditronia One buildings. Massive enough to take up most of his field of vision, the gigantic creatures before him were nightmare versions of the monster movies he loved as a kid. Except these monsters were real. His voiding bladder went unnoticed as he watched in awe the things emerging from huge holes in both the field and the daycare parking lot. Another booming roar split the air, this one a deep bellow with a gravelly edge to its beginning and end.

Cars making it past the major pileup caused by the rolling truck raced by him on the exit ramp, as well as on 694. Jason was oblivious, his eyes on the colossal beings to the east. Double roars

183

continued assaulting his eardrums, and the raging headache he received as a result made him wince in pain.

The first daikaiju pounced onto the freeway like a cat, pinning a semi-trailer and crushing it into the asphalt. The creature had to be a dozen stories tall. Hunched over, the thing looked like a huge monkey, a prehensile tail protruding out behind it. The dark, furry tail undulated in waves as it wagged back and forth. It leaned back, revealing its face. The top half above its mouth was simian, but where a primate's mouth should have been, instead was a gaping set of jaws, like a shark. The bottom half of its ragged mouth was seemingly sunk into the kaiju's neck.

Mammalian eyes darted back and forth at all the little moving metal boxes and the screaming, warm-blooded things that ran for their lives. Its hands and feet all had long digits that ended in a fat, round blob of a fingertip, like a tree frog. The frog comparison held true for the webbing that stretched from between each finger on its hands and feet. One of its feet was still planted on the back end of the crushed semi-trailer.

Then a new sound emerged to further torture Jason and Tobe's ears.

Click-click! Click-click!

An armored monster longer than the Jaws Monkey was tall plowed through the piled-up traffic behind the monkey-fish-frog monster. The black arthropod demon's chitinous claws slammed together like castanets, but with deafening volume.

Click-click!

It had a long, plated body like a lobster, but its carapaced head was more like a crab -- wide and broad at the front. Two giant, rainbow-colored eyes swiveled on long eyestalks protruding from recesses on top of the crustacean horror's face. It looked around as it crawled over houses and small businesses on the other side of the road. Its tail swung up in the air, arcing straight up in a curve behind it, as a scorpion would. Unsurprisingly, a stinger emerged from the tip.

Click-click!

The clicking monster continued attacking everything in its path, its giant claws snipping and snapping at the organic and inorganic alike. People who tried fleeing were turned to puddles of gore by the spastic arthropod behemoth. It continued south, paying no attention to its fellow giants.

Meanwhile, Jaws Monkey leapt from the crushed trailer, sailing so high into the air it blocked out the sun beaming down on Jason's car, where he cowered with his barking dog. In the Jaws Monkey's place stood the biggest of the mobile gargantuans that had emerged from the ground.

The deep bellowing kaiju towered over the monkey-fish-frog like a father to his ten-year-old son. Jason could not even see the head from inside his car. He guessed it was at least twice as tall as the monkey beast. Smooth, dark blue skinned legs that were as thick as fuel refinery storage tanks seemed to float across the landscape as the monster cleared the interstate with one stride, coming down in the middle of the residential neighborhood the crab-lobster-scorpion had already begun demolishing.

In a blur of motion, a long thick tail came up from the ground and whipped around the creature's left flank. A horizontal whale's fluke pulverized a nearby department store, the sign's red dot and surrounding ring shooting through the air and landing on a restaurant half a mile away.

Jaws Monkey landed in the lake further south from the destroyed store, flooding the houses nearby with waves displaced from the small body of water. Like a kid in a shallow pool, the simian kaiju sloshed around loudly, screeching before moving on with the demonic whale kaiju. As the larger daikaiju's head finally came into view from where he sat in his car, Jason's eyes widened.

A massive whale's head, like Moby Dick, protruded neckless from between its shoulders. The thick mass of skull and flesh stuck out and forward from its body. A head that looked like it was made for ramming. A large eye was positioned on each side of its head, its brown irises surrounded by a slightly green sclera. The eyes were definitely not those of a whale, given the size and color. Jason could see even from where he was that they were intelligent eyes, watching everything around the creature. Jason was thankful he could not see the human-like being's front.

Ewww, he thought. *Whaleman dong.*

Bright green movement in his periphery caught Jason's eye. He snapped his head back towards Meditronia One. A giant vine was growing out of the final square hole in the ground, its verdant shoots violently wrapping around each other to gain purchase on the ground. The vines snaked towards the main three buildings nearby and split into hundreds of smaller tendrils that quickly covered the triple set of structures like a web.

Tendrils poured out of the ground, growing up and around the spherical center building until it became a dense scrub brush of vines. Jagged leaves and thorny brambles had swiftly grown in and formed, reaching out to the other edifices as well. All of this happened within the space of a minute, as the other monsters stomped south, undeterred. Jason started his car and plunged into the panic-fueled madness on University Avenue at the bottom of the exit ramp, he and his dog escaping the chaos with their lives.

***

The dense thicket of aberrant growth continued snaking hundreds of vine tendrils in and around the new rooting grounds, strengthening its main trunks as Flora 313 grew and moved like it was also fauna, but at a supernatural rate. Without warning, seven large vines shot out of the monster plant's base and rose into the air around the main mass growing out of the center building. Waving warily back and forth like cobras with their hoods up, each vine ended with a bulbous, pitcher-like formation, like a huge chin. With red dermal tissue coloring each round formation, the pitchers angled up, tapering slightly to an opening surrounded by jagged, toothy jaws.

They resembled the mouth of a Venus fly trap, but with three mandibles instead. Each jaw ended with curved, tooth-like spikes which interlocked when the mouth closed, the teeth snapping shut vertically. The two main mouth flaps lay flat and wide, opening like flower petals with pointed barbs for teeth that angled up towards the sky. The third top jaw was much skinnier than the two side jaws, not much more than a strip of green, fibrous flesh with downward pointing teeth. Its sole purpose was to lock the two horizontal jaws shut once they closed, as well as seal up any remaining gaps in the teeth. A locking bar of sorts.

Anything inside was then subjected to the intoxicating vapors of the digestive enzyme soup filling the pitcher portion, eventually slipping down the slick, angled ridge inside. The juices below sedated their victims and devoured them through a slow, gruesome digestive process.

The four formerly concealed doors that had released the creatures started closing. As the aggressive plant's escape hatch grew smaller, the vine pulled the last of its roots up and out of the vertical tunnel just in time, preventing the mechanical door from severing it. The tail end of the plant monster retracted back into its main mass that encompassed the buildings nearby. As all the hatches slid back into place, the gargantuan kudzu beast started growing again.

Thousands of creeping vines slithered out from the verdant epicenter. They poured over the property and beyond, into nearby neighborhoods and the ruined department store across the freeway. The rampant growth covered everything in leafy tentacles that thrashed and rubbed against each other. Within minutes, a half mile radius all around the daikaiju was filled with an impenetrable mass of newly formed brambles from hell. Tree-like spires shot up out of the brambles, reaching heights of fifty feet or more. The expanding monster had created a dark maze of the aggressive shoots.

The new sea of vegetation hardened into bark within minutes, the green sea turning brown under the forest green leaves sprouting out all over the top of the tangle bloom. Each was the size of a cul-de-sac. Thick, dark veins ran through each leaf, looking more animal than plant.

The pitcher trap sentinels, still wagging back and forth in their serpent-like way, began to buzz. The incessant droning noise increased in volume, sounding like hundreds of different insects all trapped in a room and extremely agitated -- then the sound amplified tenfold.

The insane buzzing abruptly ceased. However, the relative silence that followed was short-lived. All around the plant daikaiju, a different but similar buzzing grew in pitch. Swarms of billions of insects filled the sky all at once, the army of invertebrates called by the giant, carnivorous vine heads. Flies, mosquitoes, wasps, dragonflies, beetles, cicadas, bees, and over a thousand more species darkened the sky above. The massive cloud of bugs obscured their summoners from view, the flytrap pitcher vines seeming to disappear, along with the overgrown complex that used to be Meditronia One. The cloud descended onto the plant kaiju, and the legion of bugs consumed the strange monster's pollen nectar.

The mutations began immediately.

In her wet prison, a woman who was hardly Miranda Shepperton anymore smiled.

***

Deep below the earth, on sublevel six, Strand and company looked on as all their camera views from above were snuffed out by the rapid, angry growth. When the last camera was crushed from existence by the expanding tendrils, he looked at Keene and Curran with a surprised look.

"Shit. That was fast!" Strand erupted with a series of hearty guffaws, drawing looks of confusion and concern from his colleagues.

He noticed their quizzical, worried faces. Then his face instantly became serious again.

"What the long faces, my faithful sidekicks?"

"Uh, I don't understand how *we* are getting out, Ivan," Keene said nervously.

"What for? Our control mechanism… er, I mean *Miranda*, is a priority. Besides, we are perfectly safe here, my friend!" Strand said with a smile. "There is five years' worth of food and drinking water down here, more generators than you can shake a stick at, and plenty to keep us occupied. Why I have several portable hard drives full of the best movies and TV shows from the last twenty years."

"Not to mention this," he continued as he walked to the nearby laptop on the conference table, navigating the mouse and clicking on an icon marked "TV."

Dramatic music queued up and a helicopter camera shot displaying the coast of some tropical island filled the screen. A man's voice started up, yelling out a line everyone in the room knew.

"*This season, on* Survivor…"

The three stooges groaned from over at their hired goons table, where they were playing five card stud now. Keene and Curran looked at each other and rolled their eyes. They had just unleashed monster hell upon the Twin Cities metro area, and they had to sit on their asses in an underground facility and watch that damn old-ass reality show with a madman who absolutely loved it. Keene got up and walked around to the fridge, removing several beers and passing them around.

Strand had already found a chair and was instantly glued to the screen, not looking at the others. As Keene sat back down, Curran was bringing up the other camera views they still had access to, those outside the wall of vines and freshly mutated insect abominations surrounding the gnarled terror above. He found several acceptable views of the area.

Satisfied he was still able to keep an eye on things, he gave in to the reality TV ridiculousness his boss was so engrossed in. As the title music ran across the laptop screen that Strand had moved to the kitchenette island's counter for all to see, Strand suddenly turned to Keene and Curran. He giggled happily, infecting the five other men's arms with rippling gooseflesh.

"This season is going to be awesome!"

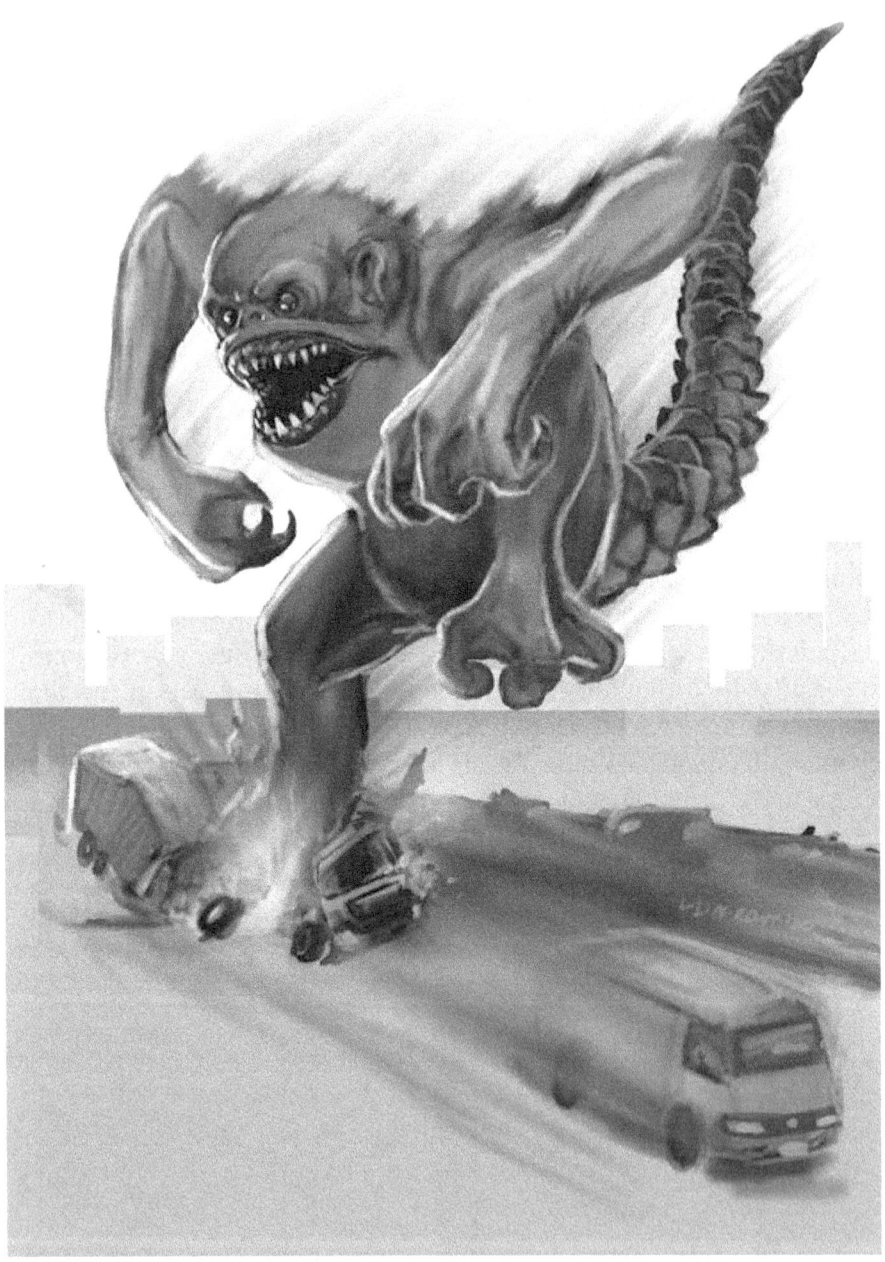

CHAPTER 15

Trench Town
Monterey Canyon

Burke Reiser stared down at the three severed fingers lying in an expanding pool of blood on the floor next to the chair he was bound to. They had previously been attached to his right hand -- his good hand. The bastard Masao had cut two of them off with a pair of large, diagonal pliers he had pulled from his backpack, one lopped off for each incorrect response he had given so far.

After the Orphan team had taken him down with their modified flashbang, he was handcuffed to the chair Natasha had been, but he was still facing the panel of screens depicting the many things happening at that moment in the Midwest of America. The most prominent feed was the destruction of Chicago, but recently had begun to include the emergence of Bionautics' retort to Hidora Neo's creations. He took note of the impressive, expanding portion of Minnesota rapidly turning into a verdant nightmare and the three giant monsters veering towards the Windy City, trashing most of the Twin Cities on the way.

The scientists responsible, led by Dr. Ivan Strand, were being called rogues and getting credit for all the monsters seen so far. Burke had laughed between screams when he had heard that, right after Masao cut off his right middle finger. The same news had incensed his four captors, their organization's credit stolen by

Bionautics. Curses in more than one language had ensued, the ethnic differences between the Orphans suddenly obvious.

Natasha had cut off his right-hand ring finger herself, after he refused to tell her the truth about his murder spree in Trench Town. Then she shoved it in his screaming mouth, gagging him. He spat it out onto the floor, where it landed next to his index and middle digits.

It didn't matter in the end, though, he thought.

Burke had contacted his superior just before he had been flash-banged in the hallway. Now he would at least try to die with any dignity he could, still hoping the team that had already been on their way had picked up the pace.

"Why did you send Nautilus Rex and the Terror Griffin to San Francisco, Reiser?"

Mackenzie MacElroy stood in front of him suddenly, fists on her hips, the giant Chinese *thing* with the spiked helmet by her side. Natasha stood off to his right, next to Masao seated at the far end of the table Burke was chained to.

"If you aren't cooperative this time, I'm cutting your shriveled little balls off myself. Then I'll feed you to the prototypes out in the hallway," Mackenzie said.

She stepped up to him and ran her painted fingernails down the side of his face, digging in harshly about halfway. Blood dribbled out, and Burke winced more.

"One of them ate Chucky up like it was a woodchipper, you miserable piece of shit."

"I did it simply for the distraction, you dumb bitch," he said, matter of fact. "I just picked two and let 'em go!"

"But why did you bring them back and return them to stasis?" Masao's voice filled his right ear.

"So, the world knows they are being controlled," Burke said through clenched teeth. Blood gushed freely from his mangled hand, spattering the floor. "Now with their recent unveiling, the world thinks Ivan Strand and his lab monkeys are *the* people behind it all. Not you."

This last part was emphasized heavily when Burke snapped his head up and stared Mackenzie in the eyes with conviction. She rewarded him with a left hook, loosening his teeth and causing him to chomp down on his tongue hard enough to bleed. She shook her hand in pain, yet it barely showed on her face.

"Not for long, Burke. My mother will set the world straight upon her return from afar."

Burke chuckled meekly, blood loss affecting him. "Mother. That's a good one. None of you knows what a real mother is. May you all rot in Hell with that twisted woman. Also, who the fuck says 'afar?'"

Yao approached him slowly, towering over him in his chair. He grinned at her like a desperate maniac.

"Are we going to snu-snu now, you ugly troll?"

Dropping down to a bent knee, Yao put her other leg back behind her and pushed off the floor. Her lower stance and extra boost from her leg push launched her into Burke's pretty white face. Her pin cushion head obliterated his good looks, the dozen or so spikes embedding instantly into his fleshy mug. A small grunt of surprise was all he had time to get out before being facially pulverized.

"Dammit, Yao! We weren't done with him," Natasha cried out. "We still don't know what their plan for this station was!"

"He wasn't going to tell you anything useful," Yao said as quietly as her deep voice allowed. "You know that. Anyway, I've been planning to do that since we walked in."

The big woman had undone her helmet to stand up again, her long black ponytail spilling down her back. Her spiked headgear remained a part of Burke's face, blood running down and covering his clothes and the floor.

"It's better this way in any event," Masao said. "There are reinforcements on the way, and we need to prepare."

He pointed to the proximity sensors and sonar display. A small object the size of a mini-sub was approaching, fast. Mackenzie sat down at the computer array that controlled all things kaiju related in the complex. Her fingers flew as she typed quickly, re-programming the implants located in all the daikaiju that Trench Town housed.

"There's our failsafe if this doesn't go smoothly," she said as she clicked the mouse once more dramatically and rose from the chair. "Seattle is going to have a helluva day tomorrow."

Mackenzie pointed around the room at its contents. "Let's use the furniture in here to make some cover in case those fools get past the welcoming party."

They moved the few cabinets at the back of the room, making places to duck down behind. Leaving Burke's corpse cuffed to the large steel table in front of the monitors, they flipped it up on its side. The body flipped over and dropped down on the tabletop side of the improvised barrier, its feet just hitting the floor with a loud double tap. Yao grabbed the corpse by the shoulder and yanked at the helm sticking out of Burke's ruined face with her other hand. It came out after two pulls, revealing a train wreck of gore. Mackenzie winced at the sight and turned to Natasha.

"Here, take Chuck's M4 and cover us from that corner. If they all come in at once, blow them to Hell with the launcher." She handed the large assault rifle and grenade combo to the Russian woman, who accepted it immediately.

"Yes, ma'am," she said, though Mackenzie was not her superior.

Natasha made a small box blind of sorts on the back-left side of the room from three filing cabinets. She jumped up and over, landing inside her makeshift pillbox.

Masao and Mackenzie ducked down behind the table, while Yao had gone between the series of shelving units on the right side of the room. These contained specimen jars, various drugs, tools, and some of the equipment necessary in the growth and cultivation of the giant beasts slumbering in their dens.

The six shelves were five feet apart from each other and stretched twelve and a half feet in the air, leaving a yard or so between the tops and the ceiling above. Each shelf was illuminated by light strips running along the front of each tier. Even with her black body armor, Yao's bulky frame was hidden by the lights reflecting off the clutter of objects adorning each row of storage. Until they were able to see down her aisle, of course. But by then, it would be too late for them.

The computer system's feminine, yet monotone voice announced that airlock two had been engaged, accompanied by faint mechanical noises from the other end of the complex verifying this. The four tired Orphans waited. Listening.

A cacophony of angry roars and screams intermixed with gunfire signaled the invaders' introduction to the prototypes that were still loose in the large hallway outside the cafeteria. The Razorback Rex was the most audible, its squeals and grunts penetrating the thick metal walls separating Mackenzie's team from the new arrivals.

Something exploded, shaking the whole building in its place within the Monterey canyon wall, and setting off sensors all over the base. Alarms screamed, and warning lights flashed from the main console in the room. A loud rushing sound slammed into the door that served as entrance to the control room they were hunkered down in. All four knew what that meant. The station's walls and structure were compromised. Ocean water rushing to meet them was the loud noise they had heard hitting the door.

"I'm activating the failsafe now. I'm sorry I've failed you all," Mackenzie said as she ran to the computer and clicked on the onscreen button that initiated her program. A cliché timer popped up on the monitor, leaving less than two minutes for the rest of their lives.

"It was not your fault, Mackenzie," Masao said.

Natasha and Yao nodded their agreement.

The four siblings from different countries abandoned their posts and gathered in the middle of the room by the overturned table. They hugged each other and sat down together on the floor. Mackenzie spoke into her headset, giving a final report on their situation, before transmitting it to Sadako and Captain Hodder at Ripley Station, Cunningham in Nevada, Tsuburaya in Japan, and Dr. Brown at Superior X.

Then the explosives planted all over the base exploded, letting millions of gallons of seawater rush in the unflooded sections, causing chunks of the underwater installation to burst out. In seconds, the effective detonation snuffed out the lives of the four Orphan soldiers. The end of Trench Town also released the smaller prototypes, as well as eight full grown daikaiju, including the Nautilus Rex and the Terror Griffin.

This time, they were headed for Seattle.

CHAPTER 16

Minnesota

Trapped inside of her cold elliptical prison, Miranda Shepperton was learning to handle the agonizing pain shooting through her body. Anguish that was being inflicted on her by the dozens of needles and wires that were embedded in her flesh -- cables, tubes, and cords of all kinds trailing from them. These snaking lengths all ran out of the back of the chamber. Connecting her to Ivan Strand's machines, they pumped her full of some ungodly concoction that was taking the place of her food and water consumption. She also was immersed in some kind of musky smelling soup. The slimy stiff filled half of the chamber

She knew it was Ivan Strand's deviance that had put her here in this place. The memory of the bastard throwing a bottle at her face was murky but ever present in her mind. Her nose still hurt like hell, but the blood that had been encrusted around her nostrils had since turned back to liquid in the incredibly humid container she was locked up in. Miranda was Strand's unwilling pawn in whatever twisted game the cracked, sociopathic genius was playing this time.

Whatever his *true* intended purpose of the insane device she was plugged into was, it made her able to communicate with and control -- in a way similar a hive mind – Bionautics' monsters of mass destruction. Horrific at first, when her humanity had still retained control, it quickly became second nature, and something that connected her in a motherly way to a litter of semi-sentient lifeforms that were capable of reshaping the world.

Cruelly denied the ability to create life in her own body by the very man responsible for her current situation – she was completely devastated when she found out her part in a secret fertility experiment she had been completely unaware of. One she sure as shit had not signed up or volunteered for.

He had stolen eggs from her many times while she had slept. She would often sleep in the labs after working late. He had drugged the hell out of her -- she still wasn't sure how -- and had also added an experimental fertility hormone in her morning coffee every Monday for ten months. Miranda found the bottle in his trash, the label plain for all to see proclaiming the name of a hormone she had been involved in the lab testing of a year prior. Paranoia and her unexplained grogginess as of late had led her to her suspicions. Finally finding the hair-thin incision healing up on her belly confirmed her worst fears.

The ill-gotten result was an attempt at asexual reproduction, according to that bastard Strand. Something that he had only fessed up to once she had found his despicably cruel journal. Enraged, she had cornered him in the labs one night with a loaded .38 Smith & Wesson. She deeply regretted not killing him that evening. But hindsight was always 20/20, after all.

Now Miranda knew most of his real intentions with her embryos. He had used them to make the abominations that were her frightening children, each of them possessing her genes in some form or another. Through that biological bond and her bastard boss' infernal machines, she was now entwined with their brains through a process she didn't completely understand but was certain it was one her employer had acquired from… *diabolical* sources. She could *feel* the Evil. With a capital "E." Evil that was starting to feel normal to her.

Strand had always been a major occult, cryptozoology, and paranormal fan. His collections of rare tomes, artifacts, and "evidence" was insane. He had built a modest second house on his property to reside in after turning his multi-million-dollar mansion into a private museum -- guarded heavily by an assortment of competent goons. Miranda had heard stories of the company he kept, from those who had supposedly practiced the black arts, to experimental scientists known for crossing many ethical boundaries in their work, and even some of the very private one percent of Americans who helped rule the world behind the scenes.

While she could not figure out the who's, what's, or how's that had allowed him to become so successful at growing giant beasts -- especially in such a brief time frame -- she had suspected otherworldly influences without a second thought. She could feel the dark presence in the body fluids flowing through her, trying to silence her fears of what she was becoming and instilling a sense of justice in her while she coaxed her monster babies into doing her bidding. The influence worked.

It made her feel whole again.

She still had her own agenda, however. Oh, yes. Strand would pay for what he had done to her. But first, she would play along, destroying the monsters razing Chicago and any of the military forces that interfered.

The verdant force that was the plant/animal hybrid kaiju had expanded quickly, creating a thick forest of giant brambles and excessive vegetation that swarmed with steadily mutating insects and the like. While Flora 313 was busy turning acre upon acre around Medtronia One into a hellish new world, Miranda's three fauna Daikaiju had nearly reached Minneapolis.

The Twin Cities metro area was in a state of panic and hasty evacuation. News quickly spread of the monsters' emergence and path of destruction south of the 694-corridor, the strip of freeway that acted like a northern border for the fraternal twin population centers. Many lives were lost in the ensuing devastation. Military forces focusing on Chicago spun on their heads trying to react to these newest threats, and so close to still populated areas.

Miranda's monstrous children carved a path of annihilation south, soon reaching north Minneapolis. The trio made short work of the outlying suburbs and the unfortunate stragglers still trying to get out of harm's way. Old duplexes from the early 1900's fell to the beasts' advance toward downtown and its skyscrapers.

The whale-headed giant Cetacea Magnon thundered through the neighborhoods, crushing everything in his way. The titan's tail flew back and forth, levelling more homes and small businesses with its horizontal fluke, while pounding the streets into rubble as he made a beeline for the city's taller structures that were lining the Mississippi River and Highways 94 and 35W.

Jawkey, the jaws-monkey-fish-frog that Miranda had initially dreamed up as a joke, bounded south on the same path, but he took the city on the eastern side of the river. He was bouncing southeast as he landed indiscriminately on buildings, cars, and even some of the unlucky people still present with every leap he took in the air. His gritty screeching and screaming ricocheted off the nearby high-rises and skyscrapers.

He reached Columbia Park, destroying the landscape as he landed. His monkey-frog feet tore up the soft earth with each pounce. As he charged through a major trucking distribution center just past the park, the third kaiju, Gonzalez, was making its way down the river.

Named after one of Strand's favorite horror series authors, Gonzalez surged through the waterway, flooding both sides with the polluted Mississippi water as it did so. Its giant, crustacean claws were thrust up above its head. With gusto, the sharp, serrated crab appendages snapped twice to let everyone around know it was there.

Click-click!

In one savage swing, both claws came down on the arched Lowry Avenue bridge, taking it out with such force that a small shockwave spread out from the impact. The din shattered windows nearby and woke up a number of car alarms. The stampeding lobster/scorpion/crab kaiju continued along the river through Minneapolis, torrents of water buffeting the shore in its wake.

Miranda felt her children's rage. They were made from *her,* after all. The kaijus' feelings and her own fueled her anger, and she urged them to destroy everything in their path. As far as she was concerned, everyone would pay for what was done to her and bow to her beautiful monster offspring.

With every smashed building or destroyed bridge, she would reward them psychically, the endorphin releasing encouragement more than enough to drive the kaiju forward. The praise of their tiny, imprisoned mother was everything to them. Each emotive signal she gave elicited bizarre, cooing noises from the creatures, mixed in with their normal roars and trilling.

Spurred on by this, the colossal whale man Cetacea Magnon bellowed almost jubilantly as he happily destroyed the houses along Interstate 94 where it started to veer away from the river. Wrecked vehicles and chunks of buildings flew up through the air like a field of grasshoppers evading a person jogging through at the end of summer. His desire to reach Chicago and battle the kaiju claiming the major city was evident with each step of the detour they took through Minneapolis. He could feel the creatures' presences, even from several states away, including their alien blood, and it enraged him more. Miranda knew these feelings like they were her own.

Jawkey and Gonzalez, not possessing the same level of sentience, were led by their larger, smarter sibling. The giant, sperm-whale-headed daikaiju -- also inspired by a horror series -- surpassed them as they reached downtown. Miranda smiled at the determination of her eldest son, pushing her twisted love out to him for his conviction. A warm, happy feeling rebounded back to her and she felt his own version of emotion, animalistic but still conveying the adoration and connection she now thrived on. The other siblings echoed this the best that they could, though theirs was more simplistic -- like a dog or cat's love for their master when they return home from work.

As Cetacea Magnon reached the city skyline of downtown Minneapolis, he made short work of the warehouse district that preceded Target Field stadium to the south. Upon reaching the overpriced home of the Minnesota Twins, the metal bleachers reflected the sun's rays, blinding the daikaiju. He roared louder than ever before, and the broad tail swung around like a whip, its fluke slicing through the baseball park horizontally.

As the severed supports split apart, the upper decks collapsed, falling on top of the lower decks. An entire sidewall toppled onto the field with a dust-filled crash of metal and stone. Fuel lines running through the building for various uses ignited and exploded up and outward as the whale giant bellowed in response, holding his arms up victoriously as a human would.

The blast blew out from under the collapsed upper decks, and the tiers of metal benches scattered all over the city, the majority crashing into nearby structures. Cars abandoned in the streets were flattened by some of the raining debris. Cetacea Magnon moved onto the Target Center basketball stadium across the highway from the ruined baseball field, where he happily obliterated the older arena. Miranda praised her son with affection through their strange biochemical bond. He grunted in response, his satisfaction present in the emotions Miranda received back from him.

Slightly jealous of their bigger brother, Jawkey and Gonzalez were not to be outdone.

She was bombarded by excited feeling from both of them, their broadcast thoughts saying, *"Mom! Look at me!"*

The jaws-monkey's display was to tear into a staggered grouping of churches from several different religions that were across the river. Then he moved on to rip apart some restaurants lining the streets to the south. A fuel station in the middle of them went up in several balls of flame as Jawkey stomped on it, bouncing up in the air again when the gas pumps blew, screeching like the primate he partly was. His smoldering fur added the stench of burning hair to the list of horrible scents in the air.

Gonzalez, meanwhile, simultaneously reduced Nicollet Island to smithereens with the lethal claws and massive scorpion-like tail. The island's high school was soon a flaming smear on the south end. Luckily, school was out for the summer. Miranda felt an overwhelming sense of pride for her other two children and let them know this through the link they shared. Their reactions were nothing but positive, finally getting the attention they were craving, like giant, spoiled brats.

Cetacea Magnon reached the skyscrapers of downtown Minneapolis. The closest buildings towered over him, yet easily collapsed under the pummeling fists of the mighty whale monster. His thick, bony knuckles toppled 600-foot plus structures that plummeted to the streets below.

The falling rubble released immense clouds of dust and smoke that were littered with flames. His attacks were relentless, going for the building supports each time. Within minutes, Cetacea Magnon had eradicated most of the taller buildings, including the larger Capella Tower and Wells Fargo Center. This made him one of the tallest things still standing in downtown, washing Miranda in waves of his victorious joy. When he was finished, only four buildings remained standing taller than the kaiju. The Carlyle and U.S. Bancorp centers, and the Foshay and IDS towers.

Jawkey launched across the river, and in two bounds latched onto the side of the nearly 800-foot-tall IDS Tower, digging all four of his webbed primate claws into the side of the tallest structure in the state. Then he climbed, quickly scaling the building like a bigger King Kong and perched at the top like he belonged there. Screeching in an ear-piercing staccato of shrieks, Jawkey raised his arms above his head, taunting his larger brother on the ground below. The building beneath him was physically protesting his position, cracks and pieces of it rained down on the streets below as the structure threatened to either collapse or topple.

Cetacea Magnon roared and bull-rushed the structure, smashing completely through it and knocking his gloating sibling from his perch. Jawkey yelped as he landed on the U.S. Bancorp center just southwest of the fallen IDS tower, a dust cloud concealing his mass after obliterating half of the 467-foot structure upon impact, adding to the spreading haze from the destruction. Cetacea Magnon let loose a series of deep, short barks, very much like laughter, and his whale's tail wagged almost comically while adding insult to injury to the ruined buildings behind him.

Gonzalez, meanwhile, had left the riverbed after running over St. Anthony Falls. The ruined dam released torrents of water that rose up over the banks and flooded much of the city on both sides of the river. The giant arthropod slammed its girth into the Carlyle building that had been still standing close to the river's edge, turning it to ruins. The armored kaiju then made its way toward Foshay Tower.

As the monsters triple-teamed the rest of downtown Minneapolis, a massive force of planes and choppers approached from the east, letting loose a barrage of missiles and rockets. The slew of projectiles hit their targets, but also a lot of the still standing buildings around them. A large part of the decimated city was ignited again in a series of explosions. Plumes of brilliant orange, red, and yellow flames erupted everywhere, yet the cries of the daikaiju were still audible over the blasts. Miranda writhed in agony in her chamber, grinding her teeth in response to the pain she felt as they were blasted by sidewinder missiles and hydra rockets.

When the smoke cleared, bloody wounds and charred flesh were visible all over each monster's body. Cetacea M. belched a cone of flame reflexively, his surprise breath weapon coating several aircraft with unnatural fire as they passed overhead. Three jets took nosedives into the ruined city, two of them exploding shortly after impact, the pilots ejecting only moments before crashing. Four flaming Apache choppers veered off at odd angles and eventually came down hard at separate places in the city, two going right into the mess of a river called the Mississippi. One of the helicopters exploded in a huge fireball. The other pair of Apaches joined the decimation on the ground, crashing down without explosive incident, though each would become a burnt-out husk as the surviving soldiers inside ran to safety. Wherever that was.

Miranda pushed telepathically to get the giants to turn their attentions toward the Windy City, and the kaiju who were taking it over. Even with the relentless assault of the remaining aircraft and their fusillade pounding them, the trio complied, changing their direction and heading south. Gonzalez obliterated the geometric eyesore that was the Minnesota Viking's stadium in the blink of an eye as it continued through the city towards the 35W bridge. Miranda was not sure if it was her influence on them that they seemed to hate stadiums. Not too concerned with it, she smiled at the quirk as the Crustacean Horror reached the rebuilt steel truss arches spanning the width of the Mississippi.

In a tragic event, the bridge had collapsed back in 2007, making America consider all of its aging bridges. The new bridge now seemed to be at risk for also being destroyed. In a strange twist of fate, however, the black monster went around it completely. Gonzalez instead fell in line behind Cetacea Magnon and his gigantic strides through uptown Minneapolis. From there, they proceeded south towards the Mall of America. Jawkey followed, bouncing around his monstrous kin with what seemed like glee.

After destroying the famous mega mall and all the businesses that had sprung up around the major tourist attraction, they turned southeast again. Now they were heading toward Illinois and their awaiting playdates. Their mother was starting to believe she was influencing their targets. Miranda encouraged them toward Chicago with a touch of sternness. She was anxious to see her children in battle, confident they would make her proud. Then she turned her attention to the still growing monster foliage that had sprouted from the grounds beneath the Medtronia One complex.

The all-encompassing swarm of insects still protected their new master, the plant kaiju's pheromones and enticing pollen-nectar concoction ensuring the undying loyalty of so many six-legged servants and slimy, crawling things. Their servitude was assured by ample supplies of food, water, and enough biochemically brainwashing, physically altering substances in both to keep them faithful until death.

Inside the twisting coils of thorny brambles that made up the center of the immense plant were the ruined buildings that had once been the corporate headquarters of the medical technology company. Redwood thick loops of overgrowth had woven around and punched through each floor of the three largest structures like metal piercings through faces at a death metal concert.

A scattering of employees had survived in the ruins. The survivors had hid in any nook or cranny they could find that wasn't already conquered by the savage growth, mutated insects, or the hideously (*beautifully*) transformed people that had flooded the area. Miranda could still feel each survivor's life force through the simplistic senses of the giant kaiju, and by the humans' fear. Fear was something she had come to love the taste of. A new trait that likely stemmed from the blood coursing through her veins. Blood that was partly stolen from Hell's children.

Pitying the trapped mortals, she prodded Flora 313 to help them to adapt, so they didn't have to *just* die. They could serve her afterward and be *reborn*. Thin, snaking vines began to seek out the trapped, hiding people in response, wrapping around those the tendrils found like constricting snakes. Once the person was bound,

207

the vines would start secreting a substance around them that encased their bodies in a quickly solidifying, milkweed-like cocoon.

Inside each cocoon, the human captives were transformed, their pain and fear disappearing as they morphed into something else. Soon, after they had matured and hatched, the former people would be new and improved. Miranda would use them through 313 to find Strand and his bastard crew of minions in the underground labs -- where she assumed her and her damned cell were also located.

There would be no mercy for the cruel man. Her hybrid grandchildren would kill them all and set her free... if she did not first do it herself. She had felt the powers inside her growing for a while now. Powers that had gone from feeling violating to *empowering*. Once she was free, Miranda Shepperton -- no, *Mirashen,* her human name was meaningless garbage now... Mirashen and her kaiju would put Sadako Sōzō and Hidora Neo down like the rabid human dogs they were.

In her prison, the thing that had once been Miranda Shepperton laughed.

***

Lake Superior
Much Later

Volk'narr was roused from his nap by a new lifeforce signature alert; three of them, actually. He cursed out loud in his alien tongue when the causes revealed themselves on the screen in front of him. The locations were in various places across the globe - South Pacific seas; the Himalayan Mountains; and the North American Southwest.

They had all moved.

They were beginning to awaken. All three of them. Things had progressed further along than he had thought, the Apocalypse had begun. Unless Volk'narr stopped it first, ensuring the Behemoth, the Leviathan, and Ziz went back to sleep, thus sparing the Earth from its doom a little while longer.

He looked at his version of a clock. Volk'narr had been asleep for *hours.*

Shit! he thought in his own language.

His many limbed, mechanized warrior suit -- daikaiju-sized for his protection -- broke out of its lake bottom burrow. Countless rocks, sediment and detritus blasted everywhere. He was cruising straight towards Superior X and the three unsuspecting Hidora Neo scientists running the show down in the Windy City with their monsters. *Time to end this facility and any kaiju within.*

Volk'narr selected another album, this time a musical group named Metallica, the album titled *Ride the Lightning.* His wicked robot fighter continued along the bottom towards the deep-water location of the hidden beast nursery. The fast guitars, drums and throaty vocals fueled his adrenaline. These human musicians knew how to get pumped up! Not that he really understood the words. Regardless, he grinned, and his sharp mandibles stretched wide open and snapped together three times. He had been waiting for this for so long.

The alien warrior's sensors suddenly reacted severely while en route to his destructive date with the Superior X station. At the bottom of the planet, the life signs of the Elders had skyrocketed, sending the continent into a splash of the crimson color assigned to their race. Cursing yet again, he halted his giant robot's approach to the unsuspecting Hidora Neo scientists in their underwater facility.

Creations that had doubled in number? He double-checked and sure enough, four more had arrived while he was napping.

Shit! Shit!

Seven kaiju who were in the process of meeting Miranda's children, the latter making excellent time getting to Chicago. They were accompanied by a swarm of attacking combat drones sent in lieu of manned aircraft -- an effort to spare lives and still do something against the daikaiju. So many kaiju in one location also sent his sensors into an uproar, almost as much as the Elder-infested continent. He quickly looked from place to place, trying to pick the more threatening source. Volk'narr should probably deal with the Elders first, but, oh.... how he longed to fight some giant beasts! He eyed up nearby Chicago on the map screen, two distinct enemy colors threatening to blur together. It seemed silly, especially when he could end half of the kaijus' controllers right now.

All he had to do was shoot the shit out of that trench just ahead of him. He would end them without any fighting. Without any *fun*. He would probably also devastate the surrounding eco-system, and maybe even drain a portion of the lake. That would not be fun, either.

With a sharp retort that was an equivalent to "screw it!", Volk'narr took the mech straight up, shooting out of the lake and streaking up into the atmosphere until he had reached a less detectable zone. The Elders would have to wait, he wanted to beat some kaiju bloody first. It had been a long hibernation, and he wasn't ready to fight Elders yet. They were usually difficult to battle and it always got really messy. It might also require him to leave the mech to fight them. Not an ideal scenario, given his lapse in combat the last 50-60 million years or so. He would be rusty on the ground. In his suit, he was damn near *invincible*.

He knew the humans behind Hidora Neo were down there on the frozen land as well, and he was inclined to leave the sinister aliens' nature free to run its course before he stopped down for a visit. The blotches on the map were not going anywhere, they were concentrated under a mountain range not too far from a human settlement – McMurdo Station it was called – yet they were far enough away at the same time. Antarctica was in its winter season, the temperatures deadly cold. Surely, the Elders would not leave the safety of their underground sanctuary. He could afford to be selfish a little longer. He had no love for the humans that had caused his activation, anyway. They were the enemy, after all.

Volk'narr changed his music yet again, the previous one having finished during his deliberation. This time he chose an early '90's band named Pantera, and their album, *Vulgar Display of Power*. The anger started fast and kept coming. The lead singer's shredding vocals partnered perfectly with the instruments that were dominating his ear canals.

Ahh, yes. He liked Pantera. Volk'narr flew toward the monster mash thousands of feet down, in the Windy City. This called for a dramatic entrance.

Then it was time to get fucking hostile and kick some kaiju ass.

END

Wild Hunt Press will unleash batch 2 of *Primordial Soup* soon.

Prepare for Volk'narr versus the daikaiju G.M.O.s. Don't forget to leave an awesome review!

ABOUT THE AUTHOR

Dustin Dreyling is a lifelong native of Saint Paul, Minnesota. A fan of almost all things Sci-Fi and Horror, he lives there with the love of his life, Melissa, and their fur and scale babies. A devout fan of authors like Jeremy Robinson, Jeff Strand, Brian Keene, and Tim Curran; their works have been a large influence to him. These are in addition to horror greats like H.P. Lovecraft and Stephen King. So far, Mr. Dreyling has had stories published in the Wild Hunt Press anthologies *The Experiment, Duel of the Monsters Volume 1,* and *Attack of the Kaiju Volume 2: The Next Wave. Primordial Soup: The First Batch* is his first novel.

ABOUT THE ARTIST

Elden Ardiente is a graphic designer, creature artist, and illustrator based in Sydney, Australia. Visit ldnrdnt.com to see his work.

ORIGINAL CONCEPT ART FROM 2014

Here are my first two attempts at a cover, both of which I made with GIMP. The first is a tad busy!

I took the picture of the *Carcharodontosaurus* skull at a travelling exhibit that was visiting the Science Museum of Minnesota. It was a fantastic exhibit that I would love to see again. The skull in the busy cover was also from that visit to the exhibit.

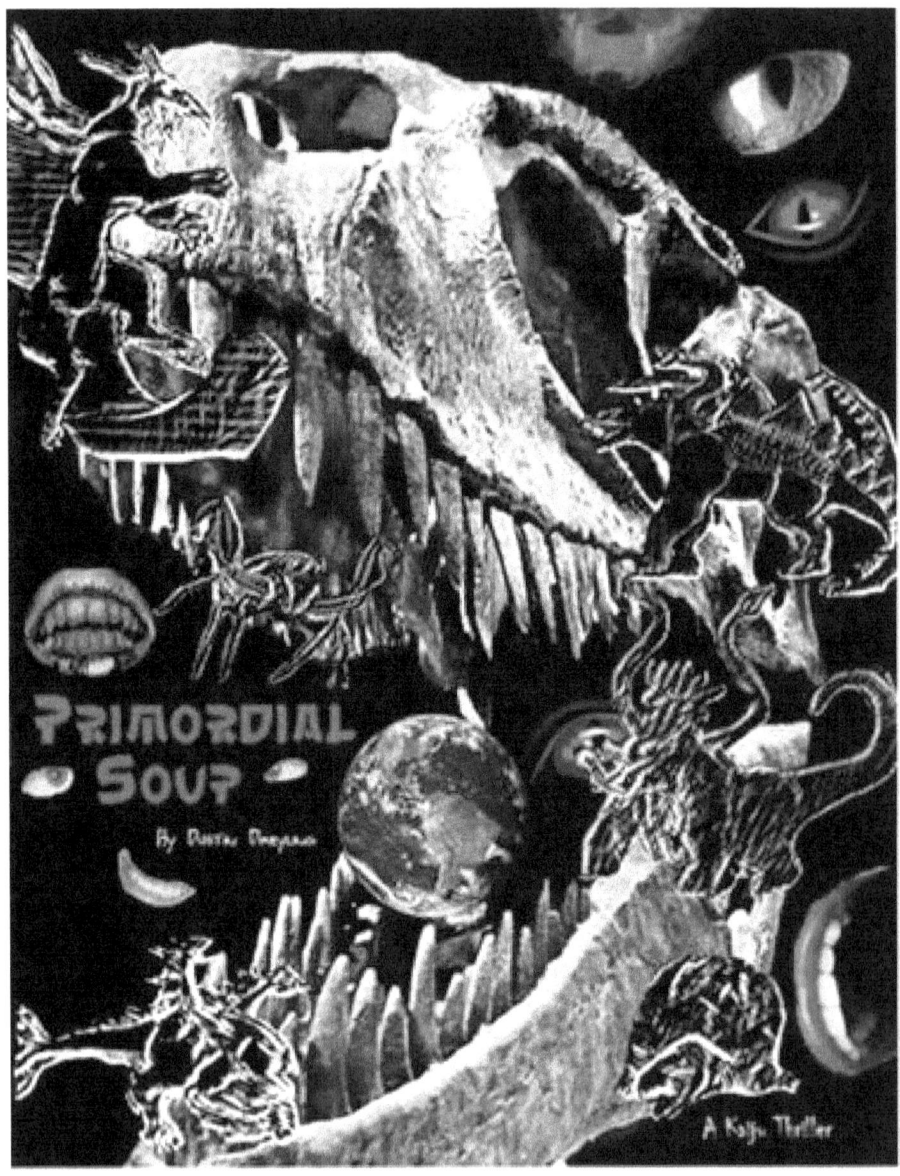

My original drawing of Rampage as a quadruped with three heads.

My first drawing of Conquer.

My first drawing of Pirahnex.

Original art for a daikaiju not featured in this book, King Pachy! (Yes, it's a teaser – Coming soon.) And on the lower right is my thumb.

The Flock's war with mankind has triggered their species to evolve. They hatch their first offspring with an armored hide and opposable thumbs. The Flock fears he will pollute the bloodline, but mankind sees his adaptions for what they are — an improvement. Both man and beast are out to destroy the baby kaiju. The race for survival is on.

Grab your copy on Amazon.com

www.ingramcontent.com/pod-product-compliance
Lightning Source LLC
Chambersburg PA
CBHW070622130626
46556CB00001B/441